About

Tony Black is an award-winning journalist and the author of some of the most critically-acclaimed British crime fiction of recent times. His Gus Dury series features: *Paying for It*, *Gutted*, *Loss* and *Long Time Dead*, which is soon to be filmed for the big screen by Richard Jobson. A police series featuring DI Rob Brennan includes: *Truth Lies Bleeding* and *Murder Mile*. *The Storm Without* (published by McNidder & Grace) featuring Ayr's very own Doug Michie, has also received much critical acclaim. He is also the author of five novellas and two short story collections.

Visit his website at: www.tonyblack net for all his latest news.

Praise for TONY BLACK's writing

'my favourite British crime writer'

IRVINE WELSH

'excellent'

THE TIMES

'the punk rocker of the Scottish crime scene'

DAILY RECORD

'bleakly beautiful'

THE GUARDIAN

'exceptionally compelli

MIRROR

D1300926

'simply superb'

STONE

'a master writer'

KEN BRUEN

'dead serious and deadly accurate'

ANDREW VACHSS

LAST ORDERS

TONY BLACK

M^cNIDDER | &
GRACE

Published by McNidder & Grace
Bridge Innovation Centre,
Pembrokeshire Science and Technology Park,
Pembroke Dock SA72 6UN

First Published 2013

A catalogue record for this work is available from the
British Library.

ISBN: 978-0-85716-056-0

Designed by Obsidian Design

Printed and bound in England by CPI Group (UK) Ltd,
Croydon CR0 4YY

Last Orders –
an anthology of short fiction

Last Orders

a Gus Dury story

'We spend our lives in flight from
all that is painful and real.'

Paul Sayer, *The God Child*

I thought I'd seen it all. Maybe that's why I couldn't
bring myself to open my eyes. I was lying in bed at my
Easter Road flat-cum-kip house when I heard the postie
rattle the slot and drop some mail onto the mat below. I had
a thought to test one eye on the clock but then routine, the
old leveller, kicked in. The days of posties showing before
2 p.m. in this city were well over so the only question
kicking me out of bed during daylight hours was who the
fuck could be interested in writing to me?

I shifted onto my side, provoked an ear-splitting cough
that sent knives stabbing at my lower back. My first thought
was to reach for a smoke, but I could see the soft-pack of
Marlboros crumpled on the floor by the scuffed foot of the
dresser. I was all out of luck again.

It was cold. I felt the chill from the loose, condensation-
wet windowpanes on my bare shoulders. A shiver passed
through me – my mother would have said someone was

walking over my grave and the way my chest felt I wouldn't have argued the toss; I could already be in it.

I was rubbing the outside of my arms, trying to suggest some warmth into my pasty-white Scottish limbs as I caught sight of a mirror to mirror reflection. My heart started as I imagined the image was of someone else in the room with me. When sense returned I realised the door to the wardrobe had my back on display as I clocked myself in the dresser mirror. I was shocked by how prominent the gnarled length of my spine looked, sticking out at sharp angles, like a bust bike-chain lying twisted in the gutter. I turned and took in the toast-rack chest and the full hit of high-ribs exposed like tiger's stripes down my sides.

'Jesus, Dury ...' I mouthed towards the gaunt, coughing cadaver in front of me. 'I've seen more fat on a chip.'

I reached for the Wranglers hanging on the chair's back and slotted myself into them. They felt loose, the old leather belt settling on the last notch. I couldn't face the prospect of catching another glimpse of myself, so covered up fast with an old Nike hoodie and headed for the door.

There had been a time, back in the day, when I had a dog that would have been wagging his tail at the sight of me. The thought of the rescue dog I'd christened *Usual* – a name he picked up at the pub – dug at my heart. My ex-wife had claimed him; said I wasn't fit to look after myself, never mind an animal. I couldn't argue with that.

There were two letters on the mat. I opted first for the manila oblong that spelled business-post, or worse, a bill. I liked to get bad news out the way. I ripped into the top and tore out the white letter; an NHS logo was the first thing to grip me. It wasn't a demand for cash, I was relieved at that, but I could afford this demand less:

'Blah, blah ...' I read, 'requests your attendance at the Hypertension Clinic.'

My blood pressure was through the roof. The result of a damaged liver and a scarred heart. Apparently, the letter stated, I needed bi-monthly checks at the clinic to make sure I wasn't going to cark it.

'Christ, no ...'

I scrunched the paper in my hand. If there was one thing in the world I couldn't handle it was hospitals. I had too many bad memories of seeing the ones I had loved there; and they weren't out-weighed by the good memories of seeing the ones I definitely didn't love going there, usually at speed.

I threw the ball of the letter at the wall, it bounced back and rolled its way down the carpet towards the bedroom.

'Fucking Hypertension Clinic ...'

The second missive was a mystery. It was the same shape as the first, but a long white envelope this time. I checked the franking over the stamp and recognised it came from East Ayrshire.

'Burns Country ...' I was scoobied, knew not a soul there.

I tore in. The letter inside was on cream paper, thick and water-marked, obviously expensive. The hand looked careful, not quite copperplate but in the ball-park.

I felt my pulse quicken as I read. Don't know why, maybe it was something about the tone. If I had to go for a tag, I'd say: reverential.

The opener was a *Dear Mr Dury* – couldn't say I liked that. When I see the honorific in there, I start thinking someone's confused me with my father. The bold Cannis Dury was no man to be confused with.

I read on:

I hope you will forgive the impertinence of my enquiry but your name was forwarded to me as a man who may be able to assist in my most desperate hour ...

I rolled eyes to the ceiling. It was the *Help me Obi-Wan, you're my only hope* line again. This was happening more and more now. My reputation going before me. I'd been a good hack, handled some big stories but that was behind me. How I got lumbered with the investigator for hire rep was something I couldn't work out. Life was funny that way, though. Man plans, God laughs.

... I will, of course, meet all necessary expenses and you will not find me ungenerous in this regard. I shall spare you the formality of details at this juncture and await your telephone call at my Edinburgh Hotel.

He was staying at The Balmoral. The only place in town that stationed a fawning, kilted, Glengarry-wearing twat on the door. 24-7 this stereotypical shortbread-tin evacuee tugged forelock for the likes of Sean Connery and the dour millionairess who wrote about that bloody boy wizard.

'Elegant slumming, it has to be said.'

I looked at the cream-coloured paper once more, felt confused enough to scratch my head but resisted. I didn't know whether to be petrified by the haughty tone or flattered by the potential Wonka ticket in my mitt.

I drew a still breath, exhaled. The interior of the flat was so cold I could see the white cloud escaping my lungs.

The telephone number for The Balmoral was written beside the name – Urquhart. It didn't ring any bells, but there were a few strings of my curiosity being tugged. I trousered the letter and made my way back to the bedroom to get suited and booted. There couldn't be any harm in a call and it wasn't like I was flat-out, or even had something else to do.

I'd flung my Crombie over the back of the couch the night before; as I retrieved it now I could see it was covered in all the dust and crap that the hoover didn't reach. I needed a coat-brush. Fuck it, I needed a hoover. The coat looked just the job, for a jakey; as I tied a scarf around my neck I could already sense the stares. Ones that said 'low-life'. There was a time I might have been rattled, cared even. Not now. I pointed my Docs in the direction of the door and got moving.

We had some weather, the usual Edinburgh kind. If it wasn't rain, it was the threat thereof. I looked up to the grey skies and crossed Easter Road between the gridlocked traffic. I was headed for the Coopers Rest pub, couldn't say it held any special attraction for me. It was a Hibs bar through and through and, being painted green and white, didn't wear its credentials lightly. I'd been drawn to it lately because of the actions of a cheeky Jambo roadworker. He'd set the winning Scottish Cup scoreline – Hearts' 5-1 drubbing of Hibs – into the tarmac with a mosaic of chalk chips. I wasn't a Hearts supporter myself but I was a big fan of chutzpah in all its guises.

A slow-blinking old bluenose was hocking up a dose of phlegm for the pavement, directing it carefully with a hanging drip from his drooping lower lip. I could see this taking off, like the Heart of Midlothian on the Royal Mile. We'd have Japanese tourists filming themselves here before long. I smiled at the irony on my way through the door.

There were one or two old soaks propping up the bar, hardy enough old boys with tractor tracks cut in their brows. One of them had a nose you could open a bottle with, a heavy physique that had once been impressive but had now gone south. He was supping a pint of Tartan and tapping the top of a pack of Berkeley Superkings that made him a metronome for the smoking ban. I ordered up a pint.

'Guinness, please ...' My eyes flicked onto auto-pilot and chased the line of optics all the way down to the low-flying birdie. 'And a double Grouse chaser.'

The barman nodded, said, 'You're as well hung for a sheep as a lamb.'

I didn't answer. The early moments upon entering a Scottish pub are a telling time. If you give away too much, you're liable to be engaged in chat. I was in no mood to pass the time of day about the state of the nation and the Tories' role in robbing us all blind or what seventies telly-star was going to be next on the sex-offenders register.

I took my drinks and headed for the corner of the bar. The pint of dark settled a craving, greeting me like an old friend. I was eyeing the wee goldie when I heard the hinges of the front door sing out.

A middle-aged man, tallish and heavy-set, stood in the lee of the door and looked unsure of himself. He was wearing a wax jacket, mustard-coloured corduroys and brogues. His type have a name for the colour: ox-blood. I was wearing Docs, same colour, but I call them cherry. Go figure.

I put the bead on him, knew at once he was Urquhart. My hand went up, slowly.

He nodded, then looked upward. I could tell he wanted to bolt, turn on his heels, throw up his hands. In the days of Empire, I'd be flogged for failing to look the part. That's when I noticed the tweed cap in his hands. He twisted it like he was wringing the neck of a pheasant on some country estate. Everything about him boiled my piss. I'm working class, c'mon, it's in the contract.

He strolled over; his voice was high and full of affectation. 'Mr Dury, I have come a long way and ...'

'Stop right there.'

His eyes ducked into his head.

'Call me Gus. I hear the mister in there, I think you're after money, or worse.'

He looked to the ceiling again. Huffed. Was that a tut?

I let it slide. I sensed his distaste at the way I talked, not my accent, though that was bad enough – heavy on the Leith – what got him was what riled teachers in school, made them say, 'The temerity!'

I motioned him to sit; the barman brought over a bottle of mineral water that Urquhart had ordered and placed it on the table with a few coins of change beside it.

I eyeballed him as he pocketed the money; could tell we weren't going to get along, we were too close to polar opposites. I said, 'Your letter didn't tell me much.'

He checked himself; two yellow tombstones bit down on his lower lip. His pallor was grey as concrete. His reply came slowly, 'I believe you are a man of some ... reputation.'

I allowed myself a blink. But no more. I feared if I gave in to temptation I'd be exposed as a man laughing himself up.

He went on, 'You have, I understand, some background.'

'*Background*?' I was scoobied.

'I took the liberty of, oh what's the demotic? Checking you out.'

The hand again. I blocked his words. I was acting out old habits. 'And how did you manage that?'

He shifted in his seat, started to unzip the front of his wax jacket. As he became more settled, he removed his scarf, revealing a dog collar. Suddenly my previous question lost its relevance.

'You're Church?'

'I am, yes, Church of Scotland ... that makes a difference?'

The short answer was, 'Yes', the easy one was, 'Should it?'

He said: 'That would be an ecumenical matter.'

I picked up my pint again, supped, said, 'I believe you're right. Perhaps we should skip it and get down to business.'

'Indeed.'

His full name was Callum Urquhart. A Church of Scotland minister from the East Ayrshire town of Cumnock.

The place had once been a thriving mining town, I knew Keir Hardie had been a union organiser there once, but that was quite some time before Thatcher got her hooks into the miners and started to dismantle 'society'.

Urquhart seemed agitated and eager to offer an explanation. 'I'm a little unsettled,' he said.

'How come?'

'I have what you might call, no good reason to be here.'

'Should I get my coat?'

'No. No. Please, if you'll indulge me, Mr Dury.'

I raised brows. '*Gus*.'

'Of course ... Gus.'

He played with the lid on his mineral water, Highland Spring, *still*. Sparkling just too exciting an option. 'I have reason, but in no way can it be described as good.' He sighed, 'I have a daughter and she is no longer contactable through the proper channels.'

The proper channels ... he spoke of his daughter like he was some ponytailed ad-man at a PowerPoint presentation.

He went on. 'I'm afraid, she has, erm, well ... it's rather embarrassing, gone missing.'

Embarrassing? Somehow, that didn't seem the right word. A daughter gone from home was a cause for sleepless nights, not a cause for losing face. I eyed him cautiously over my pint, gave him some more rope.

'She got herself mixed up with the wrong crowd some time ago. My parish is a very poor community, we once had some settled prosperity but it's long gone and I'm afraid in its wake came some rather extreme views.'

I knew pit communities had it tough, they lost their livelihood so an old bitch could prove a point. Some got paid off, a few grand to piss up the wall, they called them six-month millionaires. It didn't sound like a recipe for strong community.

'Extreme?' I said.

'Well, yes ... anarchists.'

'Go on ...'

He poured out his mineral water, drank deep, he had quite a thirst on him now. I knew the territory. 'My daughter, Caroline, she was a very wilful child and ...'

'Whoa, back up ... was? What makes you think we're talking past-tense here, Minister?'

He bridled, removed a handkerchief and wiped his palms. 'A figure of speech, I have no reason to believe ... I mean, I have nothing to go on, Gus, that is why I have come to you.'

I'd say one thing for him, he had my attention. These days, my situation, wedded to a bottle of scoosh and forty, scrub that, sixty, smokes a day, that was no mean feat. I pressed him for some details and made a mental note.

'I'll need five-hundred in advance and another five when I conclude.'

'Conclude?'

'That's right ... I don't have a crystal ball, Minister. If I go digging, what I find is what I find. What I get is a grand for my trouble. Do we understand each other?'

He nodded and took out a cheque book.

I bit. 'Cash.'

'I'll have to go to a bank.'

'Then, let's.'

I drained my pint and rose from the table.

On the way out the door, Urquhart placed a hand on my elbow and spoke softly, 'One more thing, I neglected to mention ...'

'Yeah?'

'My daughter, I believe, is ... with child.'

The newspapers had been full of scare stories coming out of the hospitals. We had a swathe of superbugs rampaging through them. Resistant to treatment, so the red-tops said, it was a new plague. Before I tired of the endless wanky grandstanding of millionaire comedians – and the TV set got taken to Crack Converters – I'd watched a rare documentary about the issue. Doctors were in the clear, apparently, and so were nurses; the blame was being planted firmly at the feet of immigrant workers. I'd been a hack and knew a beat-up story when I heard one. Papers played to the gallery as much as anyone else and the country was bankrupt so we had to find someone to blame all our ills on. Everyone needs a scapegoat. Welcome to Scotland, scapegoats a speciality, we've a history littered with them.

The last time I'd been in hospital was far from voluntary. I'd been drunken insensate and mowed down by a mobility scooter with a Ferrari upgrade. I couldn't remember being admitted, only waking up with a drip in my arm and a banging in my head Ringo would have been proud of. I'd got up and walked. I don't do hospitals as a rule. I didn't make the rule, it was made for me the day my ex-wife miscarried our only child.

I traipsed through the main doors of the Royal Infirmary and picked out the maternity ward. It was all depressingly familiar to me. The memory of Debs's slow, fragile gait towards the door on the day we left, childless, stung me. She had managed to get all the way to the car without tears but the sight of the empty babyseat in the back had brought on a gale of sorrow. I still felt that day's chill wind blowing all around me now.

I shook myself and approached a nurse as she passed me in the corridor, 'Hello, there …'

She eyed me with suspicion, the result of my tramp-like appearance no doubt, said, 'Yes.'

'I was wondering if you might be able to help me.'

I fell into the gaze of a full head-to-toe eyeball, 'Visiting hours are six till eight.'

'No, sorry, I'm not visiting. I'm just looking for someone.'

'Looking for someone?'

'Yes, a girl ... her name's Urquhart and she's about sixteen.' I knew her father must have tried the place already and the chances of her using her own name were slim to none, but chanced it. And with nothing else to go on, I needed to start somewhere.

The nurse twisted her face to the side, surveyed me over slit eyes. 'Are you a relative?'

She was suspicious, likely even onto me. But the boat was out now so I pushed it further, 'Yes. I'm her brother.'

As soon as the words came out I saw at once she wasn't buying them. I might have been able to pass for her brother once but the sauce had added a few years to the dial of late. Knew I should have said uncle; Caroline was only sixteen, after all.

'Do you have any identification?' said the hard-faced nurse.

I stalled, reached into the inside pocket of my Crombie. 'Can I show you a picture?' Urquhart had supplied a photo, a few years old I'd say. Caroline was still in school uniform, one of those dreadful posed, say-cheese numbers that everyone has tucked away in a sideboard at their parents' home. Not me, though, all I have tucked away at my parents' home are skeletons.

The nurse took the photograph from me, looked at it, said, 'This girl has red hair.'

'Yeah?'

'And bright-blue eyes.'

'You caught that.'

'If you and her are related ... I'm a monkey's uncle.'

I snatched back the picture, there was a line and she'd just crossed it. 'Are you in charge here?'

'I'm the ward sister.' I didn't know what that meant exactly, but I sure as hell knew a fucking jobsworth when I saw one.

'Well, look, *sister*, this young lass is missing. Her father is very concerned and if I don't find her soon who's to say what might happen to her.'

Hands on hips, I got hands on hips from her. 'I'm calling the police.'

'Y'*what*?'

A hand came off one hip and a finger got pointed at me. 'If you're not off this ward, and out of this hospital in the next thirty seconds, I'm calling the police.'

I focussed on the short, scrubbed fingernail beneath my nose and slowly pocketed the photograph. 'Nice bedside manner you have there.'

The same finger was pointed to the door. 'Out!'

I turned, and fired out a parting shot. 'Don't worry, I'm gone.'

As I went there was a torrent of words whipping my back, I caught only a few but they were enough.

'Come in here stinking of drink ... The state of you, as well ... Think I was born yesterday.'

I knew in a flicker I'd reached the end of one line of inquiry.

There was a time in my life when I was full of piss and vinegar. Lately, I'd lost some of the vinegar, if not my craving for the other. I headed to The Artisan pub on London Road, feeling slightly more comfortable back in my own neck of the woods.

The Artisan could have been renamed The Utilitarian. It had no style, which was just my style. I ordered a pint of dark from the dour barmaid who seemed more than annoyed to have to put her nail file down and return to the taps.

'Anything else?' She was Polish, that much I clocked right off. Her countrymen had developed a reputation in town for being as miserable as the natives – I wondered if they'd brought that with them or picked it up by osmosis?

'Yeah, put out a wee birdie?'

'A what?'

'Grouse ... double.'

I took my drinks and checked the clock on the way to the other side of the bar. My Docs were sticking to the carpet with every other step. When I sat down there was a pair of old jakes to my side, they were gambling on an iPad – the Paddy Power site taking the place of the ScotBet up the road.

I was shaking my head and wondering about the state of the universe, the disruption of chi that showered billions on a few Internet entrepreneurs and ass-fucked the rest of us, when I caught sight of a familiar face making his way towards me.

Fitz the Crime stationed himself at the bar momentarily and then eased himself off his elbow. He was shaking his head as he approached my table, 'Christ, where do they find them?' he said.

I nodded. 'The city has a great shortage in hospitality staff, Fitz ... haven't you heard?'

'Hospitality, is that what they're calling it. Christ, yer wan couldn't bloody spell it.'

He was still shaking his head as his pint arrived, deposited on a Tartan beer mat, a few millilitres of suppage evacuating over the edge like a prod for him.

'Fucking hell ... you see that?'

'You could ring out the mat, I suppose ...'

He didn't like that. 'I'll ring your neck if you're not careful.'

Fitz the Crime and I went way back. In my time on the paper I'd kept a couple of his indiscretions out of the headlines. Plod tends to turn a blind eye to its own lot's peccadilloes in private, but seeing them in print is a whole other matter. There was a time when he was grateful but it didn't last long. I'd well and truly overstretched the favour with my own subsequent requests for payback. Fitz had arked up and reminded me just who carried the weight in the relationship, but to his credit, he also displayed an unerring sense of justice that seemed out of all proportion with the world we currently lived in.

'How's the family?' I said.

He put down his pint and thinned eyes. 'What are ye after?'

I smiled; it forged itself into a low laugh. 'Did someone steal your toffee today, mate?'

The pint was raised again, a longer draught taken this time. 'No, I am just what you might call inveterately suspicious by nature ... especially when the bold Gus Dury contacts me for a fly pint when there has been no contact since ...'

He trailed off, eyes chasing a ghost about the ceiling. We didn't need to reference our shared past to know why sometimes it was better to ignore each other for long periods. Edinburgh was a small city, its Medieval streets winding and personal, but it was also a topography that favoured the incognito when they most needed it.

'Look, I need your help ...'

He turned his gaze on me. 'I thought as much.'

'It's not a big favour for you, but it's a big favour for me and a big favour for ...'

I filled him in on Callum Urquhart and his missing daughter. I laid it on as thick as I was capable. Fitz was a father, he had the territory of the heart well and truly mapped from experience.

'By the holy, it's my bollocks in a jar ye want,' he said. I let him settle, grab a hold of himself.

'I'd be happy enough with you running the girl through the system ... she's sixteen, Fitz.'

He shook his head. 'I heard you.'

'And pregnant ... did you hear that bit?'

He raised his pint again, the remaining dark liquid was a mere swirl in the bottom of the glass. His heavy thud shook the table as he let down his drinking arm. 'I said I heard, didn't I?'

Fitz started to rise, he put a finger in the empty pint glass and returned it to the edge of the bar. The barmaid watched over her nail file but didn't move. Fitz was doing up the front of his coat and staring towards the street as he spoke again.

'Urquhart, you say ...'

'Caroline, yeah. But she might not be using that name.'

He set back his shoulders and exhaled breath. 'She's sixteen, Gus, in my experience they're rarely the most forward thinking.'

'So, you'll have a squint?'

He put his hands in his pockets, looked like a car-salesman trotting out on the forecourt to flog Puntos. 'Keep your phone handy, I'll only call the once.'

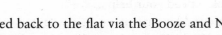

I schlepped back to the flat via the Booze and News on London Road. There was a far superior offie on Easter Road but my tastes were not elaborate, even with the fair wedge in my back-pocket that I'd taken from Urquhart.

Something wasn't sitting right with me. He was church, from that section of society that did things by the book. The filth was the obvious option for a bloke like him but Fitz hadn't heard of a missing schoolgirl who was up the peg. I wondered where the minister had got my details, but then I dismissed it: where did anyone?

I put my order in to the chick on the till. 'Case of Sweetheart and a pack of Silk Cut.'

She looked at me like I'd made a mistake. Did she remember the night before's order? Surely she was used to me changing my brand of tabs; I couldn't stick to anything.

'You're on the Silkies, now?' she said.

'Bit of a sore throat ...' It was a lie and I think she knew it. The letter from the Hypertension Clinic had put a bit of a fright on me. Maybe the trip out to the Royal was the lolly-stick in the dog turd I needed to keep me from stepping right in the shit.

'Okay,' she said, smiling.

I took the blue and white striped carrier from her and headed for the door.

My flat was cold and dark, even the shadeless 100-watt bulb in the hall wasn't enough to illuminate the grimness of the place. I took my cans through to the lounge and cracked one open. They were sweet, like they said on the tin. A tin that hadn't changed since my boyhood, I recalled a time when Hogmanay meant a sip from a can of Sweetheart Stout. The young woman on the front with the tight orange sweater was still smiling out like we were all waiting for the White Heather Club to begin.

I sparked a tab and checked my mobi. No missed calls, but there was one I needed to make. I selected the number from my contacts and dialled.

Ringing.

'Hello, is that you, Amy?'

'Gus ..?' she sounded surprised.

'How are you getting on?'

'Is this, like, a social call?' Answering a question with a question was so Amy.

'Well ... yes and no.'

A little chill entered the line. I took a sip on my stout.

'Well, it has to be one or the other ... do you remember what I said to you?'

I suddenly felt the Sweetheart Stout wasn't going to cut it. 'I told you that was all a lot of bullshit ... Amy, trust me, you were never going to be just a back-up plan for when things didn't work out with Debs.'

'Oh, really?' The tone was sarcastic, dipping perilously close to animosity. If I'd hurt the girl I hadn't a plan to. Jesus, what did I know about plans?

'Yes, really.'

'Well, you might not have consciously planned to ...'

I cut her short. 'Look, Amy ... Everyone has a plan until they get punched in the face.'

'Is that a quote or something?'

'Yeah, Tyson ...'

'Do you know any other feminists, Gus?'

She had me. 'Okay, bad example.' I stubbed out my cigarette. 'Can we start again?'

'*What*?' her voice rose like a foghorn.

'I mean this conversation ... just the conversation.' The line fizzed. I let a few seconds of static collect. 'Amy, how about it?'

She sighed into the receiver, 'Okay. I'm all ears.'

'Great. I was hoping you'd say that because I could really do with your help.'

'Sounds ominous.'

'I wouldn't ask if there was anyone else.'

'Sounds even more ominous.'

I could see I'd caught her in one of those moods, played the placatory hand. 'How about a drink ... tomorrow?'

'Where?'

It wasn't going to be in my manor and I didn't fancy the trip out to Lothian Road where she was. 'How about Deacon Brodie's, around mid-day ...'

'Christ, if you're going that touristy why don't we just go to the Sherlock Holmes?'

'It's smack-bang in the centre ... I was thinking of the ease and convenience.'

She laughed me up. 'Holy shit, Gus, you'll be buying Hush Puppies next!'

'Yeah, whatever.'

'And putting a door in the bath.'

'Yeah, good one.'

'Getting a fucking stairlift and a Big Slipper ...'

She was on a roll. I cut her off, said, 'See you there, Amy.'

Hung up.

———✦———

I spent the night supping Sweetheart and staring at the wall. I only interrupted this pattern of events to delve into a book and chug on the odd Silkie. I could hardly manage a decent draw so told myself the fags couldn't be doing too much damage. The reading I wasn't so sure about. I'd once had a houseful of paperbacks but was now reduced to doing all my reading on the screen of a Kindle. I'd been resistant at first – books were like vinyl to me, each one had history: a time and a place they were purchased, a memory of the first play or read to regale with – but now I was swept along with the convenience of a mobile library in my pocket.

I started to devour works I'd never contemplate in paperback: *War and Peace, Parts One and Two*; *The Communist Manifesto*; classics by the barrel-load. They were all free, but I couldn't help but wonder how, or why?

When vinyl went, we lost the musos. They were replaced by boy-bands and talent-show shite. It was as if the world didn't have a place for the artist anymore. Or at least, didn't want to pay for them.

We'd just about lost journalism – my profession – to a kind of corporate PR. I wondered what was next? If we lost all the artists among us – those point men for the human race – we were truly fucked. Except the corporations, of course. Jesus, it was like *The Player* all over again: '*If we can just do away with these actors ... I think we'll really be onto something!*'

I had no thought for breakfast and the last of the tins of stout lay crushed and empty on the floor. The coffee craving was on me, though, so I climbed into my Wranglers and looked for something to wear with them that wouldn't have Amy in stitches of laughter. Opted for an old Super-Dry flannel over a crisp white T-shirt. With the Crombie and the Docs I could have passed for a student – a very mature and misguided one. Perhaps just out of a marriage and trying to recapture some misspent youth. I didn't exactly want to run with the analogy.

In The Manna House I got myself a large black and felt my stomach turning at the thought of the sugary Danish on offer. Caffeine was all I needed, at this point of the day I would have mainlined it if I could. The friendly Italian at the counter knew better than to put chat on me, handed over my cup and change and smiled.

'You have a good day now,' he said.

'Cheers.' No matter how mid-Atlantic we all became, I couldn't resist a cringe sometimes. Would always be more comfortable with Scots insults dressed up as patter.

On the way to Deacon Brodie's pub on the Mile I checked my phone for any messages from Fitz: nothing. It was still early, and I'd only asked him yesterday, but I still felt a twinge of disappointment. It was a long-shot that he'd find anything on Caroline Urquhart and I knew it, but I had to ask. My *modus operandi* was always, turn over all the stones in the hope that you find the one with the gold key underneath.

The coffee was awakening the cold recesses of my brain that had been put out of action by the stout and the distraction of reading. I knew better than to brood on a case, you turned it over to the subconscious and let it work its own way out. All my actions seemed to have turned up, though, was more nagging uncertainties. I was missing something, not a piece of a puzzle exactly, more like the whole picture was blurred. I felt like I was approaching Caroline's disappearance from the wrong perspective but I had no clue what the right one was.

The Mile was as steep a climb as I remembered. The entire way sprinkled liberally with tourists dipping in and out of the tartan-tat stores. It had once been quite a thriving, lively place – for an open-air chocolate-box lid – but had now been turned into one, long outlet for cheap plastic trash from Chinese warehouses. Someone at the council must have been getting a good drink out if it, mind you, they seemed to open a new outlet every week.

At the pub I traipsed to the bar and ordered a pint of dark. I was a little bit early for Amy, which gave me just enough time to settle my nerves with a few pints. Before I got my jotters from the paper, Amy had been my Girl Friday. She was work experience, had a thing for old movies with journalists cracking big stories. Had a thing for old journalists too, but that's another story altogether. We never worked out because she couldn't comprehend my ties to my ex-wife.

I don't know what I expected from Amy, she had too few miles on the dial to understand. Christ, I was only coming round to the realisation that Debs losing the baby was such a big deal because it was also my one chance to right the wrongs with my father. And now I wasn't going to get another chance to prove I was nothing like him.

I wired into the Guinness and took up a copy of The Hun, which seemed to be replacing the Daily Ranger as the pub's paper of default. There was a story about Maggie Thatcher being sick.

'And that's fucking news is it?'

'Come again, mate?' The barman lit.

I rustled the paper at him. 'Says Thatcher's been in hospital ... nothing frivolous I hope.'

He mopped the bar top, grinned. 'She'll have been in for an oil-change, they took her heart out in the eighties.'

It was the only explanation I'd heard that made sense. I smiled and ordered a chaser, turned over to the sports pages.

On any given day of the week Amy will be dressed to impress. She sauntered in, white mules, white jeans (skin-tight) and a pillar-box red crop top that showed a stomach so flat you could eat your dinner off it. The diamanteé stud in her navel, you could argue was over the top, but who'd listen?

'Gus boy, how do?'

'Mair to fiddling.' That's a Scots spoonerism for you, does it have a meaning? Does anything?

Amy settled herself at the bar, ran her fingers through long black hair. She was a show stopper, men's eyes lit up like Chinese lanterns about the place.

She looked relaxed, any animosity for me was on the

down-low. I was delighted because I had no desire to rake over that old ground. One of my few remaining sources of pride was the fact that I'd trained Amy well at the paper. I was likely being overly-generous on myself, she was a natural. Amy had ways of getting to the bottom of things that I couldn't even fathom. And that's why – despite our recent history – I'd called her.

I said, 'I need your help?'

She leaned over the bar and ordered a rum and coke. She got the fastest service I'd ever seen. 'Yeah, help with what?'

'A case.'

A smile. Wide, a from-the-heart job. 'You're working on something ...'

'In a manner of speaking.'

'Well, that's great!'

'Calm down, I wouldn't get too excited about this one. Let's just say, I'm not overly optimistic of getting a result.'

'Work's work ... it beats staying at home and watching *Cash in the Attic*.'

'You've a better chance of scoring cash there, it has to be said. And I warn you, I don't see much scope for excitement.'

She sipped her drink, leaned towards me and planted a hand on my thigh. 'I'm an excitable girl! Try me.'

I removed her hand, she curled the red-talons round her glass again, threw her head back and laughed. It was Amy being Amy. When I gave her the details of the case, she mellowed and put on her serious face. I spelled out for her that I had some niggling concerns about just what was behind Urquhart's tale.

'You think he's hiding something?' she said.

'That I don't know.'

She shrugged at me, the immaturity of her years writ large on her face. 'He's a minister, though.'

I nearly laughed. 'There's no sin but ignorance.'

'Is that another quote?'

'Yes. It definitely is.'

I could see my point had registered. Amy was off her stool and tipping back the last of her drink, setting ice-cubes rattling on the side, before she slammed the glass down.

'Right, I'm on this,' she said. Amy was heading for the door as she spoke again. 'I'll be in touch,' she tipped her head and winked. 'I still have a few moves, you know.'

There wasn't a man in the pub she didn't convince with those words, as she clacked heels and turned for the door.

I set off down the Royal Mile, towards Abbeyhill. Downhill was a far easier schlep, I even got to fancying I might make some sense of things as I went. After all, hadn't Nietzsche said 'all truly great thoughts are conceived by walking'. He might even have been right. But I got as far as the Tron Kirk before I realised my only thought was for coffee to clear my head.

Time was, drinking on an empty stomach had been 'fries with that' to me but these days my body was waving the white flag. I abandoned my principles and ducked into Starfucks. A little protest group – one beardy student in a great-coat and flip-flops – stood outside with a banner blasting the firm for tax avoidance. I shook my head at the absurdity, but inwardly hoped he'd be picketing Jimmy Carr at festival time.

I put in my order and stood at the counter, waiting for them to ring up.

'Can I take your name, please?' said the yoof on the till.

'Y'what?'

Eyes rolled skyward, then a plastic smile. 'Your name ...'

I looked around, the queue was stretching to the door now. 'It's not a mortgage application, son ... it's a coffee.'

I felt a hand on my elbow. 'They write it on the cup, and call out your name.' It was a woman in a Boots uniform, she had the courtesy to pin down the corners of her mouth and shrug shoulders as she broke the news.

'Oh do they? ... I missed that meeting.'

The counter lad was frowning now, 'Sir, we're busy.'

I smiled, my best headlamp rictus. 'Please, call me Gus!'

I was stepping back from the counter, joining the 'collect your order here' queue as my mobi started ringing.

I recognised the caller ID.

'Fitz ...'

'How do?'

'Yeah, never better ...' He seemed unmoved by the politesse.

'Well, hold that thought because I'm about to piss on your parade.'

That was the thing with Fitz, he didn't do soft-soaping. 'I take it you ran a check on Caroline.'

He bit. 'Jesus, Dury, watch what yeer saying!'

He was always over-cautious about talking on the phone, there was no reason for it, apart from him having seen too many Bourne movies.

'Okay ... sorry. What have you got for me?'

'Do you want the good news or the bad?'

The way he was going, I wouldn't have predicted a choice. 'Well, I always like to get the bad news out the way first ...'

'Urquhart hasn't filed a missing persons for his daughter. That's the first hurdle right there. But on top of that, we've no trace of her ... Caroline isn't on our books for anything.'

With all my suspicions about Urquhart this didn't surprise me. What confused me no end was why he wanted me to find her at all. 'So, we've only his word to go on that she's even here ... It doesn't make sense.'

'Oh, she's here.'

'*What*?'

I felt a shove on my back and the queue edged forward, I was pressed against a large man in a sheep-skin coat who, from the back anyway, could have been a distant relation of the late Giant Haystacks.

'Christ Almighty ...' he said, his voice a low girlish teeter that didn't fit his scale.

'I'm sorry ...' Like I was arguing the toss.

'Gus ... Gus ... one large latte.'

I felt a wince inside me as an American accent mangled my name from behind the counter. A large paper cup was plonked down in front of me.

'Hope you enjoy your coffee, Gus.'

I didn't know whether to smile or chuck up at the sentiment. Went for a nod, paired with a conspiratorial wink that said I wasn't buying into all this false-bonhomie bullshit.

'Dury ... you still there?' Fitz sparked up on the end of the line.

'Yeah ... just grabbing a coffee.' I manoeuvred my way back onto the Mile, headed down for the crossing. 'Go on ... you were saying.'

'Caroline Urquhart is in Edinburgh ... or at least, someone her age and going by the same name is.'

'How do you know this if she's not on your books?'

He sighed, sounded like a lengthy explanation was beyond him. 'Because I ran her details with the Health Board as well ...'

'Jesus. That's a bit of a result.'

'It is and it isn't ... I don't have an address. She gave a homeless hostel as her address, but I checked with them and she's moved on.'

I stopped in my tracks. 'Shit.'

'Well, you'd think.'

'I hope you're going to tell me otherwise.'

'No, Gus, I have no idea where Caroline is.' He let a gap on the line stretch out between us and I felt my hopes evaporating, then, 'But if you have nothing better to do, I have an idea where you might, just might mind, catch a hold of someone who does.'

My feelings about being this deep in the heart of Leith were conflicted. I'd grown up here, but without the store of happy memories most people associate with childhood. Every street still hugged me like a returning son, I loved the place, I just couldn't bear being here for long.

Leith was changing, the old bricks and mortar buildings crumbling to decay and being ripped down. In their stead came the chrome and glass wank-itechture that was infesting the entire city. Most of the flats they flung up when money was cheap were unsaleable now but it didn't seem to stop them. Ever the eye to the main chance, or ever hopeful, I couldn't decide which.

I came off Commercial Street and took myself onto Lindsay Street. Fitz had given me the details of a midwife who worked out of Leith Mount. He didn't know her, or even of her. All he had was a name on a computer screen and a few details, some of which listed Caroline Urquhart as one of her patients.

There was a car park for the practice, I took a look for the white Micra that belonged to Janice Dawes, the midwife I was about to doorstep. Fitz had supplied the reg-number for her car so it was a simple matter of waiting for her to show. They were always on the go, these midwives, so with any luck I wouldn't have to wait long.

I found the car in the staff-parking bays and stationed myself under the overhang of the roof. I was sparking up a Silkie when the door to the practice wheezed open. It was an Asian woman, heavily-gone, and a doting husband holding the door for her. I couldn't halt the smile I had for them. Did I still want some of what they had? I didn't doubt it, but I knew that boat had sailed without me on it a long time ago.

I was on my fourth or fifth Silkie when the sound of comfortable shoes squelching on wet tarmac came towards me. It was a squat woman, not exactly heavy but not exactly doing the Dukan Diet either. She had that hard-won look, the one that gets some women tagged as *pushy*, or as we were prone to say in this neighbourhood, *not backwards at coming forwards*.

I watched her wrestle a bag into the passenger seat of her car and start to make her way round to the driver's door. She was opening up as I leaned over the roof.

'Hello, Janice is it?'

She thinned eyes. 'Yes.'

I tried a smile, for all the good it would do me. 'I was wondering if I might have a word with you.'

The aperture of her eyes returned to normal. She pulled her chin back into her neck, 'Do I know you?'

'No. I don't think so ...' I looked up to the heavens, tried to inveigh that familiar Scots expression of disgust for the weather. 'Looks like rain.'

I knew she'd caught me indicating the interior of the car, that's probably why she flicked the central-locking and walked round to my side of the vehicle.

'I'm not carrying any drugs, if that's what you're after.' Her tone was sharp, the look in her eyes nothing short of fierce. I pitied the poor junkie that would try jumping her.

I tried to laugh off the inference, even if it had been a particularly low blow to take. 'You have me all wrong; look, I really do need to have a talk with you ... about one of your patients.'

She looked perplexed now. The tight bun her hair was tied in seemed to grip her features into a more angular slant. 'What on earth are you on about?'

'Caroline Urquhart ...' I let the name hang between us like gunshot.

'Caroline ... Are you a relation?'

I'd tried and failed with that tack before. 'No. I'm employed by her father.'

'Her father ... she never mentioned any family.'

I could see I had her interest now; I waved a hand towards the car, held it out. 'That's a spit of rain ...'

I sensed cogs turning behind those steel-grey eyes of hers. She looked at me, then quickly back to the door of the practice she'd come out of. I could sense some concern for Caroline but I could also sense a huge dose of uncertainty for what the hell I was all about.

I stepped towards her, ramped it up. 'Look, I don't care what you think of me, but that girl and her baby need help; now either you're going to be the one to help her or we're relying on someone else out there being a very good Samaritan.'

She fiddled with the keys in her hand. She looked at me, in the eye, then averted her gaze towards the ground. A sigh, 'I haven't seen her in weeks.'

'How many?'

'Two, three ... maybe a bit longer. She just vanished ... I was very worried because she was in a bit of an emotional state.'

'How do you mean?'

'She was alone, apart from that boy, and she said she didn't plan to keep the child. She'd asked me about adoption straight away.'

'She had a boyfriend?'

The nurse's top lip twitched, she looked out to the medical practice again. 'I don't know, just a young lad. He didn't have a job, anyway. I think he was wary of Caroline coming to the hospital for some reason. The officialdom, the forms and so on ... they were both terrified of them.'

'And that worried you?'

The midwife tightened her brows and drew a deep breath, 'Yes, of course. She's due any day now, you realise.'

'*What*?'

'Yes. Very soon. I have to admit, I've been beyond worried for her ... what did you say your name was?'

I steered her back on course. 'Does it matter? ... Look, you must have an address for her?'

'A place down in the flats. I went there a few times but it's since been boarded up. I don't think anyone's living there. Do you think it was a squat, maybe?'

I nodded. 'Yeah, more than likely.'

The midwife started to tug at the sleeve of her jacket, she looked nervy now. I could see her demanding I report to Social Work with her if I gave her any more room for manoeuvre.

'Look, I really can't tell you any more,' she said.

I made to move, put my hands in my pockets. 'Just one more thing ... let me have the address and I'll be on my way.'

At one time, I'd taken to schlepping up Calton Hill to sit on a bench and watch the world go by. I admit it, I'd been known to take the odd tin or two along. On any given day, rain or shine, you could be guaranteed a host of tourists and locals alike. They were a distraction, but there was a way of avoiding them. If you got within spitting-distance of the National Monument you were screwed – and likely to be handed a camera, asked to take a photograph for someone – but there was a bench overlooking the Old Town that nobody went near.

So, I'd sit there, just clocking the sky and the concrete smear that was the city beneath. I'd become detached, near alpha-state; and that wasn't the tins.

It all went tits up for me when they started knocking the shit out of the place to develop a site next to the Cooncil offices. There was talk of turfing people out their homes with compulsory purchase orders. A Save Our Old Town campaign got going. It was Capitalism gone mad and I couldn't get my head around it. To say it soured the view was putting it mildly.

I left the bench alone when the diggers went in. The Scottish Government was putting a stop to cheap tins anyway, so that was gonna hit my recreational skite right on the head.

As I reached Leith's Banana Flats I wondered what the view was like from up there. That was the thing with Edinburgh, the scene was forever changing. You just never knew what was round the next corner. You thought you knew the place and then it surprised you with the news that, actually, you didn't know it at all.

The midwife had given me an address for a flat that was on a street I'd never known existed, and I grew up in Leith. When my brother and I were young enough to go bikes we played boneshaker over the cobbles. I couldn't see any kids nowadays doing that, unless you could get it on the Nintendo Wii.

The address was at the back of a winding row of properties that the builders had been slap-happy with.

It looked like an Airfix-kit scheme. There were tenements in the city standing the test of centuries but these boxy hovels looked to have passed their shelf-life about twenty years ago. The residents obviously agreed, ripping apart the ones that had already been burned out and chucking their charred contents on the street.

The walls were covered in graffiti. Tagging, mainly. You get your school of thought that this kinda thing ruins an area; me, I say, how much worse can they make it? Scrubbing it off's only turd polishing.

I took to a stair that smelled of piss. Even with all the windows panned in, the piss was still rank enough to make me want to chuck. I stuck my face behind my jacket and waded through the detritus of aerosols, needles and White Lightning bottles. The place I wanted was the last in the row; I wondered if it was truly the end of the road.

I could see why the nurse would think nobody lived here. I wouldn't – and I'm not the one stopping at The Balmoral. I pressed on the door's windowpane; there was no give, it wasn't opening up. As I looked in the letter box, a blast of damp hit me but I also detected some movement.

'Probably bloody rats ...'

I banged on the door.

Nothing.

Tried again on the windowpane.

A clang this time. Like a door closing.

I hollered in the letterbox, 'Caroline, is that you? My name's Gus, Gus Dury, your father asked me to find you.'

I put my ear to the slot.

There was no movement anymore. The place was grave-still – too still – I sensed there was someone in there. I toyed with the idea of putting my foot to the door when, suddenly, a whoosh of stale air came at me as the door's windowpane came through.

I caught a glance of a pot in flight.

I fell back.

My back smacked off the concrete landing just as I saw a blur of shaved head loom over me and cosh me across the face with a heavy fist.

Next thing I saw was the dancing canaries.

'Hello, can you hear me? Hello ... hello.'

My head felt like Chewbacca had taken a dump in there. I was still on my back as I opened my eyes to find a young boy looming over me with dark panda eyes.

'Can you hear me?' His Converse All-Stars slapped at the landing as he padded about my supine form.

'Yeah. Just, maybe lower the volume.' I turned my gaze away, leaned up on one arm and caught sight of the pot that had come through the window. I kicked out at it, sent it skidding down the landing.

The lad spoke, 'Are you okay? Can you move?'

I tried to steady myself but everything was spinning. 'I think so.'

'Would you like to come inside?'

'What?' I felt weary. 'Did you chuck the pot?'

He shook his head, theatrically. 'Oh, God, no ...' He leaned over and tried to help me to my feet.

My knees caved. I stumbled a little, then found some balance. I leaned into the lad and headed through the door. He sat me on an old crate, an orange velour cushion the only concession to comfort.

The lad spoke. 'I don't know who that was chucking the pot ... they come and go, you know. He was edgy, must have been on the run or something.'

He wasn't the only one. 'And who are you?' I rubbed at

my head, checked my fingertips. There was a line of blood. I felt beyond my hairline, the damage seemed minimal.

'I'm Craig. I was staying here, for a bit. I just came back to collect a few things.'

I knew the accent wasn't local, but I couldn't place it. If Ayrshire was like a condensed version of Glasgow then I could be onto something.

'Are you with Caroline?' I said.

Craig brought me a wet cloth, said, 'There's no ice. Sorry.'

I nearly laughed. 'I wouldn't have expected it. You've not much of anything.'

He gripped his palms together, looked at the floor. 'It's a squat ... what do you expect?'

I could feel some semblance of normalcy returning. At least the brighter lights had gone out, although a few dark motes still crossed my eyes.

'So ... Caroline?'

He turned away, 'How do you know her?'

I ran the wet towel over the back of my neck and tried to stand. I'd regained some balance, at least the room had stopped swaying. 'What does that matter? Look, she's pregnant and about to give birth, she should be in hospital.'

Craig's slightly-camp demeanour vanished in a second; he turned, tried to rush past me, but I found just enough strength to grab his arm.

He gasped, 'Let go of me.'

I felt breathless, dizzy. The sudden exertion was a step too far.

'Oh, fuck.'

Craig shrieked, 'Jesus you're bleeding hard.'

The pain shot through me, head to toe, seemed to touch every fibre of my being. This time there was no stopping my guts turning over. I chucked on the floor.

'I think you should have your head looked at ...'

'You're not the first person to tell me that, Craig.'

My stomach tightened again, I retched again. I was toppling onto one knee as Craig reached out for me.

'I think you're the one that needs the hospital,' he said.

I looked up, caught his eyes. 'Trust me ... Caroline needs it more.'

Something sparked in him and I had it down as humanity. If this was the bad influence my minister employer had spoken about then he needed to go back to his Bible and check his facts.

'Craig, please, take me to Caroline ... before it's too late.'

We went from a squat to a flea-pit one-bedroom flat in Gorgie. It was an old tenement that had been sub-divided so many times the bathroom was in a hall cupboard and the kitchen squashed along one wall of the living room. The heavy hardwood doors and exposed floorboards added a false air of faded grandeur to the place that a few years ago must have been close to the condemned list. TV's property porn had a lot to answer for, they'd be reselling us avocado sinks as trendy must-haves soon enough.

Craig had got twitchy in the taxi on the way over, seemed to want to confide something in someone – it didn't turn out to be me. I was still scoobied about his role in all of this when he introduced me to Caroline where she sat on the sofa in the midst of her duvet-day. She was a pretty girl with a wide, trusting face. The red hair from her photograph was now subdued by a darker blonde, but the piercing blue eyes still shone.

'Hello, Caroline ...'

She clocked me and then her eyes darted to Craig, who held up his hands in histrionic style.

'Don't even go there ...' he said, shifting hands to hips. 'He's nothing to do with me.'

Craig went over to fluff up Caroline's pillows. 'She's warned me about bringing men back, you know.'

'Oh ...' The confirmation that he was gay just added to my confusion.

'You pair aren't together then?' I said.

Caroline grabbed back her pillow, pushed Craig's fussing hands away. 'No, we're just good friends.'

If that was meant to be funny I wasn't laughing. This girl was a heavily pregnant runaway that her father had hired me to find. Now I'd set eyes on her I wanted some answers, but I sensed they weren't going to be the ones I expected.

I could see Caroline and Craig had set up home together in Poor Street and the idea didn't seem to appeal much to either of them. The impending delivery seemed to be weighing heavily, in more ways than one, on Caroline who looked to be near the end of her tether with worry.

'You should know, your father hired me to find you.'

Silence.

Craig pressed his back to the wall and slid down to the floor; Caroline had him in her gaze but he didn't look up as he buried his head in his hands.

'Craig ...' she said. Her stare flitted between her friend and myself. 'What's going on?'

I took a step forward, sat on my haunches beside her. 'Craig has nothing to do with why I'm here, I found him at the squat and didn't give him much choice but to bring me here.'

'Some mad Weejie cracked a pot over his head!' said Craig.

Caroline thinned her eyes and mumbled towards Craig,

'Bloody Florence Nightingale effect works on you every time.'

Craig pursed his lips, 'Hey, I don't hear you complaining about me nursing you!'

I felt trapped in a surreal sit-com. I rose to my feet again. 'Look, is somebody going to tell me what the hell is going on here?'

The earlier silence was joined by a rolling tumbleweed.

I pitched up the volume. 'Right, I have just about enough brain-cells left to suss that something's not as it appears here, but I'll be fucked if I can pin the tail on the donkey, so one of you better start talking or I'm on the blower to daddy ...'

Caroline kicked off the duvet; rising from the sofa was a struggle in her condition but she managed to find her feet before the red-cheeked anger subsided from her face. 'No! You can't!'

I repositioned myself a few feet away from her, she had a crazy look in her eye now and I didn't want her to hurt herself lunging for me.

'Caroline, calm yourself ...' I said.

'We came here to get away from him.' Her eyes filled with tears, she was sobbing as Craig appeared at her side and placed a comforting arm around her shoulders.

'I showed them my palms, tried to reel-in any earlier threat I'd put out. 'Okay, okay ... don't get upset.'

Craig picked up a stray vibe from Caroline and went from placid to belligerent in a blink. 'You've no idea what she's been through with him ... '

His words seemed to set Caroline off again, her lower lip went into spasm and she sobbed. 'I can't see him ... I just can't ...'

I looked back to the door, touched the sides of my mouth and wondered if I could have created more panic with a hand-grenade. When my mobi started to ring the situation went atomic.

'Who's that?' yelled Craig.

I took out my phone, I could see it was Amy. 'It's just my friend ...'

Caroline joined in the yelling, added in some more sobs. 'Don't let him speak to my dad ...'

'It's not him,' I said. 'Look, I'll ding the call.'

I pressed cancel on the phone, but at once I knew it was too late. Caroline creased up, she bent over and then her knees folded beneath her. The yell she let out went back all the way to my ancestors in Africa.

'Oh, shit,' said Craig. 'Oh, shit ... oh, shit ...'

He patted her back, tried to get her to stand.

'What is it?' I said.

'*What is it?*' snapped Craig. 'She's having the baby.'

———✦———

The ambulance ride out to the Royal passed in unreal fashion. There was some fuss getting Caroline fastened into the stretcher – her belly getting in the way – then some more when the paramedics refused to take both Craig and myself. In the end, I got the seat, because they figured my head needed looking at; I was already running out of quips for this.

I got a call out to Amy, told her where we were heading. She said she was jumping in a taxi right away.

'I tried to call earlier,' she said.

'Yeah, well, you could say I had my hands full ...'

'I see that.'

Curiosity got the better of me. 'What was it anyway?'

'I've got some news for you but it'll keep ... it's the kind of thing that's better delivered in person anyway.'

I hung up, intrigued.

When they wheeled Caroline in she was panting and gasping – I could hear her even behind the oxygen mask – it didn't look a good sign. Neither did her slapping fists off the mattress. I was less fazed when I started to hear some of the screams from the maternity ward: I imagined a Guantanamo Bay waterboarding session sounded much the same.

'Will she be okay?' I asked as they wheeled her away.

There was no answer save the boilerplate, 'She's pregnant.'

As I watched her go, some bright spark in blue-green scrubs put a wheelchair down in front of me and motioned 'in'.

I frowned, 'No chance. I walk fine.'

I managed two steps before my knees went. Seems I'd been running on my last reserves of adrenaline.

'Like I thought, that gash tells a different story,' he said. 'How much blood did you lose?'

I touched my head, felt the dried and crusty wound on my fingertips. The blood had seeped all the way down into my shirt collar, I traced more all the way to my waistband. 'Would you like me to estimate in millilitres?'

'Looks like you took quite a clatter.' If this dude was a doctor, I figured he should be putting his skills to use on someone who needed them.

I wanted to play wide, say, 'No shit, Sherlock.' But went with a peacemaker, 'Yes, quite a clatter.'

They spent half an hour or so patching me up. The wound in my head needed stitches and I landed a nice Rab C-style head bandage to complete the look of a complete jakey.

I was woozy, maybe a little drugged, when Amy brought in the news: 'She had a little girl.'

I tried to smile, but my head hurt too much, 'You know

she's not keeping the kid ...'

Amy bit her lip, nodded. 'Yeah, she said ... I could hardly blame her.'

'What ... is everything okay?'

Amy moved towards the edge of the bed, sat. 'She's fine ... been chirping away like a budgie.'

I tried to sit up but the tight, white linen constricted me, 'What about?'

Amy put on her shit-stopping serious look, 'It's not pretty, Gus ... Not in any way.'

I motioned to my head, 'Do I look like someone who needs sugar-coating?'

Amy stood up quickly, seemed agitated. She took off her coat and put it over the chair by the bed. The place was like a furnace, I couldn't fault her for that, but the rolling up of sleeves indicated an altogether different purpose. 'I checked out our minister ...'

'And?'

'Well, let's just say you were right to have your suspicions.' Her eyes burned into me as she spoke. 'He's in line to be the Moderator of the Church of Scotland.'

'Now, that's a big gig.'

She nodded. 'The biggest, comes with the Right Reverend title ... you could see why he has Oscar night nerves.'

'Indeed he does.'

Amy put her arms round her slim waist, hugged herself, 'Gus, I feel strange talking about this, but Caroline said some stuff when she, well after the birth, I think she was still under the drugs, but ...'

I pushed down some of the sheets and edged myself up. I could see Amy's distress, so motioned her closer. 'Look, if there's something I need to know, you better just spit it out.'

Amy started to cry. She was a tough girl and this came

out of the blue. I'd never seen her like this before. 'Hey, what's the matter?'

She put her hand to her mouth, 'Caroline says ... he's the father.'

I slumped, felt the air sucked out of my lungs like a punch to the gut. '*What?*'

I looked at Amy and saw the emotional dam burst. 'She says he raped her. She was coming home late, just nights on the town with Craig ... Urquhart hated him because he was gay, called him deviant, an affront to God. He said she had lost her way and he needed to set her on the right path ... Gus, Caroline ran away because she hates the sight of her father and who on Earth could blame her?' She put her face in her hands and sobbed harder, 'Gus, it's too sad for words ... just too sad for words.'

I couldn't listen to any more. I felt a burn in the pit of my stomach that I knew as anger. It was at the kindling stage just now, the worst kind. I had known anger all my life and could tell this kind, the controlled variety, was far more powerful than the volcanic eruptions. I was ready to flay Urquhart alive.

'Give me my phone over,' I said.

'You can't use a phone in hospital.'

'Fuck it. Give me it.'

She passed me the mobi, it smelled of fags, Silkies.

I dialled Urquhart's number and he answered on the second or third ring. My voice was firm, the tone as dulled as my emotion. 'Hello, Minister, this is Gus Dury.'

'Oh, hello ... I was hoping to hear from you.' He managed to make it sound like a pleasant enough social call. Like I was about to offer to drop off some cakes for a fete. 'Have you uncovered anything?'

My tone sharpened, 'You better believe it.'

'Well, that's wonderful news.'

'Is it?'

'Well, yes, I-I ...' Some of the pulpit-confidence subsided.

'I've found your daughter, Minister ...' the last word stung as it passed my lips, felt I needed to spit it out. 'But I've ran into a few extra expenses along the way.'

He played dumb, milking a reverence he had no entitlement to. 'I don't understand.'

I ramped it up, my volume, my aggression, the lot. 'Understand this, my *good* and *godly* man, the price is now two-thousand in cash by this afternoon.'

'*What?*'

'You heard, *Minister* ... You ever want to hear that Right Reverend bit upfront then you better be where I first met you at five in the p.m. And bring cash, I don't take cheques, not from the likes of you.'

I killed the line.

I'd never had a good experience in a hospital, didn't think I ever would. I knew I wasn't alone in that regard. But something stabbed at me this time, this one time that I was able to be around for the birth of a child had wounded me more than I could say.

When Debs lost our baby, I knew that was it. They told her we wouldn't get another chance. And we never did. I don't mean to bring life into this world: we had no chances left after that. The child was our last one.

It killed me to think about those days, so I didn't.

There were times when I couldn't look away, though, and that's where the alcohol came in. I wasn't drinking to forget, I was drinking to obliterate.

When people ask me why I drink so much, I know the answer: because oblivion is the only place I feel comfortable.

41

I tugged my beanie hat over the head bandage and turned into the shop on the corner of Easter Road and London Road. I ordered up a packet of Marlboro. On auto-pilot, the girl reached for Lights.

'No, give me the red-tops,' I said.

I was back on the lung-bleeders and I knew they'd be skating on the River Styx before I attended any fucking hypertension clinic.

On the way towards the Leith San Siro I felt a calm enter my blood. My father had played there, was a *kent face* all round these parts. When I thought about him now, I knew I had no feelings in my soul for him. I knew how Caroline felt, perhaps not emphatically, but I knew the neighbourhood of her hurts.

She'd never be free of what her father did to her, I knew that. She'd never lose the guilt, and the pain, and the neat store of recriminations she'd package up and take with her wherever she went, for the rest of her life.

But our time was finite and the mind could sometimes be tricked to forget. I didn't want to think about her life being written-off, I wanted to think she was stronger than me.

I didn't want to think about the child at all.

Amy had gone to see the poor mite, but I didn't want to store the image in my mind. Just now the child was merely a jumble of words and thoughts to me; I couldn't allow it to become flesh and blood. I had a dark place in my heart reserved just for these sentiments, and that's where I placed that poor child.

Amy was standing outside the Coopers Rest, oblivious to a pack of jakies' interest in the pavement scoreline. I waved from across the street and she nodded, dowped her fag on the wall.

I'd asked Amy along, not as back-up or decoration, but because she set the tone I wanted. She had edge.

'Hello ...' I said.

'He's inside.'

'Already?'

'Been here since I arrived ... why do you think I'm standing in the street?'

There was rarely an answer for Amy's questions.

'Right, then ... let's do this.'

She nodded and reached for the door handle.

Urquhart was sitting in the snug with a bottle of Highland Spring. Still. He had a pinched, grey pallor on him today. The look didn't so much say he'd been rumbled, as presented a pontifical *so what* to the world.

We made our approach slowly, but kept eyes on him the whole way. On our way he stood up, and his eyes lit on Amy.

When we were a couple of yards from his table he spoke, 'Who is this?'

Amy looked him up and down, she blew out her Hubba Bubba and popped the bubble fast. Her look said an answer to his question was going to be a long time coming. She sat down and crossed her legs towards the bar.

'You don't ask any questions, Minister,' I said. I called to the barman, 'Rum and coke, twice.'

Urquhart double-blinked but stayed silent.

As I sat down, I removed the beanie hat and spoke. 'Rum's the condemned man's drink, Minister ... would you like to join me?'

He stared at my bandaged head and then lowered himself slowly into his chair, his long thin shanks brushing the rim of the table. I could see the knees of his corduroy trousers had worn thin.

There was silence around the table. Amy eyed Urquhart with derision. Once in a while she'd blow out a pink bubble, just to put the knife in him.

'Could you stop that, please?' said Urquhart.

'Why?' said Amy.

He clammed, mumbled, 'It's vexatious.'

Amy fluttered her eyelashes, leaned forward, close enough for the minister to scent the strawberry gum on her breath, 'If someone says stop, do you always stop, *Minister*?'

His open mouth grabbed for air, 'I beg your pardon?'

Amy smiled, showed wide white teeth, 'Never mind.'

Our drinks came.

The barman left.

I spoke up, 'Now, let's get down to brass tacks. The cash.'

Urquhart ruffled, 'I think I shall have my side of the agreement fully realised before I part with any ...'

I raised a hand, only one. It was enough to silence him, 'Hold it right there.'

Amy slurped rum and coke through a straw. When she clattered down the glass her masticating jaws distracted the minister, set his attention wandering. He shuffled uneasily on his seat, 'I have had quite enough of this performance, Mr Dury. Now I engaged your services to locate my daughter and I demand to know what progress you have made towards that end.'

I leaned forward, mouthed a slow whisper. 'The money.'

Silence.

Amy slapped a palm on the table, set the glasses rattling as she yelled, 'The money!' She drew a fist and spoke again, 'Now.'

Urquhart wet his grey lips and slowly produced a long manila envelope from the inside pocket of his Barbour jacket. I snatched the package and opened up.

'There's no need to count it, it's all there.'

It looked about right. I peeled out a few fifties, gave them to Amy, said, 'Here, you've earned that.'

She didn't seem to agree, but took them anyway. I watched as she pocketed the money and returned eyes to Urquhart.

I resealed the envelope and handed it back to Amy, said, 'Take this to Caroline ... that girl deserves all the help she can get for a fresh start.'

Urquhart's face reddened with bluster, 'Now look here, I paid you to find my daughter!'

My reply was calm, flat. 'I did.'

'Then, where is she?'

I smiled, 'I never said I would tell you that.'

He made a knot of his mouth, then opened wide and started fumbling for the right words. We have a phrase in Scotland, 'Are you catching flies, Minister?'

'I-I don't believe this ... you have swindled me.' He rose on shaky legs, started to fasten his jacket. 'I'm not standing for this,' he said.

I motioned sit, leaned over and patted a hand on his chair, 'Unless you'd like me to fuck up your chances of becoming Moderator once and for all.'

His moist eyes grew wider. He glanced first at me, then at Amy. As she burst another bubble the minister returned slowly to his chair.

Amy shook her head then sighed and got up to leave. 'I've seen all I can stomach,' she said.

Time stretched between us like a great gulch as Amy went for the door. Urquhart watched her jerky movements and persistent stride like each step was a countdown to his own doom. His shoulders slumped. He seemed to deflate before me as he lowered his head and looked into the soft, white palms of his hands. 'What has Caroline told you?'

He was uncomfortable giving voice to her name, almost forcing it over his lips. I tipped up my glass, drained it, 'Everything.'

'She lies, you know.'

'Will the DNA?'

He turned his weaselly eyes on me.

I said, 'Didn't think so.'

I'd made my point, it was my turn to stand up now. I rose, glancing for the door. As I moved towards him and lowered my mouth to his ear, he seemed to anticipate my words. 'If I ever hear you have been within a country mile of that girl, I will personally preside over your crucifixion. Do you understand me?'

He said nothing. Looked away. I grabbed his face in my hand and twisted it towards my own.

'Is your hearing off? ... I said do you understand me?'

He jerked his head away. 'Yes, yes, I understand.'

As I straightened my back and buttoned my Crombie he took out his handkerchief again and pressed it between his hands, then carefully began to fold it away again.

I moved off, left him staring at the tabletop.

As I walked, I expected him to ask about his daughter, either one. But he stayed silent.

At the door, my heart pounded so hard I felt it moving my shirtfront. I turned, thought I might see a broken man, in tears perhaps. He was pouring out the remains of his mineral water. Face, stone.

Long Way Down

a Gus Dury story

I was sitting in the laundrette on London Road, just watching the wheels go round as Lennon said. Nowt much was occurring, hadn't been for a while. You get in that frame of mind, things like Generation Wuss telly and boy-band music start filling the gaps. My wet brain was already looking like something Sponge Bob would take off his Square Pants for, so another aperture was likely to set me dribbling at the mouth.

I turned over a stray copy of The Hun – had The Times tucked below, was thinking that's some heavyweight reading for the east-end of Edinburgh but I let it go, turned it aside because I couldn't face the news, for the first time in my life I didn't have the concentration for it. I couldn't face the anti-independence stance on every page of the paper either – wondered who in this whole country was falling for the 'Scottish edition' bullshit they'd plastered on the front. There was a new vibe in town; Scots dreaming of having a nation of their own will do that.

The washer stopped, clicked off after a final gut-bursting spin. I took out the pile of wet denim and captured the inevitable stray sock before tipping the lot in the drier. I was fiddling with the Elastoplast which held my crumbling iPod together, contemplating a track from The Stagger

Rats, when the temperature in the small enclosure of the laundrette ramped up. I loosened a tab from my soft-pack of Camels and headed out for a smoke. I was stood in the street, sparking up as a horn blared at me from a passing car.

'The fuck is that?' I mouthed, mid-gasp of the first draw.

A silver-grey Merc, big one – none of your shitty A-Class – flicked on the blinkers and turned into Abbey Mount. The car was parked up in the bus-stop as the driver's door flipped open and a squat, open-shirted Cockney Wanker-lookalike got out. He was flagging and waving to me, the wide-open shirt front wafting a breeze over the forest of chest hair as he called out, 'Gus, lad ...'

'Jesus Christ ...' It was Danny Murray. I hadn't seen him in years but this was already too soon. The sight of him soured the taste of my fag so I dowped it in the gutter.

He was jogging, stuffing a Racing Post under his arm as he approached. The search-light smile was the real sickner though. We've a phrase in Scotland, what you after? ... seemed to fit the bill.

'Alright, Gus my old son ...' he said. I could swear I'd picked up an Eastenders inflection in there; the man was like a bad soap-opera reject from the 80s. All Pete Beale with his tankard-behind-the-bar-bonhomie. Worst of it was, the cunt was as Leith as me.

'Danny Murray, you're coming up in the world.' I nodded to the flash motor, that's when I clocked the private plate: D Man 109. Wanted to laugh, but felt like crying when I weighed this joker's luck against my own.

'Can't complain, Gus ... doing alright.'

He was too. But not off his own graft, I'd heard he was running for Boaby Stevens and say what you will about Shakey, he looks after his crew.

'You were always into everything bar a shit sandwich, Dan.'

He tipped back his head, laughed. I could see the goose-bumps forming on his exposed arms as he shivered in the street. 'Fancy a pint?'

Now I thinned eyes. 'What?'

'Jesus, it's brass-balls out here, Gus, come on ...' he looked about, squinted down the street and over to the Artisan pub. 'I'll shout you a bevvy.'

I was averse, call me old-fashioned, but I tend to avoid the company of cock-heads as a rule. I showed an open hand to the road, 'Lead the way ...' I mean, there's principles and then there's choking for a drink and being on the skint bones of your arse.

Danny walked into the road, palms up to halt the traffic, he got a hail of horns sent in his direction but it didn't stop him beckoning me like the captain of an army advance. I let him weave his way through the stalled cars and clouds of tyre-smoke and pressed the button on the pedestrian crossing.

The Artisan was an old-school Edinburgh drinker. Set me in mind of days past, of Col's Holy Wall. I winced at the memory of my wasted effort on running the place after his death; but you put a sopping-wet alkie in charge of a public house and you can expect no less. It was a miracle the place was still standing.

The pub was dominated by a circular bar, utilitarian tables and PVC chairs dotted around the outskirts. A poker-machine – what would once have been called a simple puggie – sparked and whirred to the left of us. I nodded to the taps, 'Guinness ... and a wee birdie to chase it.'

Danny produced a wad thicker than the phone book and smiled a gold-toothed grin at the barmaid, she was as dour as a stroll out by the sewage overflows at Porty, shot him a glower and clunked the glasses on the bar. 'Bag of nuts as well, my girl ...' said Danny.

Her look said he was lucky to keep the nuts he already had.

I took a table at the back of the pub, in the darkness of a shameless bulb that was clearly on the blink. Danny followed with a tray.

The creamy Guinness tasted like courage, spiked my veins and sent my heart ramping. Another gulp and I'd be flicking the switch in my head that said keep going, don't stop. It was a hair-trigger and always at its lightest when I had little or nothing going on in the wider world to distract me.

'So, spill the beans, Danny ...'

'Eh?'

'This isn't a social call.'

He struggled to open the bag of nuts, started to get agitated. He shuffled in his seat then put the bag in his teeth and ripped open the pack. A shower of nuts descended on the table-top. 'Aw, shit ...'

'Danny ... your nuts have dropped, now man up, what the fuck is this about?'

He looked suddenly weary, a cold line of sweat pustules erupted on his brow. 'Truth be told, Gus, I've been looking for you.'

I didn't like the sound of this. 'If you've been looking for me, it's not because you want to find me ...'

'What?'

'Has Shakey sent you?'

He turned in his seat, his arse-cheeks squeaked on the PVC. 'No. God no.'

I could tell he was lying, put the bead on him. 'Danny, don't bullshit a bullshitter.'

He dropped his gaze and fingered the rim of the table. 'Well, not exactly.' He looked up, looked away. His voice flattened a little. He was a man on edge, at the end of his rope, I could see that now ... I knew the territory. 'What I mean is, well, y'know I work for Shakey and so I suppose in a way everything comes back to him but this is something I thought out all for myself.'

I liked the sound of that even less.

I fired down the Grouse. 'I'm not with you. Spit it out, Danny.'

'I have a job for you.'

I was skint. Bored as a bastard and verging seriously close to a skite. But a long way from taking work from gangsters or their shady acolytes. 'Forget it.'

'No ... wait, hear me out.'

I'd fallen foul of Shakey once before, he had me driven out to the wilds of Midlothian and strung up. 'I'd need my head tested to get involved with that fucking lunatic. No way.'

I picked up my pint, started to gulp the Guinness and rise at the same time. I had no words to say to him, but if there were any queuing in my mind they were simply: 'Get fucked.'

Danny seemed to intuit my next move was the door. He got up and stepped in front of me, his tight Farah trousers looked close to splitting as he bent down for his Racing Post. Inside the paper was a grey-to-white envelope, it was held together by an elastic band, a necessity since the contents were spilling out as he flashed them under my nose.

'What's this?' I said, lowering my pint.

'Three grand,' he dipped his head and leaned forward, 'It's all in used twenties.'

I don't know who Danny thought he was dealing with but I set him straight. 'Well that's handy, wouldn't want to be accused of money laundering transferring it to Switzerland.' I shook my head and walked past him. I was at elbows with the poker-machine when he grabbed my shoulder and spun me round.

'Gus, please ...'

'No way.'

He grabbed my sleeve, tugged tight. 'You don't understand.'

'I understand fine. And it's still a no.' I put my hand on his and tried to unclasp his fingers but he clung for grim life – it was the strongest sense yet I'd caught of his sheer desperation.

'It's Barry ...' he said. His voice so low it seemed whispered into my ear like a secret.

'Barry Fulton?' He was the only common ground we shared of any significance and he knew this.

Danny nodded. His grip still held firm. I lowered my hand and stared into his concerned eyes.

'He's inside.'

He wet his thin grey lips, 'Not anymore.'

'What? When did he get out?'

Danny unclenched his fist and let his hand fall to his side. 'Two days ago.' He raised the envelope stuffed with cash again and pressed it into my chest, 'I knew you'd be interested, Gus.'

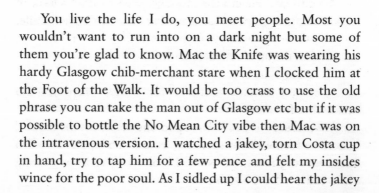

You live the life I do, you meet people. Most you wouldn't want to run into on a dark night but some of them you're glad to know. Mac the Knife was wearing his hardy Glasgow chib-merchant stare when I clocked him at the Foot of the Walk. It would be too crass to use the old phrase you can take the man out of Glasgow etc but if it was possible to bottle the No Mean City vibe then Mac was on the intravenous version. I watched a jakey, torn Costa cup in hand, try to tap him for a few pence and felt my insides wince for the poor soul. As I sidled up I could hear the jakey getting into his 'Just 30p for bus fare to visit my mam in hospital' speech.

Mac's reply was delivered deadpan. 'You want to join her? I can put you in an ambulance there for nothing.'

The paraffin lamp was on the back foot as I arrived, his sudden sobriety seemed to have been dispensed from Mac's thinned stare. It was a look that said impending violence was a cert. He was still retreating, backwards, yawing on wobbly legs as I put a palm on Mac's shoulder.

'Alright, mate ...'

Mac lit. 'Gus, lad.'

Greetings over we made our way up the Walk towards Robbie's Bar. This neck of Leith is like a kaleidoscope, sights continually shifting. We'd had the gutting of the new tram tracks close down a stack of old and familiar businesses. In their place were new pound stores and Polish grocers running a sideline in protein-shakes by the bucket. I grimaced at the over-tanned, over-muscled meat-head whose cardboard cut-out sat in a shop window.

Robbie's was reassuringly familiar. A drinker's bar. A Leith legend. It felt like home. Mac got the pints in and I nodded him towards a table by the door.

'What's wrong with the bar?' he said.

'Not today.' He got the message, even painted a look of caution on his coupon that tugged at his half-Chelsea smile.

I blew the head off my Guinness and sat down. Mac was already on the sniff for information.

'So what's the score?' he said.

'Christ, I haven't seen you for weeks. Have you no small-chat for me?'

He creased his brow. Dropped one corner of his mouth, where he seemed to be speaking from in a trippy drawl, 'Do me a fucking favour, Gus, do I look like I've been picking tittle-tattle off the allotment?'

The thought of Mac in wellies made me smile. 'If you were doing any digging it would be because there was a body to dispose of!'

He liked that, seemed to be running the visual image. 'Cemented into a new motorway flyover is more my style.'

I grinned at him; knew he was only half joking. 'Right, Mac, I need you to test a few of those contacts of yours.'

The tone turned to the serious notch. 'Oh, aye?'

I hadn't known Mac as long as I'd known Barry Fulton. There was a time in my life when I knew hardly anyone like Mac. Since my marriage went tits up, and my career followed suit, I'd met quite a few people like Mac. It was safe to say I wasn't exactly mixing with the professional-set on the squash court.

'I have this ... old friend.'

Mac shook his head, 'One of them?'

'No. Barry's a square-peg ... he just made a few wrong turns and found himself in Saughton on a twelve stretch.'

'What for?'

I sipped my pint, then: 'A counter jump.'

Mac winced. 'Must have been tooled up for a twelve.'

'He was ... shall we say, inexperienced.'

'He must've been fucking dippit, Gus ... doesn't have Born to Lose tattooed on his head does he?'

I liked the line better the way De Niro delivered it, but I let it slide because I needed his help. 'Barry would be the first to admit his mistakes, but he got fucked-over by a woman and . . .'

Mac cut in. 'This isn't misplaced sympathy, Gus?'

I knew what he was trying to say but anything Debs and I once had was now long gone. It might have taken a while to accept it and a power of drink to wash it down but there it was.

'Barry got hitched to a coke-head who became a crackhead before the ink was dry on the marriage licence. He was trying to keep house and home together when he got desperate.'

It was the kind of sob story that was meat and drink to Mac. 'My heart bleeds.'

'Yeah, well, I thought it would.' I reached into my jacket pocket and produced a thin roll of twenties. 'But there's a drink in it for you if you can help me out.'

His eyes widened then he took the roll and pushed it in his own pocket. 'Where do I fit in, Gus?'

'Simple. Barry isn't a bad lad but he's been mixing with some bad people . . .'

Mac's hand shot up. 'Whoa, wait a minute, who exactly are we talking about?'

I took another sip of Guinness, it did nothing for my nerves as I dropped my voice to the down-low. 'Boaby Stevens.'

Mac leaned back, took the roll of cash from his pocket and made a show of thrusting it back in my hands. 'You can get yourself fucked, Gus!'

'Come on, Mac ... where's your balls?'

'Where I want them ... not dangling from my fucking ears which is where they'll be if Shakey hears I've gone against him!'

I returned the roll of cash to his hand with a little more on top. 'You're not going against Shakey, I just need to know what Shakey's got planned for Barry, that's all.'

Mac crushed the money in his fist, wagged it at me. 'It's not about this, you know.'

'I know, mate.'

He put the cash away and sighed. 'What are you looking for?'

'That's the question ...'

'What?'

I put my elbows on the table, 'I ran into Danny Murray, he's working for Shakey, and he wants to find Barry.'

'Well, I'm guessing it's not to ask what he wants for his Christmas present.'

I nodded, my mouth dried over as I tried to speak. 'Barry's a good lad, like I say, we go way back. I knew him at school for fucksake.'

'So what, Gus?'

'So, I'll find him. Not for Danny Murray or Shakey or a bundle of used notes stuffed in a Racing Post. I'll find him because he's an old friend and if he's in some kind of trouble I want to know about it.'

Mac rose from the table. His pint had hardly been touched. He was doing up his coat as he spoke. 'You still on the same number?'

'Yeah, I am.'

He nodded. 'I'll give you a call.'

I tipped the dregs of Mac's pint into my own as he left the pub.

There was a time in my life when leaving Robbie's, or any pub for that matter, with only a couple of drinks in me was a non-starter. Call it maturity because I couldn't call it a lack of funds with the best part of three-grannies stuffed in my pocket, or call it whatever, but I was back pounding the pavement. And thinking of Barry.

We'd done the school together and those types of ties you don't unpick for the hell of it. He'd been Baz then, a bit of a joker and a bit of a wido, all the teachers hated his guts. We lads loved him for it. He had a carefree, cut-the-crap way about him that was always on the verge of being out of control. Some folks are never far away from the self-destruct switch, I knew the territory, but Baz took it to a whole other level. In third year I watched him implode a Bunsen burner by clamping the rubber feed. The explosion burst a girl's eardrum and set some heavy-duty school curtains alight. The fire-brigade's attendance is still my highlight of six-years' stoop-shouldered study. It was also memorable as Baz's last day – he got expelled. There was another school. A stack of McJobs after that and a power of what the Eagles might call witchy women. Katrina, or Kat as she was known, was the worst of the lot. She was still on the junk, last I heard anyway, and still in possession of the kind of nasty mouth you might never tire of plugging. She was a full-on bitch and bad news for Baz but also my best chance of tracking down the lost soul.

I took the bus out to Porty and got off outside an old-school drinker where a couple of snoutcasts were spraffing away outside about the current state of the Jam Tarts' finances. It was 'beyond a joke' apparently that players weren't getting paid. I had to clamp it when the thought of eleven near-millionaires being out of pocket for a little while bit; my old man never saw that kind of money in his whole playing career. Shudder the thought, what kind of damage would that sort of wealth have done to him; and the rest of my family? I dreaded to think. To me family was what you made it, no more, no less. Blood counted for little.

Katrina's gaff was part of the boxy high-rise that sat in Porty's main drag, it was as incongruous as a chocolate-dildo at a Morningside tea-party. This end of the town used to see the well-heeled promenading during Victorian times; you'd be lucky not to catch a crowd of hen-night scrubbers pissing in the gutter now.

I pushed the bust door-front and made my way to the first-floor gaff. The yellowing net curtains in the window of the door would have had my Mam reaching for the Daz.

I depressed the bell and stepped back. In a few minutes a hazy black shadow started to stagger behind the frosted glass and manky curtains.

'Hello, Kat ...' I said.

She squinted, dropped her neck further into her shoulders and tried to discern something in the ball-park of familiarity.

'It's Gus ... Gus Dury, I'm Barry's mate, remember?' I felt like I was talking to a child, she scrunched up her brows and started to grip at her sides with two lank arms that didn't look strong enough to lift stamps. The woman was in a worse state than I had imagined possible.

'Gus ...oh, aye,' she said. 'Barry's not here ...'

The reply came a little too practiced for my liking; this fucktard didn't have enough marbles left to crank out a reply like that.

'What makes you think I'm looking for, Barry?'

She stepped back into the flat, fiddled with the edges of her cardigan. She was too scoobied to manage a reply. I felt like putting her out of her misery, felt like ending Barry's misery to tell the truth. I pushed open the door and walked in. She managed to look surprised after I'd got to the end of the corridor and turned back to face her.

'Hey, hey ...'

'Shut the door, Kat.'

She slow-blinked in my direction, vague bloodshot eyes above heavily crenulated bags. I'd seen too many junkies to summon a single atom of sympathy. She'd given up, like they all had, but it was the rest of us that had to live in fucking Zombieland with them. And people like Barry had no escape from them; they remembered the before, the time when junk wasn't a way of life, or more accurately, death.

Kat raised a thin mitt to the door and pushed it to. She stumbled in her blue-fluffy baffies as she walked towards me. The cardigan was getting wrapped tighter and tighter round her thin waist in an effort to shield her from something: life, at a guess.

I turned into the smoke-thick living room. There was a TV stand but no television. A burst couch, spewing foam from one arm. A patchy, manky carpet and a coffee table, replete with dirty works. I looked around, thought about opening the curtains but didn't want to shed any more light on the place. The one thin sliver of a yellow sunbeam that erupted through the gap in the curtains was dust-filled, sent motes dancing in my eyes.

'I don't understand ...' said Katrina. She had a bunch of limp black hair in her hand now, she twisted it. 'I don't know why you're here.'

I knew she was lying. There was an old Gola holdall sitting beside the arm of the burst couch; I hadn't seen one of those since they came back in fashion about a decade ago. I walked over to the bag and peered inside; seemed liked Barry had been round to drop off his gear.

'Where is he?'

'He's not here.'

'Oh, aye.' I walked over to the Gola bag, gave it a tap with the tip of my cherry Docs.

She gripped her sides and swayed. 'Aye, he was here ... but he left again.'

At least she was coming clean, I didn't fancy tearing the gaff apart to look for him; not without a tetanus anyway. 'What do you mean ... left?'

She leaned on the wall, looked woozy. 'The night he got out he dropped his stuff off ... then he went again.'

I was ready to rattle her chops, took a step closer and let my impatience hit her. 'Went where?'

She shrugged.

I poked her in the shoulder, one finger, it was enough to near fell her.

'Stop that ... I don't know where he went.'

'Was he alone?'

She shrugged again.

I pointed my finger, it was enough.

'No. Some guy was with him. He said they had some business, that he'd be in touch but he wouldn't be back ... look, leave me be, he's not here!'

I didn't like the sound of what she had told me, for the simple reason that it rung true. Katrina wasn't in possession of the faculties to manufacture a cover story. She wasn't in possession of faculties, full-stop. She was near the end of the black-tunnel that all junkies travelled. Another hit, if she could find a vein capable, and she was over. That's what her days were about.

When I left her, closed the door, I knew she wouldn't remember seeing me inside of five minutes. Barry must have got the same impression when he showed, least I hoped he had; the heart has its reason, and all that.

I crossed the street to the grimy drinker with the fag-bound boyos outside; the chatter was on Rangers now, voices were being raised.

'Mark my words, this fella will shaft the club!' said the snoutcast.

I shook my head as I took the pavement, the club was already on Shit Street.

'Aye you're all right, yer all wrong ... I knew that the second I saw his name was Green.'

Holy Christ. This actually amounted to reasoning among these monkey-brained troglodytes. I stepped up to the plate. 'And here's something for you both to think about, the fella that he replaced was called Whyte!'

I saw the half-sozzled, slow-blinking eyes turn to saucer shapes. There was the hint of a cog turning, maybe the sound of the rodents working the controls in their heads moving, as they tried to piece together the significance.

I helped them out. 'Green and Whyte ... something to think about.'

I grabbed for the door and tipped the daft lads a wink. I could tell I'd kicked off a conspiracy theory already.

The bar was dark, dingy. In days gone past there'd have been a pall of grey smoke you'd struggle to shine headlamps through. Now the nicotine-stained walls and ceiling looked painfully over-exposed – the woodchip papering would turn to writhing maggots after a few scoops.

I slotted myself on a stool behind the heavily scarred and scratched-up hardwood of the bar. There were bars in Edinburgh that Stevenson frequented in his drinking days when he was known as Velvet Coat; if he ever got as far out of the New Town as Porty, I'd have sunk money on him supping here.

I ordered up a Guinness and a low-flying birdie to chase it. The bar man dispensed a gruff acknowledgement that came topped with a thin-eyed stare in my direction. Okay, I was looking rough – in the ball-park of a jakey to be truthful – but this was hardly the fucking Ivy.

The pint and chaser were laid in front of me and a hand went out, I waited for a 'make those your last' but it never came. Say one thing about the ass-fucking the Tories had given the country of late, the shortage of cash and the surfeit of those drowning their sorrows spoke to publicans like a whore with a lullaby.

I took a seat by the window and stared out at the entrance to the flats where I'd just left Baz's Katrina in a perplexed state. She didn't exactly look sorted for E's and wizz – and I'd put those stairs beyond her withered legs, she could hardly stand, never mind make ambulatory. The chances were she'd be getting a visit from Mr Fix-it sooner or later.

I downed a full draught of my pint and took out my rumpled paperback of Trocchi's Young Adam whilst the wee goldie stood sentry. In a brief moment the pint did the trick, sent my senses swirling as I luxuriated in Trocchi's dulcet prose. So what if they called him a pornographer, and accused him of pimping his wife, the guy could write and who ever said being a genius was easy? Give me some grit, someone who knows the wild side over Jeeves and fucking Wooster any day.

'Another pint?'

The barman stood over me with a white towel in his hands, he was wringing it like he had hold of a game bird's neck.

'Why not ...' I said.

He nodded and I clocked the three or four black hairs on his glabrous scalp that he'd greased back, likely with Brylcreem. He was an anachronism, the whole place was – maybe that's why I felt so at home.

My second pint was in motion, that creamy head of goodness making its way towards me as I spotted a familiar face on the street outside. He was jinxing between cars halted in the road and looking far too cocky for my liking.

'Aye, aye ...'

I turned a tenner in the direction of the barman but kept my gaze on the scene through the window. It was Weasel. One of Devlin McArdle's runners. He did odd-jobs for the Deil but I'd be very surprised if he was ever given anything more than the scrapings on the bottom of the barrel. Weasel was one of those shifting faces that attached himself here and there wherever the opportunity arose. He'd turned out for Shakey once and he was rumoured to be on the job with

Barry when he got put away. It was only a rumour because Barry would never confirm it – others would – but Barry had loyalty.

'You clown, Barry ...'

'What?' The barman was back, holding out my change. I shook my head, 'Nothing ... just thinking.'

'Jesus above, why would you want to do that?'

I smiled and took my change. 'Why indeed?'

As I turned back to the window, Weasel was taking the door of Katrina's flats. He stood with the door open, blocking it with the sole of his Adidas Samba, and looked furtively up and down the street before ducking inside.

'What are you up to, Weasel you little shit?'

I watched him ascend the stairs towards Katrina's floor; the barman was wiping a tabletop as I downed a fair pelt of my Guinness.

'Keep them coming, mate,' I said.

The low-flying birdie called out to me, singing that golden oldie that always strummed the chords of my heart.

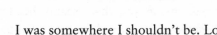

I was somewhere I shouldn't be. Locked in reverie with my beloved late brother and less-than beloved, but just as late, father. Michael had the noose round his neck that he'd taken from the clothesline, the one my mother had across her back when Cannis Dury came home out of pocket and pride. Everything was a blur that somehow burned in my eyes and my heart and my head. Someone was screaming but I couldn't make out who – was it Catherine or my mother? I never heard my sister scream, she was always locked in silence but I knew my mother's cries all too well. Jesus, who was it?

'Debs? ... Debs, is that you?'

As I uttered my ex-wife's name my eyes widened.

I was still in the bar.

A table full of empty glasses.

My heart-rate ramped; I looked about me. Only a few old bluenoses and a dole-mole nursing a pint of heavy.

My mobile was ringing. I dipped a hand in my pocket and took it out.

'Hello ...'

It was Mac. 'Fuck me, you still on the sauce?'

'What? ...' I looked out the window. Blackness. 'I mean, what time is it?'

Mac's voice rose, became lyrical. 'Gone ten anyway ... where are you?'

I had to think, tried to lace up my thought patterns. 'Portobello ... I paid a visit to Barry's missus.'

I heard Mac scratching the stubble on his chin. 'Yeah, I bet that was a waste of shoe leather.'

'Well ... something like that.' I felt my head start to reconnect with reality; my mouth had dried over, I drained the last of my warm Guinness.

Mac dropped his voice, tipped in some serious tones. 'You wanted to know about Shakey and what he had in mind for your friend, Barry ...'

My breathing stilled. 'You found something?'

'Well, that depends.'

I knew what Mac's depends meant. It could be delivered in two instalments. The first was the grim facts. The second was the grim facts and a warning dressed up as advice.

'Go on then ... spill it.'

Mac drew breath. 'Shakey has been hearing a few things about your pal, Barry ... things he doesn't like the sound of.'

I couldn't see Barry in the same starting blocks as Shakey – the idea that he might be likely to put a chink in Shakey's armour was laughable. 'What? How is that even possible?'

Mac's voice rose. 'Seems Barry made some very interesting contacts in Saughton. Heavy mob, Irish ...'

Barry was an affable bloke, he could make mates anywhere but he had the nous to shy away from the 40-watt variety of criminal. I hoped he hadn't latched on to someone as serious as the word 'Irish' suggested. 'What do you mean, heavy?'

'I mean what I say ... fucking loyalist nut-cases. You know the type.'

I did indeed. The type – if they were over here – were not getting enough action at home. The end of the Troubles didn't sit well with them so it was over the water to pastures new – expand and conquer, pick a fight.

'Fucking hell ...'

'Aye, well, that's what I thought.'

I sighed into the mobi. 'What else did you hear?'

'Jesus, Gus, your pal's about to kick off a turf war ... with some big-time players, isn't that enough?'

I couldn't get my head around it. 'What do you mean ... what exactly has Barry got himself into, Mac?'

He dropped his voice to a whisper. 'Gus, he's planning a job on Shakey's turf ... but if that's not bad enough he's planning it with some Irish hardies and that just doesn't sit well with a good patriot like Shakey.'

My thoughts started to mash. I could feel a hot band tightening around my skull. 'We need to find, Barry.'

'Eh, what's this we?'

If Mac the Knife was in retreat it was more serious than I imagined. 'Come on, Mac ... since when did you go pussy on me?'

He laughed. 'Aye, nice attempt at reverse psychology, mate ... not working.' He seemed to be moving, I heard a car door open, an ignition bite. 'No, Gus, you can count me out on this one. I don't know the guy from Adam but he must be a decent enough sort for you to stick your neck out for him ...'

'He is ...'

'Yeah, just don't go as far as slapping your neck on the chopping block!'

He hung up.

I staggered on to a Number 26 bus heading back to the east-end of the city. The air inside was rank, filled with a grim dampness that misted the windows and clung to the fabric of the seats. The grunting engine, evacuating diesel fumes, and the slow revolution of the lumpy wheels made my guts churn. Two teenies played a tinnie tune on a phone that had them laughing and guffawing like burst drains. I was tempted to turn round, blast them one, but I kept schtum. I couldn't guarantee that I wouldn't chuck up some Guinness if I opened my mouth.

The orange glow of the street lamps battered the top-deck of the bus and sent a sickly sheen all the way down to the tarmac that was taking another battering from the rain. I reached out to steady myself, gripped the silver rail, and got looks from an old giffer in a bobble hat. She had a mouth as tightly pursed as a cat's arse and I'd have been surprised if anything half as pleasant came from it. I wasn't fazed. So she had me down as another one of Edinburgh's drunken jakeys – who didn't? I'd fallen pretty far from the days of desk-diaries and pinstripes. If I'd been somebody of note once, I'd forgotten. My past was as far behind me as the reek of the Porty sewage outflows that spewed into the sea.

At Abbeyhill I thanked the driver and stepped out.

The wind was blowing down London Road, a procession of black cabs lined the street hoping to pick up those afraid of the rain. Some young girls in high-heels and tight dresses, likely heading to a George Street style-bar, took the bait and climbed in. I mean, there was no point spending an hour with the hair straightners to get pished on, now was there?

As I passed the old Station Bar I felt tempted to take another scoosh home with me but I clocked the laundrette's lights burning and remembered my washing.

'Shit, man ...'

The little Dot Cotton woman in there would have a lecture for me, like the last time, and the time before. She was what the Scots call thrawn. She was what I called an aul' witch. Something happened to a certain type of women in their bad fifties that boiled the bile in them. They just couldn't pass up an opportunity to spit out some spite.

The bell above the door chimed as I walked in. Empty. I looked around. The machines were silent, a few had the pay boxes removed. I was heading over to the counter when a small blonde head appeared through the window in the door to the back of the shop. The face lit up, a heartmelter smile. I didn't recognise the girl but I was already glad Dot wasn't filling tonight's back-shift.

'Hello,' she said. The accent was hard to place, I'd have said Italian but I'd likely have been wrong.

'Hi there ...'

'I have your things. I put them in a bag for you, I hope that is okay.'

I nodded.

She handed over the bag. Everything was neatly folded. I didn't know what to say. Christ, had she folded my boxers as well? I felt the burn of my cheeks flaming up.

'Thank you,' I said.

She smiled again, straight white teeth. The Ultra-bright variety. 'Did you forget something else?'

'I'm sorry?'

She started to laugh, reached under the counter and put something behind her back. 'From earlier, when you were in?'

I twisted my neck. Put eyes on her. 'You've lost me?'

A hand swung round from her back, produced my beaten-up iPod. 'Tah-dah!'

'Oh, I see ...'

She was grinning as she spoke. 'It must have sat there on the bench all day ... no-one even touched it!'

'Well, it's hardly a worthy find.'

She put her hands behind her back again, looked content with her good deed. 'I've seen you with it before ... I recognised the, er ...' She pointed to the sticking plaster.

'The Elastoplast ... had ran out of tape.' I tucked the iPod in my pocket.

'I played some songs through the speakers ... I hope you don't mind.'

'No, not at all.'

'I hadn't heard of Love and Money. They're good ...'

'They're great.'

'I liked The Stagger Rats too ... Fuzzy, Fuzzy.' She held my gaze for a moment and then looked away suddenly.

The conversation seemed to have bottomed out. I picked up my bag and slotted the iPod on top.

'Look, thanks again,' I said. 'Much appreciated.'

'Not a problem.'

At the door I turned back before I reached for the handle, 'Where's that accent from?'

'Poland,' she said. 'I'm from Poland.'

'Oh, I'd have said Italy.'

She turned down the corners of her mouth, sneered. 'Too sunny for me.'

'Me too, for sure.'

The bell sounded as I gripped the handle and walked out into the rain-spattered street.

My flat was on Easter Road, a stone's throw from the Hibs stadium. There was no more monolithic reminder of my father's standing in the city. The sound of the match day roar, of police horses herding hooligans in the street, all played their part in keeping me tied to a past I'd sooner forget. My father's playing days coincided with the apogee of his own egotistical form of self-destruction. We had that much in common, I was prepared to admit, only all my arrows were trained on myself. None of his were, they were trained on his family, and none of them missed.

I was slotting the key in the door when I heard the sound of a fancy car alarm clicking on. I turned to catch the blinkers flashing on and off and then I heard Danny Murray's loafers slapping off the wet flags.

'Hello, Gus ...'

'The fuck is this, Danny?'

I looked over his shoulder, back down the street.

He flagged me down. 'A friendly visit, between colleagues.'

We were pretty far from that level. And friendly was the last word I'd use to describe Dan the Man.

I shook my head and rested my laundry bag on my hip. 'What are you after, Danny?'

He eyed the open door behind me. 'Maybe we should go inside, Gus ...'

He had me on the back foot. I turned and let him follow me up the stairwell. The hinges on the door to my flat wheezed as I directed him inside. Danny made his way to the living room and stationed himself in the centre of the sofa.

I was sparking up a Marlboro from the pack on the coffee table when he started to speak.

'Well?' he said.

'Well, what?' I eased out a blue trail of smoke, it swirled towards the dim bulb in the centre of the room.

Danny put out his palms. 'What have you got for me?'

I started to remove my Crombie, dropped it on to the crook of my arm, laid it over the back of the easy-chair. I was looking directly at Danny as I took another gasp on my cig. 'Are you trying to be funny?'

He shrugged. 'Funny ... No, not me. I'm not known for my jokes, Gus ...'

He had that right. 'You just saw me this morning ... Do you think I've managed to take care of business in that time?'

'To be honest, yes.'

I reached round the back of the chair and removed the Racing Post and envelope with his cash from the inside pocket of my jacket. I had the package raised and ready to chuck it back at him as he rose from the sofa and started to fan hands in my direction.

'Whoa ... Whoa ... Gus, I'm just checking on my investment.'

I flicked some ash on the tray, shook my head. 'Investment? Do I look like the fucking Man from the Pru?'

He stopped flat. Dropped his brows. 'Gus ...'

My tone wasn't doing it. I pointed my fag like a dart as I spoke again. 'Now look, Danny, I understand you want Barry found and I understand that time is a factor to you ... what I don't understand is why you're so bloody jumpy.' I dipped my head, brought it closer to his own. 'Now what are you not telling me about why you need Barry in such a hurry?'

He stepped back, tried to laugh me off but the move towards slipping on his back-tracking shoes was clear. He didn't want to reveal to me that Shakey wanted Barry for the inside-track on the Irish mob's job. Once he got hold of

Barry and his information the boy was likely to become as expendable as pig feed.

'Gus, you get me all wrong ... I'm just anxious to find Barry, that's all. We go back and it's not easy readjusting to the street after a stretch in the pound.'

It was all very altruistic of him. And about as believable as the plot to Iron Sky. But I let him think I was as dumb as him. 'Okay, Danny ... I hear you. I want to look out for our Barry as well ...'

He smiled, reached a hand on to my shoulder. 'Good. Good ... So you'll definitely have him soon?'

'Yes, Danny ... soon.'

He put out his other hand, caught me in a pincer movement. 'How soon?'

'How soon would you like him?'

He gripped my shoulders tightly. 'Tomorrow.'

'Too soon. I have some leads but this is a big city and if he doesn't want to be found ... No, tomorrow's too soon, Danny.'

He bit his lip, dropped arms and turned away from me. 'Look, you don't understand how much ...' He stopped himself, realised his halo was slipping. Danny touched the corners of his mouth with thumb and forefinger, spoke again. 'Okay, when?'

'Give me a week.'

He bit, flared up. 'No way! ... That's far too long.'

'Okay then, you need to give me a deadline. I work well to deadlines, I used to be a hack ...'

Danny was gripping fists as he spoke. 'The day after tomorrow ... but let's just say, if you turn Barry over to me any later than midday, well, I can't guarantee to be any help to him. '

I woke with a ringing in my head and what felt like a bison sitting on my chest. I buried my face back in the pillow but the heavy smell of Marlboros had me gagging. I sat up and swung my legs over the edge of the bed.

My Levis looked too far away, hanging on the back of a chair on the other side of the room. I pushed myself on to my feet and made the pilgrimage over the manky carpet, picking up a freshly-folded white T-shirt and a black V-neck from the laundry bag. Inside ten I was in the neighbourhood of respectable – if unshaven, red-eyed and a gut-rasping cough are your idea of respectable.

I clocked my boots beside the coffee table in the living room but my stomach was too tender to contemplate bending over to lace them up; I sparked another red-top and gazed upwards as the bulb became submerged in swirling blue plumes.

'Fucking hell, Barry ...'

I had a day.

24 little hours.

Hardly any time to find him before the statute of limitations ran out on Danny Murray's patience. The thought of Shakey's unctuous errand boy calling the shots riled me but at least I'd managed to inveigle some proper information out of him. Midday tomorrow would be too late, he'd said. And that had to be because the Irish mob were planning their job then. If Barry went ahead I knew the consequences and they didn't bear thinking about. Vivisection with a rusty corkscrew was likely one of the nicer options on the cards.

I dowped my cig, reached for my cherry Docs.

The heavy footwear were a struggle to lace but once in place the bouncing soles felt the part. I picked up the rest of my fags, slotted the Camels in beside the Marlboros and made for the door.

It was cold out, but only a smirry rain that could be fended off by turning the collar up on my Crombie. I headed back up Easter Road, passed the Manna House and the posh offie, then on to the first London Road bus stop. I checked the real-time message board for the next bus to Porty, said, 'Ten minutes ...'

I waited the ten minutes.

Waited to see the final countdown turn to 'due' but the bus didn't arrive. The timer changed back to fifteen minutes instead.

'Fuck me drunk ...' I shook my head, took hands from my pockets and waved palms either side of my head.

'Those buses, son ...' I turned round on the sound of that word. My heart stung when I heard someone call me 'son'. I still couldn't fathom whether it was because I wanted to be someone's son, or didn't want to be the one person's son that I was.

An old bloke in a tweed cap, his nose a riot of burst blood vessels, joined me in shaking heads, said, 'As much bloody use as tits on a bull!'

He had their number. 'Lothian buses are a joke.'

'They try to blame the tram works.'

'Well they've axed enough of the service to pay for them.'

He shook his head. 'Aye. And if they ever get the bastards running, they'll blame them for taking more buses off the roads.'

I had a sense this conversation could go in circles all day, I clamped it down. Looked the other way. As I glanced over to the laundrette, I found myself wondering about the Polish girl from the night before; I don't know why, perhaps it was the unusual kindness. Had I even said thanks properly?

She wasn't there. I could only see the old witch, the Dot Cotton, loading a drier from a yellow plastic laundry basket. She wore a shiny tabard with pale blue checks and two pockets on the front. She reminded me of the battle-scarred cleaners who used to hoover around my desk at The Hootsman, grunting and moaning about the state of the place as an eternal Woodbine dropped ash on my in-tray.

The bus ride out to Porty was the usual trial of screaming and shouting care-in-the-community patients with backing vocals from noisy schoolchildren on the doss. There was a time in my life when I'd have hollered a few notes in their direction myself, but not now. The older I got, the more appealing the path of least resistance became. Could it be I was actually maturing enough to pick my battles carefully. Surely not.

The main access door to Katrina's block of flats was being held open by the postie for a pram-face mum with a screaming toddler on one hip and a fluorescent buggy with mag-wheels by the other. I kept my distance just long enough for the melee to pass and then I jogged for the slow closing door and took the steps.

I picked out the smell of piss and sickly-sweet Buckfast mingling on the grimy stairwell. Some of the young crew had been in to tag the walls since my last visit, and despite being a respecter of the creative urge that I am, I couldn't help but think their efforts sucked balls. Right into a hernia.

I clattered up the last step and battered on Katrina's door.

There was no movement beyond.

I ramped up the thuds with the heel of my hand.

Now some stirring. The sound of a plate sliding into the skirting, a knife and fork joining in.

I heard a light switch going on.

Then the bolt turned in the door.

I was given an inch of exposure to the flat. It was more than enough. I pressed my shoulder to the wood and my inch became a mile.

Katrina took a few seconds to register her disgust. 'Hey, what you playing at?'

I walked through to the front room. The place was in darkness. I pulled open the curtains and the grey Scottish skies brought a familiar dim pallor to the proceedings.

Katrina slumped in the door's jamb. 'I told you Barry's not here.'

I tried a few doors, more for effect than anything else. The rooms were all empty.

'I can see that, Katrina ...'

'Well fuck off then.'

'Tut-tut ... terrible language.' I walked over to the spot where the Gola bag had sat yesterday, the blue shag-pile carpet displayed a familiar depression. 'I hope you're not going to make me swear, Katrina ... do you know why?'

'Why?'

I pinned back my mouth. 'Because I only swear when I lose my temper ... I'd hate to lose my temper with you, Katrina.'

She looked at me through drooping eyelids. If there was a thought distilling behind them it deserted her. She opted for the same old. 'He's not here.'

'No, I can see that ... and neither is his bag.'

She put a hand to her mouth. Her chin became dimpled like a lemon. 'I threw it out ...'

I jumped at her. Pinned her scrawny neck to the wall with my forearm and stared into her eyes. 'Now you have crossed the fucking line, girl ... If you know what's good for you, and give half of a shit what's good for Barry you'll tell me where the hell he is now!'

Her eyes dimmed.

I roared again. 'Now!'

'He's not here ... he's not here.'

'That's not what I fucking asked you ... I want to know where he is?'

She started to whimper, struggling for breath. 'I don't know.'

'Then tell me this, Kat ... what was Weasel doing here yesterday?'

'I don't know ...'

I pressed my arm harder against her throat. 'Wrong answer!'

She coughed. 'He just brought me round a score ...'

'And took the bag for Barry?'

She didn't answer.

'I'm only going to ask you once more, then I'll snap your fucking junkie neck, Katrina. Don't think for a second I won't, there's no love lost between us and I know Barry would be better off without you ...'

'Aye, okay ... He took the bag.'

'Where?'

'Weasel's flat ... in Craigmillar.'

I stepped back and let her grab for air. She folded like a hinge before me, coughing and spewing. I didn't want to know how much grief this pathetic excuse for a human being had caused Barry.

'Get me the address ... now.'

Walking cleared the head. Walking in Edinburgh, battered by gales and likely as not rain in stair-rods, washed the head right out. After leaving Katrina's flat I took to the high street in Portobello and bought a thank-you for the laundry girl. It was nothing much, just a CD. But it set me in mind of earlier days; I couldn't say happier ones.

Myself and Debs had never worked out; the reasons too multifarious to go into. But she was still there with me – never far from the back of my mind. She was like my conscience and my caution rolled into one. If I was left to my own devices I'd be six-foot under by now. That voice though, that shrill, pedantic whine that she always berated me with at the worst of times was never far away. I could hear it now as I turned the CD into my pocket.

'What the hell are you playing at, Gus?' that's what she said.

I wasn't playing at anything. The Game of Life had long since ceased to be of any amusement to me.

I was just going with the flow.

Rolling with the punches.

Maybe I'd be lucky and get some sense knocked into me. Sure as shooting this business with Barry wasn't going to end without a few tasty blows being struck. If past form was anything to go by, then I'd be on the receiving end. The thought gored me, made me feel even more pity for Barry. He'd had it tough enough without having friends like me.

It seemed every shop in the street was selling cute and cuddly pandas. Their sad eyes dug at me. I couldn't see past the fact that they were captive beasts. There was something unsettling about a city getting so excited about having the animals locked up in the zoo. Was I the only one who saw how miserable they really were? Keeping them behind bars wasn't helping them – it was helping us. It made us feel a little bit better about having ballsed up the entire planet. In Paris during the war they ate all the animals in their zoo – that shows what they really thought of them.

From the pandas my mind latched back on to Barry's plight: it seemed like he was actually better off behind bars. He'd gone from the big house to the shit house in one fell swoop. Try as I might, I just couldn't get my head around his drop. It had been gradual, a slow steering towards the long way down but he'd hit rock bottom now. Nietzsche said you needed to strike the lowest depths before you could bounce back, but Barry wasn't bouncing anywhere from his dark pit of despair. Not unless it was back inside, or worse yet, into Shakey's hands.

I flagged a Joe Baxi and the driver in the Nigerian footy shirt tapped in the Craigmillar address on his TomTom.

'Cheers, mate ... and quick as you like, eh.'

I checked my mobi for messages: zip. Unless you call a text from my mate Hod with a link to Frankie Boyle's Twitter account a message. It seemed the Pope had made his first tweet and the bold Mr Boyle had taken his chance to address the pontiff directly about abusive priests. I smiled inwardly; there was something about the direct approach, about speaking the truth to power that I liked a whole lot.

The taxi pulled over at the foot of the street like I'd told him. I passed the fare through the hole in the safety glass and stepped out.

The rain had stopped.

That was something.

The address that Katrina had given me for Weasel was a boarded-up council flat – the affectionately termed cooncil curtains. The whole street was a tip. Awash with rubbish that had attracted a couple of scavenging dogs: they eyed me like competition for a lick at the Lean Cuisine container they'd liberated.

'Grow sense, dogs ...'

They growled.

I stamped a Doc on the road and they took off, paving the way for a feral gull to swoop down on the salvage.

I was in no rush to crash Weasel's gaff so I sparked up a cig and took myself to the sheltered side of the street where I could watch the goings on from the lee of another derelict building. I was two draws in to my red-top when my mobi rang.

'Mac ... what is it?'

'I'm glad I found you.' His voice was gruff.

'Sounds ominous.'

He took a sharp intake of breath. 'I just had word that your friend is not in a good way ...'

My mind spooled with images of a bloody and battered Barry. 'What?'

'Danny Murray's been done over.'

Relief washed over me. 'Dan the Man ... fuck me, I thought you meant Barry.'

A tut. 'Yeah, well, the only reason Barry's not being fitted for a cement overcoat I'd say is because he's managed to duck under the radar ... but that can't last.'

I was lining up my reply as a stocky figure started walking down the path towards Weasel's flat. I ducked into the ruin as the pug in trademark black leather stepped up to the door and slapped the rain from his shaven head. I couldn't help but notice the hefty holdall in his other hand had a suspicious shape.

I dropped my voice. 'Look, I have that under control.'

'Are you out your fucking tree, Dury? ... You want to drop this, now. Didn't you hear me? Danny's up on bricks at the Royal and your time's running out.'

I kept my gaze on the big biffer, as he walked to the back of the property and looked up to the back windows. When he headed back the door opened again and Weasel's skanky arse scurried out into view. They seemed to have some business to do but Weasel wanted it kept away from his door.

'Yeah, look, thanks for the tip, mate,' I told Mac. 'But I have this under control.'

He loaded in the panic. 'Where are you, Gus?'

There was no avoiding the concern in his voice, he'd had a change of heart, this whole situation had suddenly got serious enough for Mac the Knife to get involved.

'No dice, Mac.'

I clicked off. And started out for the other side of the street.

The dogs were back at the split rubbish sacks, fighting over what looked like the remains of a chicken chow mein. The tinfoil container was being torn between their chops, spilling milky yellow fluid laced with rancid rice over the street. I made my way round them quietly and quickly and slipped on to the pathway leading round Weasel's home.

The building was small, inconsequential. It could have been any one of a million Scottish maisonettes like it. The only distinguishing feature was the crumbling rough-casting that exposed the brick beneath. The pebbles from the wall crunched beneath my Docs as I paced towards the backyard.

The pug had the bag open, Weasel staring in.

'Aye, sound,' he said.

'Course it's sound.' The pug was a wido off the schemes, rough and likely useful, I didn't rate my chances.

Weasel stuffed a hand into the back pocket of his trackies and produced a bundle of notes. He charged his coat hanger shoulders as he stepped back and waved for the pug to count it.

'No need to count it, son ... You're not that daft, eh!'

The pug grabbed Weasel's jaw in his hand and shook. The little streak of piss stood there like a schoolboy being stood over for his dinner money and took the effrontery like it was due to him.

'Cool. Cool,' he said.

The transaction seemed to have concluded, I watched the pair head back for the front of the house and ducked behind a decrepit shed; if it lasted another couple of minutes without blowing away I was in luck.

'Right, well, you know where to come if you need any more,' said the big biffer.

'Aye, no worries.'

Weasel followed him halfway up the path then waved him off and returned to his front door with the heavy holdall weighing him down on one side. The fuckwit still managed to put on a swagger, for the benefit of no-one but himself, as he yawed back down the path. He was grinning, a wide toothless rictus as he took the keys from his trackies and started to scrape the edges of the Yale lock. I let him get the key in the door before I made my move.

One thing about the Docs, the air-cushioned soles can come in handy. Save a few fallen rough-casting pebbles getting crushed underfoot I was stealthy.

The rabbit-punch to the back of Weasel's napper wrapped his head off the front door so hard that the frame bounced off the facing wall and swung back with renewed force.

I winced, shook out the sting of knuckle on skull. My reactions were quick enough to push Weasel's limp jelly-body through the door and reach for the holdall all at once.

He groaned, rolled over on to his back.

'Weasel!' I heard Barry's voice from the top of the stairs, then his heavy footfalls as he descended towards me.

If he'd been tooled up, I'd have likely got my head blown off when I stuck it over the threshold. As it happened the Mossberg-pump I'd taken from the holdall was the only shooter at the party.

'Hello, Barry my old son,' I said.

My old mate stood staring at me with a look of quiet disbelief that threatened to dip into incredulity.

'Gus ...' said Barry.

I was leaning over Weasel now, tucking an arm under his oxter, 'Give me a hand with this piece of shit.'

Barry descended the stairs and got round the other side of Weasel; for a moment, as he stood at the open door, I wondered if he might bolt. He looked me up and down and seemed to clamp on to his emotions, reached for Weasel.

I was still holding the gun in my other hand. 'Right, lift away.'

We got Weasel up the stairs, he was pathetically light. Nothing but skin and bone – you'd see more meat on a butcher's pencil. In the front room we dropped him on a filthy sleeping bag that I wouldn't have let a dog lie on. But this was Weasel we were talking about; it was likely too good for him. As I straightened my back, gripped hold of the shooter again, I spotted the Gola bag from Katrina's on the other side of the room.

Weasel rolled over and groaned. I saw he was coming round, thought about delivering him another whack but Barry caught my attention. He was collecting a pack of Club from what would have passed for the windowsill, if the windows weren't boarded up. I offered my lighter and sparked up as well.

'So, what's the craic?' said Barry.

I huffed. 'There's been precious little fucking craic, mate ... unless you include the one down the middle of Danny Murray's head they're seeing to over at the Royal.'

'What?' He looked perplexed, if he was acting he was a Gielgud.

I drew deep on my cig. 'Are you shitting me? Because if you are, I can walk out on you now and leave you to Boaby Stevens' pugs if you like.'

He leaned against the wall, started to scratch his brow. 'This is fucked.'

'You're telling me?'

He looked up, eyes darting beyond me to Weasel who was groaning again.

I paced towards Barry. 'Look, mate, Danny sent me after you, I'm guessing because Shakey wanted the rundown on the job you're about to pull with some of the Emerald Isle's finest.'

He shook his head. 'It was bloody, Kat ... you know that.'

I walked away, didn't want to record his look when he started to kick off about that woman. She'd done him enough damage and if the truth be told, I didn't need a reminder of my own sorry loss on that front. If the roles were reversed Barry could have been Debs talking about how I'd screwed her life up on a colossal scale.

'She told me she was clean, you know that?'

I shook my head in disbelief. 'And you went for that?'

'No. Well, I hoped you know. We were making plans, for when I got out.'

How you made plans with a junkie whose only ambition was the next fix on the horizon, I'd no clue. 'And what went wrong?'

'She had a house full of crack-heads when I got home. I had to turf a mob of them on to the street. But she has a mouth you know, it runs away with her, the junkies were all trying to butter me up about some big job I was on, she'd fucking blabbed.'

You didn't need to join the dots to see how Shakey got hold of the information. 'So what then?'

'I just split. Didn't even take my gear, sent Weasel round for that. I'm finished with her, Gus ... truly.'

I looked over my shoulder towards Weasel; his hair was stuck to his forehead where I'd flattened him against the wall.

'And this job?' I said.

He shrugged, looked away.

I fronted up. 'Barry ... the job?'

He still couldn't look at me. 'Well, y'know, I'm committed now.'

He fucking needed to be committed. 'They're Irish, power lunatics you do know that?'

'Of course I do, why do you think I'm going ahead with it? Once you're in they're worse than the Foreign Legion, I'd get my head in a poke if I backed out.'

I felt my adrenalin spike. Fight or flight, whatever. I wasn't taking any chances with my chosen course of action. 'Oh, you're backing out, Barry ...'

Now he fronted up, squared shoulders and put the bead on me. 'Oh, aye, who says?

I poked the shooter in his chest, 'In the words of Napoleon Dynamite – a frickin' twelve-gauge!'

He stepped back. 'Gus, now wait a minute, you don't understand who you're dealing with here.'

I looked at my watch, time was getting tight. I didn't want to be around when the Bedford van packed with brick-shithouses pulled up. Gun or no gun, I didn't rate my chances. I took out my phone, scrolled the contacts.

'So, just who are we dealing with here?' I said as the line started to ring.

'What? ... Wait a minute, who are you calling?'

'I'll ask the questions, Barry ... Now I want names and I want the full story on this job including the exact where and when.'

He grunted, near spat. 'You're off your fucking head.'

'No, I'm as sane as they come. But I know a man who is as complete a radge as you're ever likely to meet.' The line connected. 'Hello, Mac, I've a favour to ask ...'

I sent Weasel on his way once I was assured he was a third wheel in the overall scheme of things and then I sat listening to Barry's sorry sob story about how the Irish took him under their wing in Saughton. They'd heard all about Barry keeping schtum on the counter jump and taking a twelve-stretch. They had this thing about informers over there, liked a man who could hold his tongue. The way he told it, they really rated him, but I wasn't so sure. The Irish were all over this city now, but it wasn't their city. It was Barry's, however, and that had its uses, especially where the local faces were concerned.

'Barry, you must have known Shakey would ark up,' I said.

'Of course, I'm not thick.'

I resisted the obvious reply. 'Well why get involved in a job in his fucking backyard?'

He took a last draw on his cig, stubbed it. 'I told you, I had plans, I was going to take the money and run.'

'With Kat?'

He looked away. 'Yeah, with Kat.'

'Well that's not going to happen now, so why am I babysitting you?'

He stood up, 'Look, they're a serious outfit … you don't just walk off on them.'

I knew what he was saying and it made sense to me. But he was deluding himself if he thought that the Irish lads would offer him any cover when Shakey got hold of him. It struck me as fairly obvious that Barry had carved out a life for himself that he was wholly unsuited to. There were reasons for that, wrong turns and so on, but he didn't have any chances left, save the slim hope I offered him now.

I reached into my pocket and removed the envelope from inside the Racing Post, chucked it towards him. 'Take that.'

He caught the package, looked inside. 'Gus, what's this?'

'Just a few quid … for you to get yourself set up in a new town.'

A car's horn sounded from beyond the cooncil curtains and Barry stuck an eye to the gap in the wood. 'It's a wee white van ... A burly fella's getting out.'

'That'll be Mac,' I said.

'Mac the fucking Knife?'

I nodded, as I stood up to face him I could sense Barry's apprehension. He was lost, confused and ready to place himself in the hands of his maker. For want of that option, I stepped in, 'Look, take the money and get far away.'

'But ...'

I flagged him down. 'No buts, Barry. You're getting in that car with Mac.'

Three loud thuds clattered on the door. Barry's eyes widened.

The door's hinges sung out, 'Hello ...' It was Mac. His footsteps sounded on the stairs.

'Gus, I don't know ...'

'Don't even think about it, Barry. Just do it.'

The living-room door opened and Mac stepped in. He stood with his feet splayed and shoulders back, his broad chest seemed to be filling the room with threatening rays. Barry looked at him, then back to me. If there was a doubt in his mind that Mac was a man to be messed with it evaporated on first sight.

'Alright, Gus,' said Mac. 'This him?' He tipped his head in Barry's direction, Mac managed to make him look like something he'd just stepped in.

'Take him south, no stops, and don't let him out your sight,' I said handing over the shooter. 'And ditch that on your way home.'

Mac trousered the pump-action. 'How far south?'

'Far enough that he can't get back in a hurry.'

Mac nodded. 'I'll take him to fucking Brighton.'

Barry rolled his gaze towards the ceiling. 'Oh, Jesus.'

'Well he's not going to help you,' said Mac stretching a hand out towards Barry's shirtfront.

Hospitals set me off. Too many bad memories. The familiar smells, the disinfectant, the industrial floor-polish; they all just stick painful pins in me. I walked to the front desk and took directions from a sister called Agnes who had hair like a crash-helmet, there was a tin of lacquer somewhere sitting empty that was to blame. Still, she smiled widely enough and that was something to be grateful for in Edinburgh these days.

I followed the signs to Danny Murray's ward and hoped I wasn't going to be greeted with too much of an eyesore. Shakey had a reputation for being thorough. It was just Danny's bad luck that he was the one who had been sent to find Barry – but then the Romans would have killed the messenger so maybe his luck was in.

The ward was split into a series of private rooms, almost cell-like; he must have loved that. I turned the handle and went in.

'Hello, Danny,' I said.

He looked at the brown paper bag in my hand. 'I hope that's wet.'

'Grapes, actually.'

He looked away. I spotted the monitor at his bedside and the drip attached to his hand. His head was bandaged tightly but there was little or nothing the medical staff could do with the bruising and cuts on his face.

I pulled out a chair as Danny directed the remote control to the small television in the corner. Jeremy Brett as Holmes faded to black on the screen.

There was an uneasy silence for a moment or two and then Danny spoke, 'What are you doing here?'

I sighed. 'What are any of us doing here, mate?'

He shook his head. 'Bloody riddles.'

I offered the grapes, they were refused. I placed the bag on the bedside table. 'I thought you'd like to know that I found Barry ... like you asked.'

He huffed. 'Fat lot of good it's going to do me now.'

The plastic chair was stiff, I eased my back further into it. 'Fat lot it was going to do you in any case.'

He turned, a wince crossed his face. 'What the hell are you on about, Dury?'

'You didn't want Barry, or should I say Shakey didn't want Barry ... it was what he had you were after.'

Danny looked away, held firm.

I leaned forward a little, lowered my voice. 'The job, Danny, you were after the details of the job.'

He turned to face me. 'And?'

I grinned all over him. 'Don't worry, I have all the details for you.' I fished in my pocket for the piece of paper where I'd written down the particulars of a horse trader called McCarthy with a property in the wilds of Midlothian.

Danny pressed himself forward in the bed, the stiff white linen creased. 'They're turning over a fucking stables, are you kidding me?'

I shook my head. 'McCarthy sells all over the place, it's all cash too, they reckon he's holding three-quarters of a mill' at any one time.'

A pained smile crossed Danny's face, 'Aye, bet he's selling to all those bloody Irish tinkers!' He leaned towards the bedside cabinet and retrieved his mobi. 'Christ, Shakey will love this ... hates horsey types at the best. All those fucking wax jackets and wellies ...'

I let him dial the number and headed for the door.

At the jamb I turned. 'Put in a good word for Barry, eh.'

Danny nodded, then started to tell his tale.

It was getting dark when I jumped off the number 26 on London Road. A black lab shook itself and showered me with the water on its coat. It was that time of night when people started to rush about. The end of the day. Time to be home. You could be jostled, elbowed, knocked on your arse if you weren't careful. I trudged into the Booze and News store and picked up a copy of The Hootsman; there would be nothing in it but old habits die hard.

As the lad on the till rung up the paper I eyed the neat rows of bottles on the shelf behind him. They had The Famous Grouse, my favourite brand, but I declined the instinct to indulge.

'Keep a clear head, Gus,' I told myself, sotto voce.

'I'm sorry, sir?'

I was jolted back to reality. 'Eh, twenty Benson's, mate.'

The young lad turned for the smokes and rung them up. I added a pack of mint gum from the rack and passed over a twenty: the last of Danny's pay packet.

On the way out I ducked under an old woman's umbrella – a stray metal insect leg stabbing at my eyes without mercy. She was unaware or didn't care. I kept on with a craving for a cig on me but the smirry rain was back. I opted for gum.

The traffic was backed up all the way to the lights at Abbey Mount. I could see the bloke from the little art shop wrestling with the shutters. The windows of the laundrette were bathed in condensation, too much to tell who was holding the fort, but I stuck my hands in the pockets of my Crombie and trudged in that direction anyway.

Arthur's Seat was still visible between the gaps in the tenements – like a gloomy old man crouched on the edge of the city, and passing judgement, no doubt. I tipped him a wink, we were almost brothers in arms after all.

As the bell above the door chimed I walked into the laundrette and looked about. It was empty, at least I thought that at first. I was turning back for the door when the Polish lass appeared at the far end, her face pressed into a paper tissue.

'Hello there,' she was eating, her mouth half-full.

'Hi again.'

She wiped the edges of her mouth, lost some lip gloss. 'I'm just feeding my face!' She smiled, spluttered a little. 'I have cake, would you like one?'

I shook my head. 'No, thanks anyway.'

She walked behind the counter and dropped her tissue in the waste-bin. She was smiling again as she rose up on tiptoes to take the stool. 'You don't have washing with you.'

I removed my hands from my pockets, 'No ... I, eh ...' The CD was inside my coat, I handed it over. 'Well, here, as a thanks for the other day.'

She looked embarrassed.

I felt embarrassed.

She spoke first, 'The Stagger Rats ... thank you.'

'You said you liked them, so I thought, y'know ...' I was getting tongue-tied. It was time to depart. 'So, anyway, thanks again.'

She wagged the CD, 'There was really no need. But thank you.'

I turned for the door as I reached for the handle I caught her turning over the CD, reading out the tracks.

'They're playing at the Caves this weekend, you know,' I said.

'Oh, really ... Are you going?'

I shrugged my shoulders. 'Don't know, maybe.'

The bell clanged as I pulled the door wide.

'Then maybe I will too.'

R.I.P Robbie Silva

a novella

If I had to say when it started, when the shit really broke, I'd go for the day I met Gail. I was sitting in a drinker at the foot of Leith Walk tanning Tennent's – roughly one hour out my stretch – and retelling the morning's main event. Trust me, after nine months in the pound, a thing like this was an *event*.

'So, I walks out the gates and goes into the first shop I sees, asks for a pack of smokes, I was *gasping*, like.' I got the nodding dog from Wellsy and Bandy Rab. It had been a while since I'd held court with the old crew – boys looked like they were right into it as well – I can feed a yarn with the best of them, known for it.

'And the guy at the till, he's some fat fucking Jambo sitting on his arse with a gut spilling over the counter. Y'know the type, most exercise he gets is doing a couple of scratch-cards a day ...'

Laughs. More nods. Bandy Rab shifted onto his other arse-cheek, leaned into Wellsy, making his pint shoogle in the glass; Wellsy gave him a wee frown that said *cool the beans, man*.

'So, he gives me this look ...' I made the look, that's when I caught sight of the blonde with her eye on me; she was leaning on the bar, pushing out a belter of an arse in cut-down Levis, or was it hot-pants now I think of it? There was definitely a bit of a glossy pout about her lips anyway, I remember that, that and a fair rack as well. I've always been more of an arse man, but well, you notice a thing like that, don't you? She was with a couple of lads, an older bloke that looked a bit of a player and a some gimp with a mullet and an AC/DC T-shirt.

I splayed arms, made the gesture – funny how an audience will improve your performance – continued: 'Then he goes ... *back the way you came*.'

'Eh?' I said it the way I told him. 'And he's up out the seat, goes, *I'm not serving you*.'

I felt the heat rising in my chest, the return of the red mist, as I retold the story – this guy had got my goat. Fucking sure he had.

'So, I looks at him and he turns away, flags me off with the back of his hand like I'm some Calton Hill cock-washer or something.' I mean, I'm six-two and 15 stone. I'm solid too, all muscle, no jelly on me. I went inside this time with a 44-inch chest and bench-pressed it up to 46. Jed the Press they were calling me, no-one could fucking out-press me in there.

I copied the Jambo's dismissive gesture for the boys – they shook heads, knew the score. I saw the blonde was still all eyes for me as well. Made me want to smile but you can't encourage them, makes you look too keen and that's the last thing you want, nothing'll blow your chances faster. A hoor of a business.

I started up again: '"*I don't serve your lot,*" he goes ... *My lot*, I says, and what the fuck would that be, mate?'

I stood up at this point, fair getting into the swing of things, has to be done. It was a big deal to have anything to tell them; fuck all had happened in Saughton that's for sure and certain.

'Now he's on his feet and fumbling about the counter, saying: *Don't call me fucking mate, I'm not yer fucking mate, pal*. He actually calls me *pal*. The fanny. Typical fucking Jambo – he's all right, he's all wrong. But then he arks right up, hoicks out this shooter, old fucking war heirloom ... and the cunt points it at me.'

I hold my finger out in front of me like it's a gun and Wellsy and Bandy Rab get off the nodding dog patter and onto the Ren and Stimpy eyes, staring, just staring. It's a look that says *and where the fuck's this going?* Y'know, like they're not quite sure they aren't sitting with some serious radge that's gone and offed somebody in the last hour. No danger. I mean, I've no fear of doing another stretch, life on the out isn't that exciting at the best of times, but c'mon ...

"*I'm warning you,*" he goes, and I'm like in total shock, disbelief y'know ... I'm half-an-hour out the fucking pound and this cunt's pointing a shooter at me ... Holy fuck, I says, stroll the fuck on mate ... but, he's a Jambo – a fucking fat one 'n' all ... even by Jambo standards – so the reactions can't be so fast, I'm thinking ... I swing my arm round and snatch the shooter out his mitt. He's staring at me now, got that glaiket look that says, *just-how-the-fuck-did-that-happen* and *is-this-bloke-maybe-fucking-Robocop-or-something*?'

The lads lapped it up. Though maybe they were just so relieved that I hadn't offed this prick. Got laughter and back slaps. Wellsy near choked on a bit of swally that came up and out his throat. I watched them sink back in their chairs, wiping their eyes; Wellsy supped a bit of Cally Special to clear the pipes.

That's when the blonde bit turned round fully and put her tits out, leaned back on the bar. Stop the lights, man, I was thinking ... she was giving me the diddy eye. Pure mad for it so she was. Then she caught me staring and a bit of a smile spread on her face, a kinda crooked smile – knew she had the hook in – there were bright white teeth shining out from behind her glossy lips. That's when the mullet-gimp grabbed her arm, tried to turn her round. The old boy was having none of it though, slapped the gimp down. The bold old dude looked a useful sort and the wee man stepped back, looked almost shrunken. I wondered had I seen this big grey-haired guy somewhere before – inside maybe? He had one of those time-done stares, but it was the bit of stuff I was more interested in. I clocked a tattoo on her belly. A wee green clover, like the Tim badge or something, just above the belt-line of her hot-pants. I was thinking, *Christ, no' a Pape* ... hoped she didn't have a beard like Danny McGrain's down there!

'So what did you do then, Jed?' said Bandy Rab.

'What do you think I did? ... Got my fucking smokes and got the fuck out of there. Kept the gun, like.' I lifted up my shirt and showed them the old Webley tucked into my denims. The handle was wooden, scratched all to buggery it was, sorta looked like I had a table leg stuffed down my keks ... I was thinking that can't be a good look but then the blonde bit seemed to straighten herself, pushed off the bar and started to walk over. She had one of those model walks, exaggeratedly crossing her legs one in front of the other at every step. Her deep brown, rounded eyes shone as she got closer, but it was the rack I was focussed on ... it was like something you'd see on the front of *Loaded*.

Could hardly believe my Donald Duck!

Wellsy and Bandy Rab nudged each other under the table as she holed up in front of us.

'I heard what you said about that guy,' she went.

I played it cool. 'Oh, aye.'

'Yeah ... I know him.'

That threw me a bit, played a safe ball: 'That a fact?'

She leaned over the table, widened those big eyes even further, but my own slipped down the V of her tank-top.

There was more said, but whatever it was I paid so little attention that I couldn't tell you what ... except for one thing: her name was Gail.

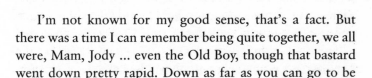

I'm not known for my good sense, that's a fact. But there was a time I can remember being quite together, we all were, Mam, Jody ... even the Old Boy, though that bastard went down pretty rapid. Down as far as you can go to be honest, in my books anyway.

Jody might not have agreed, but Mam would have if she knew what I knew after she passed away; Jody was just too kind-hearted for her own good, that was her problem. I never had that option. I sometimes think, when you're dealt a shit hand it's all you can play. I mean, you can spend a year and a day weighing up different options, trying to persuade yourself out of the obvious, but you're only delaying the inevitable. You can't deny your nature, who and what you truly are. That's the way I see it anyway, always have. A hoor of a business.

As Gail invited herself into our company, Wellsy and Bandy Rab took the hint – clever boys – and went for the early bath.

'Want to go for a ride?' she said.

I nearly ate my chips backwards.

'Y'*wha*–?' Thought my luck was in for sure. Then she produced a chain with a car key on it and grinned all over me. I felt like a right tube.

'What about your mates?' I said.

'Who?'

I nodded to the pair she'd just left standing at the bar. They looked away when they saw there was some attention on them.

She laughed. 'That's my *half*-brother and my old man ...'

'Keep you on a tight leash, do they?'

She arked up a bit at that, turned tail and headed for the door. As she went she clocked me over her shoulder, nodded follow. I downed the last of my Tennent's (I know, I know – but I'll be fucked if I'm drinking that Hun piss McEwan's) and wiped my mouth with the back of my hand.

When I think about it now, I must have looked a wee bit too keen on the prospect ahead of me because Gail started to laugh as she went, her shoulders bobbing up and down so much that she lost her footing and staggered into a table ... funny creatures, women.

The BMW started first time.

Nice set of wheels. Always loved these Beemers, but I was thinking this was a hell of a lot of car for a girl of her age and station ... though I really hadn't a scoobie about her station at this stage. She looked all right, I mean dressed all right and all that, she could have been working in some office, one of the Standard Lifers or what have you, but this was the middle of the day. She was no dole mole that was for sure so she must have been collecting a wedge somewhere, somehow. There's a few of that sort in Edinburgh – strangers to a day's work – though mainly they're English students doing a masters in daytime telly and hand-shandies at mammy and daddy's expense. Chuggers, town's full of them.

'Nice motor,' I said.

'It's a fucking heap!' She flicked her hair back, those dark-blonde curls making waves over her shoulders. She didn't seem overly interested in anything I had to say; seemed like she was already decided on me without having sussed me out much at all. Or maybe she had; thing I found out about Gail later was, she liked her split decisions. I watched her turn the key in the ignition and then she went,

'I'm hungry, let's eat.'

She took us to Maccy Dees on London Road. I felt like a lottery winner driving down the road in a flash Beemer with a fit bit. The fun factory seemed a long way away. The road that had led there was even further away, forgotten, wiped out. I wanted to be spotted by some of the old crew – Jamie Dees or Whitey or Fanny Bass – anyone that knew me, just to have them turn head and give them a wee bit of something to yak about in the pub later on. I'd have got a blast out of that back then; showing off. Boys are all about showing off.

'What you want?' said Gail.

I was a bit low on the green-folding stuff, had been lifted with a wad of Jimmy Denners and forty Regal but came out with two-bob and a fag-coupon. Fucking screws. All thieving bastards, I tell you. If they're not introducing you to the slippery steps, they're rifling your pockets for snout and coin. Said, 'I'm all right, thanks.'

'Not even a Coke?' she promptly produced a stack that would have settled a small nation's debts, said, 'Sure? ... It's on me.'

I smiled, 'Maybe a Coke, then.'

She ordered herself a Big Mac, sprung for the 'Go Large' option when asked. As she leaned over she exposed her lower back above her hot-pants ... how did she stay in shape and eat like that? Something wasn't right there ... was she for real? Was any of this?

On the way out the gates of Saughton I was as flat as a tack: expecting a long stretch of sofa surfing, maybe hawking my arse for a labouring job on some new rabbit-hutch housing site in Midlothian or somewhere if I was lucky, but here I was in a flashy motor with this Gail bit and ... well, it was beyond the beyonds.

We drove to Holyrood Park, pulled up next to the swan

pond. Tourists were taking pictures, scores of them headed for Arthur's Seat in a long shaky ant-line. I shook my head. Some things never changed about Edinburgh; some things changed all the time ... like the Hibs managers. My mind wandered onto the current back-four; game these days was all about defence. A hoor of a business.

Gail devoured the burger and fries, then set about washing it all down with the Coke. She touched her chin as a few droplets of Coke dribbled down. I could count the number of words I'd had out of her by this stage on my fingers and toes. I was waiting for some kind of a breakthrough, bit of proper chatter, y'know, a groundbreaker, but then she said, 'I think we should have a word with our friend ... '

'Our *friend*?'

She took the lid off the Coke cup, sucked the drips out of the straw, then took out an ice cube, said, 'Jambo prick that wouldn't serve you.'

I looked at her. She was pouting, sucking back the ice cube.

'He's had his ...'

She let the ice thin a bit more, then swallowed. 'Nope, he's not.'

I played along, lifted the top of my jacket, exposed the Webley's handle. 'I have his shooter.'

Gail's eyes widened; they were dark pools, intense. She reached a hand over and took out the gun. I watched her hold it in her hand, play with it. It looked too heavy for her, lolling from side to side in her grip; but the power-trip seemed to make her happy. 'I have an idea,' she said.

'Oh, aye.' I wasn't sure I liked the sound of this, but there was something about watching her pat the shooter off her St Tropez-tanned thighs that had me wondering how bad could things really be.

'You just stick with me ... I'll show you a thing or two!'

I didn't doubt it. She lifted the gun, kissed the stalk.

Inside I liked two things: watching Hibs hump Hearts; and the other, well, it was a more solitary affair ... Gail climbed over the gear-stick, popping another ice-cube in her mouth.

'*Mmh-hmh,*' she said, passing the cube from her mouth to mine.

'It's broad daylight,' I said.

It didn't seem to bother her, not in the slightest.

There was a Bon Jovi CD stuck in the Beemer's player.

'Bon-*fucking*-Jovi?' I said.

'It's my prick brother's – *half*-brother! One of Daddy's fuck-ups, anyway ... he's no taste in music, or anything else ... Daddy couldn't get the CD out the player. He lost the head every time he drove it after that ... so, that's why I got this car?'

I double-blinked. 'Hang about ... never heard of garages, with mechanics, folk that fix these things.'

The idea had her scoobied, seemed a stupid suggestion.

'Daddy has heaps of cars ... he isn't bothered.'

An old phrase hit me – *man alive* – said, 'Okay, whatever.' It fairly twisted my melon that someone would turn over a motor to their daughter because they couldn't be bothered having the fucking CD player fixed but I quickly sussed there must have been more to it; was Gail bullshitting me? There was certainly more to this girl than met the eye ... but what did meet the eye wasn't half bad so I let it slide.

We headed back out through the city centre, hit the Corstorphine Road. Gail fumbled for a pack of smokes, sparked up. I took one, opened the window and had a hit on the red Marlboro. The clear white trail that escaped the window had me smiling at the thought of my new-found freedom. Did I really want to take any risks with that? Christ, life was a risk ... and short too, experience over the last few years had taught me that. Perhaps it had made me a bit reckless as well. I mean, what was it all about, eh? When I think about being banged up and my Old Man ... and Jody, well, I try not to think about that. It's easier to just say *fuck it* ...

'So, this Jambo ... what's your problem with him?'

I got a look, those eyes again ...

'It's personal.'

I tapped the dash, 'Hey, if we're about to stand the cunt over ... we can get a wee bit personal.'

She smiled, placed a hand on my thigh. 'He caught me fucking round the back of his shop.'

'*Wha–*?'

'On the crates round there.'

I took a draw on the tab. 'And ...'

'He, like, took it kind of personal.'

She needed further prompting. I raised brows, said, 'Called the filth?'

'Not exactly.' She looked at me, those black eyes sunk further than I thought possible. She was seriously ratted with this guy; I knew the territory. 'He threatened to tell my Dad ... if I didn't suck him off.'

I didn't know what to say. For some reason the thought actually upset me. For the first time since I'd met Gail, I wondered if there might just be some depth to this girl, something beyond the hot-pants and the St Tropez tan. She wasn't all surface. I felt myself draw closer to her. I don't know why, it was just one of those things.

Some people you meet don't mean a thing to you. Seriously, you couldn't care if they lived or died. And others, they strike a chord. I don't know what it is, they remind you of something or someone maybe. There's a connection, like when you were a kid and you spent every day with your best mate who wore the same clothes as you, swapped footy stickers with you and got upset at the thought of you ever moving away. Yeah, I felt myself draw closer to Gail; I also felt myself draw closer to beating the living crap out of this fat fucking Jambo.

I'm not saying there was no doubts. No way. I had plenty. But, y'know what, there's a point where I just switch off to all that – the wee voice of reason. One that tells you, *hey Jed man, calm your jets*! This isn't a new thing with me; it's been brewing, in my make-up you might say, for a few years.

I had this square-peg psychiatrist bloke come round when I was in the pound and he asked if there was anything that made me angry, called them *triggers*. I'd never really thought that deeply about it before so I said I supposed there was but this wasn't enough for the cunt.

He asked me what they were, had me making a list ... actually fucking writing them down. Well, at first, the list was pretty short, things like, when Jimmy Hill called David Narey's goal against Brazil a toe-poke and just the sheer sight of Charlie Nicholas on the telly or in the paper. But, naw, that wasn't good enough for him.

He made me add to the list. Wanted personal things. I started with some shite about the way every bus in Edinburgh is a number 26 and that's fine if you're going to the top of the Walk, but when you're wanting to get to the southside for a quiet jar with the boys it's a right pisser. He didn't buy that, asked me to delve deeper.

I wasn't into it. He could see that but that didn't bother him; he was on a fucking mission; you get square-pegs like that.

So, I told him about this time I was heading home through the Grassmarket late at night. It was after seeing Liverpool hump Newcastle on the big screen. There's nothing like watching fat Geordies crying, so it had turned into an all-nighter. It was well gone chucking out time when I spotted this young lassie puking herself inside out in the street. There was these two biffers trying to hold her up. She was just a young lassie, a schoolie likely, and this pair were holding her arms – one carried her stilettos – and letting her chuck but they were laughing and nodding at each other as they did it.

They got her straightened up and started walking her down the road. I watched her pull her arm away and say she was going for a taxi but this pair of cockheads were having none of it, nodding and laughing away to each other. I saw where it was going and I knew it was none of my business but for some reason I started following them, slowly like.

The lassie was all over the fucking road, limping and leaning into walls. She could barely stand and this pair were copping sly gropes at her arse and tits but she was just too rubber to even notice. Then they headed her up a close, one of those dark vennels, the go-nowhere ones you get all over the Old Town.

I felt my heart beating faster as I retold this story to the square-peg; I remembered my blood was pounding in my head when I got round the wall of that close and saw the pair of biffers wrestling with the young lassie. One had her skirt up over her head and the other was holding her wrists. Her head was jerking about like a puppy in a sack before she passed out.

When I showed up, I shouted out to them – they looked stunned, shocked to see me. All I saw was the whites of their eyes widening. They were big lads, but I was game. I went in with the head and decked one, the other, a big ginger holding the girl's arms, dropped her on the ground; she fell like a sack of tatties. He went to gub me and caught me on the cheek. It was a good swipe but I brushed it off like swatting a fly and laid in about him. It was all kidney punches, must have been dozens of them because when I was finished I was sweating and panting; I realised I'd been holding him up as he slumped down the wall of the close.

I was wrecked, right out of it. Puggled.

The girl was lying on the cobbles; she was gone too. Looked like she was curled up for sleep. I got her on her feet and back to the road; flagged down a Joe Baxi.

Her name was Susan and she lived in Pilton; I told the square-peg that. He didn't have anything to say about my story though. There was nothing about triggers or such shite and I never got to see what he wrote down in his wee pad about me.

I couldn't have given a shit.

She parked the Beemer up at the kerb; a reverse job slung in there sweet as a nut. Quite the driver, Gail. When she pulled out the keys she hit me with a wink, was like a shutter closing over the big baby brown eye for a second then it was sparkling once more.

'You ready?' she said.

'I was born ready.'

That got me a squeeze of the thigh and a snatched kiss before she was easing out the door backwards. I took off my jacket and threw it under the passenger seat.

It was a little access road about three, maybe four, hundred yards long. At the end was a garage, place that did motorbikes and by the looks of it, the odd dodgy spray-job; streaks of paint testers running down the front wall. There was nobody out the front of the garage and the street – split into the kind of boxy wee rat-hole flats and bedsits you get all over Edinburgh – was quiet as the grave. Must have been Giro day. Or that prick Jeremy Kyle was on.

I took a good deck up and down for signs of life. I knew the routine. This type of lark is okay for kicks when you start out, a good buzz, bit of an adrenalin high, but after you have your collar felt a few times the pitfalls dawn on you. There were blaggers in the grey-bar Hilton lived for that kind of thing; got a blast out of being hunted and rumbled. They were long-term lags though. Hitting fifty-five or sixty with thirty years of it parked up inside. Nut-jobs. They'd sit in the yard yakking about doing over a post office and living like kings, holed up in a Travelodge with the bedspread scattered in notes. They'd no sooner land a few grand than they'd be blowing it in Scotbet or splashing for rounds in some skanky drinkers. Like I say, I've no fear of landing another stretch – meat and drink to me – only thing I can't take is the stoat the balls. Paedos, kiddie-fiddlers, beasts ... whatever you call them, they're all sub-human filth. Leave me alone with one of the bastards for a few minutes and they get a taste of their own fucking medicine. But, like I say, I'm no fucking idiot either. Careful does it. A hoor of a business.

Gail called out to me, 'What's up?'

I was stood in the street, checking out the locks on some heavy wooden gates leading through to a communal drying area, said, 'Nothing. Just coming.'

As Gail headed to the end of the road, I leaned back onto the gates. The locks heaved, squeaked a bit; the wood creaked. When I leaned back I saw the rusty screws holding in the lock had separated from the rotten wood. One kick, maybe even a shove would put the gates through.

When I caught up with Gail she was easing herself off

a wall; she looked calm. This was unusual. Most folk get hyped-up before something like this – Gail looked like she was up for another day at the office. I'd seen people piss themselves, puke their guts up, start shaking uncontrollably, but the ones with no nerves were the ones you had to watch. Pound to a pail of shite they were likely to go scripto on the job and end up lamping some poor old cunt who was only in for a Daily Record and a packet of Pandrops.

'You sure you know what you're doing?' I said to her.

A smile, broad one. 'You're kidding em on, right?'

I shook my head.

'Look, Jed boy, you don't need to worry about me.' She leaned forward, hooked an arm round my neck and slipped her tongue in my mouth. She'd managed to reassure me.

When we hit the shopping concourse, I touched the shooter's handle, made sure it was tucked into my waistband well enough. It was. There was a shoe shop up on the left. I pointed it out to Gail. 'Nip in and get a pair of Pretty Polly's, eh?'

'You're shitting me.'

I shook my head. She sparked, 'Why me?'

'Because it looks a bit odd a bloke buying that sort of stuff, don't you think?'

Her eyes narrowed. 'Okay. American Tan, I take it?'

'Aye, whatever.'

When she got back from the shoe shop, Gail handed me the packet of tights and I stuffed them in my back pocket. I saw the Jambo's store now – it gave me a bit of a rush. 'There it is,' I said.

Gail smiled; her white teeth dazzled me. 'Let's do the bastard.'

'Hang about.' I held her arm, waited for a woman with a tartan shopping trolley to go past.

'*Wha*–?'

'Didn't want her going in there and us ending up dancing around that fucking trolley on our way out.'

I let the old wifey get a few yards past the store and then I nodded Gail over the road. The building was home to a block of flats and the entry was a blue door beside the Jambo's shop front. I pointed Gail over there. We stood in the hallway as I pressed the top button on the buzzer; it read 'Davis' in an immature hand. A whiney English accent answered. 'Hello.'

'Fed-Ex for Smith ... the buzzer's out.'

He buzzed us in.

I pushed the door and Gail followed. Inside the grey hallway I took out the tights, ripped the legs apart and handed one to Gail. She pulled it over her face. I shook my head.

'Pull it down when we get right outside. Just leave it on the back of your head, okay.'

'You sound like you've done this before,' she said.

I grinned, thought about saying 'Aye, once or twice,' but held schtum.

I took a few deep breaths, checked the shooter again, then looked at Gail. She hadn't altered one bit since we'd been in the pub.

'Ready to roll, then?' I said.

'Fucking right!'

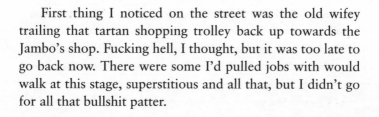

First thing I noticed on the street was the old wifey trailing that tartan shopping trolley back up towards the Jambo's shop. Fucking hell, I thought, but it was too late to go back now. There were some I'd pulled jobs with would walk at this stage, superstitious and all that, but I didn't go for all that bullshit patter.

I hugged the outline of the shop front, moved fast. Just before I reached the door I pulled down the stockings and removed the shooter. On the way in I upped the aggression immediately.

'Hands on the till now, y'cunt!'

The Jambo had a skinny wee roll-up in his mouth, obviously just about to go for a sly gasp. When he saw me his mouth widened and the rollie dangled from his lower lip. I didn't give him long enough to recognise the shooter, brought it across his coupon and split his cheek. The rollie went for a flier.

'You fucking deaf or stupid, cunt? Eh? Eh?... Money out the till now!'

There was no-one in the shop but some movement behind me started to tug at my attention. I made a cardinal error, turned away from the Jambo. Behind me Gail was turning over the shelves, tipping tins and Weetabix packets onto the floor. I stood watching in disbelief. In a second she ran past me, mounted the counter, her hot-pants sliding on the shiny surface as she grabbed a bottle of Smirnoff off the rack.

I was frozen. Didn't know whether to shout at her or run. My mind blanked. I watched as she brought the bottle down over his head and then he crumpled on the floor, blood gushing from a serious head wound.

'The fuck are you doing?' I yelled.

Gail started to kick at the Jambo, stamp on his face. Her blows were too insubstantial to do much damage but before long the soles of her shoes were covered in blood and she slipped about on the slimy floor.

'Cunt ... fucking cunt ...' she yelled. She had the stocking off her face now, turned up so she could get a better look at him. It made me scan for cameras but I didn't see any.

As I gazed about the shop something kicked in me and I

got sense enough to turn the till around and rifle it. I filled my pockets with cash. Must have been the best part of a grand in there. When I was done I looked back to find Gail had righted herself; she turned to the cigarettes counter and pulled down a can of lighter fluid, started to douse the Jambo with it.

'No ... fucksake ...' I shouted out to her but she was gone on some nut-job trip. I put the shooter back in my jeans and tried to grab the canister off her but she was beyond my reach. I turned to mount the counter; heard the Jambo coming round, moaning. Then I heard the match strike. I was over the counter as Gail dropped the flaming match. He went up like a lantern.

'Jesus-*fucking*-Christ, girl ... what are you doing?'

She was laughing now, lolling her head back as she said, 'He had it fucking coming ... he *so* had it coming!'

———✦———

There's been a couple of times in my life when I just seemed to burst out my skin. You run on some kind of weird energy that doesn't seem to be yours. It's like when you hear about these folk in car crashes and they have a kid trapped inside and they find this super strength to lift the motor off its wheels to free the nipper ... this was one of those moments.

I grabbed Gail by the waist and flung her over the counter out of the way. She didn't land right and staggered into a stack of Ariel washing-powder boxes. The lot went flying. There was a puff of powder raised as my arms swung back over the counter. I grabbed an old anorak that was sitting on the back of the chair by the till. I wrapped the navy and red hood around my hand and started beating the fat Jambo with it. The flames shot out the sides and then there was a black escape of smoke and they were gone after three or four swipes. When I was done, I dropped the jacket.

The Jambo looked fucked, but he was alive. I was grateful for that. I propped him up and he yelped a bit. His arse-cheeks squeaked on the floor as he went and a brown streak appeared on the lino – he'd shit himself; I didn't blame the cunt.

I was about to ask if he was okay when the door opened and an Asian bit came in and started screaming. Her hands were up at her face, but she didn't seem to be moving anything else; it was like she was frozen to the spot. Just screaming and bawling.

I knew I had to mush.

I ran round the counter and grabbed Gail's arm. She didn't like that, wanted to fight me. I showed her a fist, said, 'Move. Or you're going cold.'

She got the message.

The Asian bit's screams brought in people from the street. A workie in Adidas trackies and, behind him, the old diddy with the tartan shopping trolley lolled into the doorway. This was the last thing I needed. The workie looked like he was thinking of squaring up to me, so I sorted that problem out first. I grabbed his left ear and brought his head forward as I sunk mine into his nose – a fountain of blood escaped as he fell to the ground.

At the door I fronted the old dear, said, 'Excuse me, love.'

She didn't get the message, so I put my hands on her shoulders. She smelled of lavender as I motioned her to the side.

Gail was already on her way out when I hit the street. I'd side-stepped the shopping trolley but the handle caught my foot as I went and the day's messages – fucking kilos of spuds and a frozen chicken – keeled me over. As I went a few tins of mushie pees rolled out in front of me. I picked one up and, in blind rage, threw it out into the road.

There were cars stopped now. People staring. Gail shouting, 'Get off your fucking arse.'

I was ready to kick her own arse into her fucking neck for this turn of events. It was all her fault, but then I spotted a suit on his mobi and I knew we had to nash. Proper fast.

I got on my feet and shook off the shopping trolley. Gail was already heading over the road. Cars screeched as we went; a few daft cunts sounded their horn at us. I was raging. I'd scraped my shoulder in the fall and it stung like a bastard. Those fuckers can count themselves lucky they didn't get a good leathering or at least a few holes in their windscreens.

'Move it! Move it! Move it!' yelled Gail.

I ran after her. She was on the other side of the road now and heading back for the side-road. I caught her up. The square-pegs on the pavement pinned themselves against shop fronts as we went. It was almost funny; I mean, thinking back I can laugh about it ... but at the time it was a fucking disaster movie in progress.

I got my stride, hadn't realised how muscle-bound I'd become in the pound; my thighs were rubbing together and the friction was painful. At the top of the side-road I looked back to see if anyone was following. They had more sense.

As we turned the bend, I removed the stocking. Gail took hers off too and dropped it on the street.

'Pick it up!' I said.

'What?'

'Pick it up ... think the Filth won't find that?' Jesus, these days, you can't be too careful. Don't need to watch CSI to get the fucking message ... one hair and you're done.

She picked it up, started to jog, but I hauled her back. We settled into duckwalking towards the car. I was still pumped, sorely pissed and ready to cane Gail's arse for her, but experience had taught me to keep it together at times like this.

I was clocking the garage, looking for signs of life when I heard the beep-beeping. Up the road – where the Beemer was parked – a HGV was turning. Fuck! This was all we needed. I saw from the driver's face that he was lost, had taken a wrong turn and was trying to manoeuvre himself out of trouble. I knew the fucking feeling.

'Shit ... what do we do now?' said Gail.

I grabbed her wrist, walked her towards the wooden gate I'd checked earlier. When we stopped I pressed my back against the panel. The locks were rotten and the screws rusted. I leaned my weight there for three or four seconds but it didn't shift.

'What's wrong?'

I didn't answer.

The gate was stronger than I thought.

The beep-beeping continued up the road. The driver was embarrassed. He waved, thought we'd stopped to look at him. I gave him a nod; as he turned back to the wheel I put the force of my shoulders into the gate. It sprung.

'Right, this way ...' I said.

The last thing I heard as I eased through the gap was the beep-beeping being replaced by the sound of sirens. It was the filth.

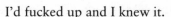

I'd fucked up and I knew it.

Normally on a job like this there'd be two motors – one from Sam's Hot Car Lot and a change-over car that's near-as-damn-it to legit. But Christ on the bloody cross, I'd dived in with only the one car ... and one we couldn't get to at that. A hoor of a business.

The filth were on the main street now, couple of squad cars by the sound of it. I heard some randomers shouting at them – probably directing them to our whereabouts. Gail looked a bit grim; she was panting hard and there was sweat on her brow and her top lip.

'What do we do?'

'Follow me.'

It was a back yard to a block of flats, what you might call a drying green. I ran to the edge of the wall and took a deck at the path; it led nowhere.

'Fuck.'

'What's up?' She was panicking.

I took off my shirt and threw it on the grass, told her to do the same.

'What?'

'Don't fucking question – do!'

She stripped and I ran to the line, hoicked down a couple of white shirts – they were obviously some square-peg's … was a good drying day after all.

'Here, get this on!' I said to Gail.

As she buttoned up I scooped up our old clothes and ran them over to the dumpster. I was thinking about the next move the whole while; in a few minutes plod was going to come rumbling up the side path and right into us.

'What about the car?' said Gail.

'Leave it … you can come back when it's dark. Or better yet, get someone to collect it for you.' We were smack-bang in the middle of no-man's land. There was no way of blagging a motor in a hurry and I'd ran right out of time to think. 'Right, over here.'

I put my fingers together, gave Gail a punty up the wall. She could hardly reach the top with her fingers but when she got high enough I put my hands under her shoes and lifted her over. She climbed up on top and sat there. 'Jump

... fucksake, jump.' This girl, I was coming to realise, was either utterly reckless or utterly dippit. Either way, if she didn't find sense in the next few seconds, we were fucked.

I followed after her. The wall was a good ten-feet high but I'd been doing the chinnies inside and the arms were well able to get me over. As I reached the top I spied a curtain twitching in a second-floor window of the flats. Looked like trouble. I could see myself hauled down the nick, being ID'd by some fucking busybody. I rested a moment to see if the cunt would show his face – you get a look at them, a good look in their eye, and they think twice about shouting out – but no-one showed.

I eased myself down the wall; Gail was biting her lower lip now. I heard the filth close by. There was the sound of cuffs rattling on belts, then the sound of walkie-talkies. Gail started to whimper; tears welled in the corners of her eyes. I watched her lips curl down and then she showed her bottom row of teeth. I knew that she was a heartbeat away from full-on bawling and that would be that.

I grabbed her round the neck, put my hand over her mouth, whispered, 'Now look, shut the fuck up, right?' Her eyes widened; there was fear in there; I knew the territory. I grabbed her, lifted her clean off her feet and eased us into the wall. The walkie-talkies were inches away from us now. All that separated us from the long arm of the law was the width of two rows of brick. I nodded towards the wall; Gail's eyes started to fully moisten, pools gathered on the lower lids then began to run over the rims. Black-mascara streaks trailed down her cheeks. I felt the hot tears on the back of my hand.

'No sign of them here, Sarge ... over,' said plod.

The walkie-talkie let out a static crackle.

'Right. Got that.'

I waited for a moment, frightened the pounding of my

heart might give our place away over the wall, but then the radio sparked again.

'Take the through-road with Mike, eh Davie ... Over.'

'Okay, boss. Over.'

I heard plod holster his walkie-talkie, then call out. 'Mike ... back this way.'

I heard their cuffs rattling as they ran. I waited for the bang of the gate, then let them get a few yards up the road before I turned back to Gail. Her eyes were scrunched up now. I didn't feel confident enough yet to release my grasp, said, 'You have to keep it down, right?'

She nodded.

I let her go.

Gail stepped back from me, then doubled over and puked.

'Jesus,' I said. 'This really is fucking amateur hour.'

I was still shaking my head as she straightened up, wiped the back of her mouth.

'What now?' she said.

I pointed to the water butt sitting next to the fence on the other side of the back green. 'There, up and over.'

She turned and started for the wall; I called her back. 'Uh-huh ... stick to the line of the building. Slow and casual, right? They're looking for a pair on the run so don't let's fucking telegraph it for them.'

As we set off I heard more sirens coming into the next street. They had us just about surrounded. For some reason a song I fucking detested started in my head ... *I need a miracle, I need a miracle ...*

Over the fence I did a quick recce of where we were. There was little or no room for manoeuvre, I knew that.

I figured getting onto Gorgie Road would be our best bet. Would fucking have to be, we had nothing else going. I had a mate in Dalry; figured if I could at least get to a payphone I could bell him for a pick-up.

Moosey owed me.

We'd been cellmates a few years back, but Moosey had started his stretch off in the worst possible way. He was a swooper – one of those cons that case the yard for fag dowps, dropping like gulls on them. I had to tell him straight if he carried on like that he'd never develop any cred, would likely end his days in there as some fat cunt's bitch. He got the message, eventually. But Moosey was one of those dafties you really needed to look after; like I say, he owed me.

When we hit Gorgie Road I tried to convince Gail that we needed to look as casual as possible.

'Grab my waist.'

'Eh?'

I put an arm round her. I was smiling, a wide-old grin, was trying to look the part. 'Snuggle up, hon.' After my earlier outburst the poor girl still didn't know whether she was about to get a slap. I said, 'We need to look the part ... The filth's flying about all over the shop.'

I was still sweating, felt the shooter slipping in my waistband as the moisture collected there. I tried to nudge it into place by contracting my stomach. Last thing I needed was a gun slipping onto the pavement and blowing the scene.

We got as far as a little Chinese carry-out place that was open for the lunch-time shift. Slipped in and prayed for a phone, nearly felt ready to kiss the little dude behind the counter when I saw the yellow payphone on the wall.

I popped in a few coins.

Ringing.

More ringing.

'Christ, Moosey ... pick the fucking phone up.'

The Chinese bloke slit his eyes at me. I smiled back, turned away. I knew he was getting suspicious. I nodded Gail towards the menu board. She took the hint.

'Hello ... ' It was Moosey.

'Moosey, mate ... how y'doing, there?'

'Jed ... that you?'

'Aye, the very same. Look can't talk right now. Need a bit of a lift, in a hurry like.'

A gap on the line. Moosey's voice came back low and flat. 'This a lift *lift* or are you up to your nuts in something there, Jed?'

I turned back to the counter; the Chinese bloke had gone out the back. 'Look, Moosey, I need a fucking pick-up on Gorgie Road, now! ... You fucking owe me, so move your arse.'

'I don't know, mate. I mean ...'

I upped the ante. 'Look, Moosey, there's a nice drink in it for you. I'm at the Chinese ...' I looked at the menu. 'Red Dragon.'

There was a gap on the line, then a sigh. 'Aye, okay. But I'm not driving you anywhere. I'll leave the keys in and then you're on your own.'

'No worries. What kind of motor is it?'

'Dunno ...' he paused for breath, sparked up a tab, 'haven't nicked it yet.'

The Chinese bloke made a reappearance. I made a big effort to get on his good side right from the off, ordered up a chicken chow mein, barbecue spare ribs and a few tubs of rice, prawn crackers, shit like that. He jotted the lot down, shoved the order chit through a latch at the back of the shop.

'Fifteen minutes,' he said.

I nodded, turned back to Gail. She had a sour look on her puss. She twitched as two more police cars, sirens wailing, sped up the road. I put a hand on her arm; she pulled away.

'Look, we're half-way there.'

She stared me down, said nowt.

I tried again. 'A mate of mine's coming out. He's dropping us off a set of wheels, then we're going to get out of here.'

She didn't buy it. I felt like leaving her to it. I mean, this had all been her doing. But I knew I had to front it out; hadn't bailed on a crew yet, even if it was a bullshit one like this.

As Gail sat there, head down towards the floor, I caught sight of an expression I thought I'd seen before. It was on Jody; she wore that look when something was wrong. I remembered seeing it once after I came home from working my first proper job. Oh yeah, work, a proper job.

I'd been a mechanic's mate, fucking grease monkey. We were both still at home then. Well, Jody and me, and the old man. Mam was gone. Jody hadn't left school yet. She was in one of those grey V-neck jumpers that kids used to wear to school back then. Her hair was tied back in a band and there was a spread of school books sitting on the dining-room table, like she'd just tipped out her school bag.

When I walked in Jody was staring – just like Gail – off into space. It sounds so run-of-the-mill, so everyday, but it wasn't a look like you get on some square-peg's coupon in a post-office queue or some old grunter at a bus stop who's just bored out of his tits and looking for an excuse to kick off about something or other. Nah, this was pained.

Only way I can describe it, pained.

I went over to the table but Jody didn't even look up. She just sat there, motionless. I eased out a chair, trying to be as quiet as I could, but the action gave her a start and she jumped. Her face seemed to whiten, then she let out a little squeal. I'd scared her and I felt gutted by that.

'Jody ... Jody ...' I said. 'It's only me. What's the matter?'

She froze again. The stare was gone but the look was one of terror now, animal terror, like when you see a wild creature trapped. 'Jody ...'

I got up, tried to comfort her, pat her on the back, put an arm around her, but it only made her worse. She screamed out and that's when the old man came stomping in from the kitchen.

'The bloody hell's going on in here?' he blasted out.

'Nothing ... it's Jody, look.' I pointed to her as she sat there, trembling all over. She looked away from us both, towards the radiator on the wall and seemed to be shutting us out.

'There's nothing wrong with her,' said Dad.

'But ...'

'No, I mean it ... don't pander to her, she's just being a stupid little bitch!' He turned to her, roared, 'Aren't you?'

He leaned out and grabbed her arm, yanked her from the seat; my sister yelled out and I felt myself take a step back in shock. As I cleared a space on the carpet, she pulled her arm away from my father and ran from the room. When she was gone, my old man stood shaking his head. I heard Jody sobbing in the bathroom.

I fronted him, 'You didn't need to make her cry ... couldn't you see she was upset about something.'

'Crap!' he snapped. 'She's just being a typical lassie.'

I didn't know why he was being so harsh; I was ready to duke him out for acting this way. I felt my heart pounding; my hands started to curl into fists.

'You upset her ...'

He looked at me, stared in my eyes. His moustache moved above his lip as he grinned. 'Don't be getting above yourself there, son.'

I didn't want to be his son.

'You made her cry.'

'She fuckingwell made herself cry ...' He raised a finger, pointed at me. 'You're just a fucking boy, you don't know what you're saying. She's a woman for Chrissakes. They're all about setting men against each other. Have you not figured that out yet? Watch the dogs on the street and learn something!'

He turned away. His eyes were wide and bright as he went and then his jaw tightened as he left through the door.

I knew he was wrong. He always was. I never thought like him, not once. Not ever.

Even looking back now, even seeing his face in my mind for the briefest of moments, made me want to puke. Or hit out. Hit out at something, anything.

When I remembered the look on Jody's face then it brought a pain to my chest, a heartscald, hurt. I never knew why she was looking that way, why she was crying. Not then, I never. But, I did now. The memory burned harder with the knowledge that I could have done something to help her. But I didn't. I found out too late what it was that caused Jody's pain.

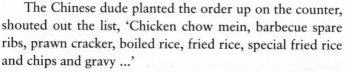

The Chinese dude planted the order up on the counter, shouted out the list, 'Chicken chow mein, barbecue spare ribs, prawn cracker, boiled rice, fried rice, special fried rice and chips and gravy ...'

I stood up. Gail got up with me. My first thought was,

shit, Moosey isn't here yet. I took a deck up the street; there
was no sign of movement.

'Look, that's our order, hon,' I said.

Gail failed to enthuse.

I walked for the counter, made a show of taking in the
fridge-cabinet behind the bloke. 'What you got there in
bottles?'

He turned, waved a hand. Could hardly blame him for
being a bit of a cock; his job, I'd last five minutes before I'd
be lamping some cunt with a two-litre bottle of Diet Pepsi.

'Okay, how about an Irn-Bru ...'

He turned, opened the fridge up and reached in for the
Irn-Bru.

'Eh, no ... diet please, squire.'

He looked like I was taking the piss. Diet, with that
order? He swapped the bottle. I watched him tot the lot up
and then he said, 'Is £27.55.'

I pinched my lips, whistled out. 'Pricey order.'

He didn't bat an eye.

I started to count out the cash and then there was a
knock on the window; I spun to see Moosey smiling at me.
He pointed over to a blue Ford Focus sitting in the bus lane.

'Fucking nice one, Moose!' I muttered.

I turned away from the counter, was nearly at the door
when I realised I'd left the food and hadn't paid; went back:
'Sorry, mate.' I dropped a twenty and a ten-spot. 'Here,
keep the change.'

Gail was at my side as we ran for the car.

The guy in the Chinese stared out the window as I got
in the driver's door and pushed back the seat. As I chucked
a U-turn in the road I saw Moosey heading towards the bus
stop. I made a point of not acknowledging him. He'd done
me a good turn.

As I glanced at Gail her head was pinned against the

back of the seat like she was waiting for take-off in a F-16. She seemed to be thawing, but I hated to break it to her, we weren't in the clear yet.

The window on the driver's door of the motor was out; Moosey had likely shattered it with a spark-plug, part of the kit he carried. Though as I looked inside I saw he hadn't needed his steel rule – the ignition had been started with a screwdriver. Fucking car was a biscuit tin. I upped the revs and started to fly through the gears on the way to Gorgie.

'So, you want to go home?' I said to Gail.

There was a pause, some lip-biting before she spoke. 'I could do with a drink.'

'State you're in, I'd be steering clear.'

I took a hairpin right, rolled the box into a tight side street to avoid the heavy traffic on the main road. Gail was winding down the window, trying to catch some air. 'What do you mean by that?'

'You're hyper ... probably tipped a bucket of adrenalin into your blood. You take one sip, you'll be pished out your face!'

She looked at me, sneered. 'What's wrong with that?'

'After the day you've had ... I'd sooner you went home and had an early night.'

She turned to face me, got riled: 'Don't you trust me or something?'

Was that a real question, I mean after the way she'd performed in the fat Jambo's place? No never. That was a conversation for another day.

We'd cleared the scene, couldn't even hear the sirens anymore. I was beginning to feel we'd been lucky. Relieved almost. But we'd caused a lot of damage, some proper fucking carnage. Plod was going to be scoping for us, for sure and certain.

'Gail, hear me, go home. Settle down for a few days,

keep a low profile.'

'I'm not fucking stupid, y'know.'

That was one for debate too. 'Then do as I tell you, right?'

She folded her arms, huffed.

Something told me this girl had more grief in store for me.

Jasper was a good lad, type that would always sooner do you a good turn than a bad turn. We'd shared a cell in Kilmarnock a few years back. He'd been lumped in with me after the bloke he was sharing with had been tea-bagged in the yard; they'd left this boy with more perforations than PG Tips, but Jasper knew nothing about it. He'd been under suspicion because the screws found a chiv in his cell but it turned out to be the victim's – obviously hoping to get his retaliation in first hadn't worked out.

Jasper was doing a two-er and I was on a five that got cut to 18 months on appeal but in the time we struck it off we became firm mates and ended up running a snout ring; on the out we had enough of a bundle to set ourselves up with a gaff. The situation worked out a treat because we kept ourselves to ourselves and never got in each others way. When Jasper heard I was on the out again, he was good enough to offer to put me up once more.

I hit the button for the buzzer – hoped it was the right address because I'd left my jacket – and the piece of paper with Jasper's details – in Gail's Beemer.

'Hello.'

I recognised the voice.

'All right, mate ... it's Jed.'

'Jed boy – I'll buzz you in.'

Jasper's flat was two flights up; when I reached the landing he was waiting for me with that shit-eating grin of his. 'Jed, you old bastard!'

He grabbed me in a bear hug.

'Whoa, watch my ribs.'

Jasper looked me up and down. 'You been boxing?'

I gave him the *as if* look, marched indoors. 'Hope you've got the kettle on.' I tried to make it look like I hadn't just seen a shopkeeper torched, then made my escape in a hot motor, which I'd dumped in an industrial estate on the other side of town before legging it by bus and hoof. But Jasper wasn't buying it. He'd seen the look too many times before.

I sat myself in front of the gob-unit, flicked a few channels whilst Jasper put on the kettle. He was playing it cagey. 'So what's it like to be out?'

'Yeah, y'know ... same as I remember it.'

A conversation killer if ever I had one. Thing is, talking about the inside when you're on the out is a no-go. You want to move on, get away from all the shit that fills your head in there. You have to block it out, and that means removing the differentiations. A hoor of a business.

'I heard from wee Rab this afternoon.'

'Bandy Rab?'

'Said you pulled yourself a nice little blonde bit in the pub.'

I exhaled; my breath escaped louder than I imagined it would. Came like an awesome sigh.

'Fuck, that bad, eh?'

I looked up to see Jasper standing in the door jamb. 'You could say that, yeah.'

He dried off the cup he was holding, returned to the kitchen. 'That's the kettle boiled.'

'Great. Got any biscuits?'

'Fucking hell, you getting your feet under the table already?' said Jasper.

He had me there. Funny how you always look at your old friends as a kind of extended family – or in my case a substitute one – I wouldn't want to be relying on any of my kin to look out for me. Not now.

Jasper came through from the kitchen with the two teas and a pack of Kit-Kats tucked under his arm.

I took my tea, swiped the chocolate biscuits, said, 'Ah, nice one.'

'Thought you'd appreciate it ...' He nodded at the Kit-Kats. 'Be a fairly decent score in Killie, eh?'

I smiled, tucked into the two fingers of confectionery heaven.

I was in two minds about whether to tell Jasper about the afternoon's events with Gail. I felt sure I could trust him and he would stand by me no matter what; but I was a professional standover man and keeping the puss tightly buttoned was an old habit I'd never got rid of. It was a case of what he doesn't know can't harm me. I knew if he had plod busting his chops he wouldn't be too pleased but fuck-tae-fuck, it was a career hazard that Jasper had already grown used to, many years ago.

'So, you still doing a bit of fencing, bit of dealing?' I said.

He tapped the side of his nose, gave me a wink. 'Got a new line.'

'Oh yeah.' Now this did interest me. Jasper had always worked the lower end of the criminal spectrum; his first stretch was for kiting. Had been a good earner but got too hard to work it when people stopped paying with cheques. He'd progressed to running lists on junkie hoisters – at one stage he had a spare room full of Gillette Sensors, Fahrenheit aftershave and Touche Eclat. The supply chains proved too erratic though, with his junkie partners dropping down dead or getting busted every few months. 'So, what's your latest venture?'

He smiled, run a finger down the middle of the Kit-Kat wrapper and split the biscuit in two. 'Shipping.'

'Y'*wha*–?'

'You heard. Shipping.'

'You, on a boat?' I laughed him up.

Jasper's smile slid off his face. 'Yeah, what's so funny about that? My old man was a fisherman, y'know, it's in the blood!'

'Just sounds like a lot of hard work ... now you fannying about on a yacht, I can see ... going a pedalo in the Costa, I can just about imagine but a proper fucking boat!'

He chomped on the Kit-Kat; I watched the jaws go hard at it, then, 'Well, that's where you'd be fucking wrong, mate. I've been at this caper for six months and let me tell you, it's a fucking payer ... best I ever had.'

I leaned forward, pried, 'And what are you ferrying?'

He grinned again. 'This and that ... mainly that.'

'Dope?'

'Maybe, maybe not ... all depends. See, this boat I have is useful for many a bit of business let me tell you, Jed. Many a bit of business ...'

I didn't want to hear any more. I was tired and coming down from the day's antics. Jasper's tales of woe would have to keep for another day. As I sipped my tea I suddenly took a start – a loud wrap on the door.

'The fuck's that?' My tea spilled down my jeans as I got up.

'Calm down,' said Jasper. 'Just cool the beans, eh?'

I watched him walk towards the door. I looked out the window to see if there were any police cars pulling up in the street; he was back before I could register the scene.

'Jed, it's for you.'

I recognised him, and the suit, from the off.

He stood for a moment and looked at me, then back to Jasper. He was holding a carrier bag and as he opened it, leaned inside, Jasper got jumpy.

'Whoa, watch yourself there, mate.' He placed a hand on his arm, leaned over and peered into the bag. He seemed to be satisfied there was nothing dangerous inside and gave the nod.

The bloke in the suit smiled, said, 'Think I'd walk in here with a threat?'

Jasper shrugged.

'I'm long past that, not my style anymore.'

'That right?' Jasper was playing up; he *was* the type to duke it out.

The suit grinned; I spotted some gold in his teeth. 'If I wanted to do you over, my mate ... I wouldn't waste a good whistle.' The accent was London; I didn't like that. When he pulled my jacket out the carrier bag and threw it at me I knew at once how Gail's old man had found me.

'You aught to be careful, lad ... leaving a forwarding address behind.' He held up a crumpled piece of paper that I'd left in my pocket. It had Jasper's contact details on it.

'The fuck's going on here?' said Jasper.

The gadgie smiled, balled the paper and put it in his pocket. 'Looks like I'm in time for tea.' He moved over to my side of the room and picked up a Kit-Kat. 'And biscuits too, lovely.'

I saw Jasper was ready to lamp the cunt, but I gave him the look, one that said I'd explain later and he retreated into the kitchen for another cup.

'Now, you must be wondering who the fucking hell I am, I shouldn't wonder.'

I knew he was Gail's old man. 'Go on, surprise me.'

He held out a hand. 'Robbie Silva. Pleased to meet you.'

I vaguely knew the name.

'To what do I owe the pleasure?'

He smiled. I caught sight of some more gold; it sparkled under the bare bulb above his head. As he leaned forward he tapped my arm. 'Call me Robbie.'

'If you say so.'

He laughed; a piranha smirk spread across his coupon. 'I do, lad. I do. I mean, after your exploits with my daughter today, it should really be me offering you the tea and tiffin!'

I wasn't so sure about that.

Jasper returned with a mug of tea, set it down. Silva smiled again. I'd already grown tired of his grin. It was wearing.

I took up my own tea, took a sip, said, 'Jasper, give us five minutes, eh?'

He looked at me, frowned, then turned to the still smirking Silva. Jasper shook his head and left the room.

'Thanks, my friend, much appreciated,' said Silva. 'Now, we can have ourselves a nice old chat, eh? ... One old lag to another.'

The mug of tea was hot; I placed it on the arm of the chair. I wondered where Silva was going with all this. I mean, I'd dragged his daughter – nah – let's get this straight, she'd dragged me, into a daylight robbery situation. Either way, we'd had a close call. Silva was looking like a bit of a player; I couldn't see him being happy about my involvement with his daughter. I could expect a good kicking ... if I was lucky.

I bolded it: 'Look, what the fuck is this?'

Silva leaned back, crossed his legs. I noticed he wore white sports socks with his suit; so you can take the crook out the east-end but not the other way about. Figured. He crossed his fingers, tried to look like he was starring in some fucking gangster movie or other. He might have been big time, but I'd seen it all before.

'I hear you just got out of the shovel,' said Silva.

I hated the way these Londoners used that fucking rhyming-slang. But they were all the same. 'And?'

He uncrossed his legs, leaned over. 'What'd you do?'

'Got caught.'

He laughed, sat back. Christ, he was easily pleased. It unnerved me that I was getting on so well with him. He clearly wanted something; either that or he was very grateful I'd got his daughter out of a tight spot.

'I've done my fair share of time in the shovel.'

I saw where this was going; cue the macho-boasts. I played up to him. 'Yeah?'

'I did a stretch in Albany on the Isle of White in the eighties, fucking hard stretch ... was stabbings every other day of the week back then. Not like these cushy fucking hotels they put you up in these days.'

I looked out the window, toyed with the idea of sparking up a tab.

He went on, 'So, what I'm saying is ... we've both been around.'

I took out my snout, started to tap on the box. Silva got the message.

'Anyway, my point is, I hear you done good today. You got my girl out a tight spot. You're obviously not some ten-bob blagger.'

I put the tab in my mouth, lit it. The smoke escaped in a long thin trail towards the ceiling. I watched it for a second or two then turned back to Silva. 'And ... let me guess, you might be able to put a bit of work my way?'

He leaned back again, crossed fingers. He had a bit of a gut on show as he spoke, 'Well, likely as not I can put some work your way and it'd be good work. I'm stone ginger on that.'

'Y'*wha*–?'

'What I'm saying is it would be proper work. Not just bread and butter.'

I played him. 'No thanks.'

'Now, hold on, don't be hasty. Be a good few shekels in it for you. I'm known on this manor, ask about.'

I huffed, said, 'No thanks.'

His eyes widened; the rims were red. 'Are you fucking mugging me off?'

I took another drag on my tab, exhaled. 'Fact of the matter is, mate, I've seen how your daughter operates, and you know what they say ... the apple doesn't fall far from the tree.'

I'd given Silva a choice: he could go postal, put a heavy threat on me, or, put a lid on that temper of his. I didn't think he had it in him. I watched as he took breath, narrowed his eyes and looked out into the street. 'Is that a fact, Jed Collins? See, I did a bit of research into your background and I'm sure you wouldn't like to be punting a similar philosophy there.'

I got out my seat, had the arm hooked ready to land one in his puss; he rose fast, fronted me. The smile was back. 'Have a think about what I said, lad.'

I eyeballed him. He kept a stare on me too as he dipped in his pocket and removed a card with his number on it.

I took the card but my mind was awash with old images, thoughts. I wanted to smart mouth him back. But, he had me.

As Silva walked through the door he touched his brow. 'Thanks for the cuppa.'

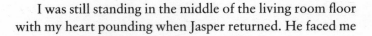

I was still standing in the middle of the living room floor with my heart pounding when Jasper returned. He faced me for a few moments, then ran fingers through his hair. His expression told me he was searching for the right words.

'The fuck is going on here, Jed?' he said.

My mind was still all over the shop; my blood was racing. 'What?'

'Have you turned my flat into a fucking flop? ... Have you just come from a fucking job?'

I didn't have the marbles to answer him. I shook my head. I knew Jasper had picked up on Silva's comments about the jacket. Shit, he'd find out soon enough, soon as he turned on the TV news.

'Look, I got roped in ...'

Jasper slouched, then slumped in the chair. 'Fucking hell, *fucking* hell.'

'It was supposed to be a nothing job ... it just got out of hand. I didn't think it was going to amount to anything, but ...'

'Yeah, but what?'

'Jesus Christ, it was this mad bit, she lost it on me and, well, that was that.'

Jasper stood up and paced the room. 'This is out of order ... totally out of order, flopping at my fucking residence, after pulling a job.'

I tried to stop him pacing; he shook off my hands. 'What if the filth run you down?'

'They won't ... I'm in the clear. Man, I wouldn't have come here if I thought ...'

'Aw, thanks a fucking bunch, mate. Nice of you to think of me.'

I let Jasper rant and rave for ten minutes; he silenced himself, seemed to get over the initial outburst.

I was off on one myself though, broke the silence. 'The cunt!' I said.

'Eh?'

I nodded to the door. 'Our visitor.'

'Who the fuck was he anyway?'

I drew breath, felt my hand reach up to my mouth; I wiped away with the back of my hand, prepared for Jasper to go scripto once again. 'Robbie Silva.'

'Fucking hell ... Long Dong Silva.'

'Wha–?'

'That was Long Dong Silva? ... In my flat! Holy shit!'

I'd heard of him but I'd been off the grid for so long I hadn't heard this handle before. 'Why do they call him that?'

'He's a top fucking man now, that's why. Came from nowhere to be one of *the* swinging dicks in the last few years. He's big time, Jed.'

I turned away from him, went to look out the window. I saw Silva crossing the road and getting into a black Audi. The car sped off.

'So what's his angle?'

A huff. 'Fuck knows. Used to run porn rings a few years back – everyone said he'd road-tested the slags himself. He's got a big crew around him now though, I'd say he's into everything.'

I moved back towards my chair, sat. 'So what's he want with me?'

Jasper squinted, tilted his head. He lifted a palm, waved it in my direction. 'He offered you a bit of work, eh?'

'Something like that.'

'Think he knows you?'

'Dunno ... knows of me, maybe.'

'Well, if he's been asking about he'll know you're a good jump man.'

'Aye, and he'll know I work alone. Folk at Silva's level don't go jumping counters!'

'So, where's he coming from?' I rubbed my thighs

through my jeans, it was a nervous movement and Jasper sussed it. 'Jed, what's the go here?'

'I wish I fucking knew, mate.'

I put myself up in dock for a few days. Lot of shitty daytime telly. Fucking Trisha, reruns of Quincy and The Rockford Files. The afternoon news was a showstopper though, nice little item about a Edinburgh shopkeeper with third-degree burns after a bungled raid. Jasper had been out taking care of business when that little item ran, so I was chuffed to bits about that, but Christ I was getting bored. Was sure I felt my brain softening inside my skull. There's a point, for me anyway, when sitting about makes me tip over. I mean, in the pound you get used to it, but when there's a big bad world awaiting you and no locked doors holding you back it can do your nut in. A hoor of a business.

I was cautious about going out so soon. Took a scarf off the rack and an old golf umbrella – big job – was one of Jasper's numbers from his days in the casuals, had the point sharpened for self-defence, or pure agg, purposes. I doubted the fucking thing had ever been opened. Might have opened a few heads in its day though.

The street was quiet enough, lot of old dears with shopping trolleys though – made me think of the one back at the fat Jambo bastard's place. The telly news bit had said he was in a 'stable condition' whatever the fuck that meant. I couldn't see Gail being too chuffed about that – she was out to off the cunt. The thought had simmered in me for a few days; Christ Almighty, if I'd known she was so completely Radio Rental, I'd have steered well clear. Thinking with the boaby, though. Never a good idea.

These last few days I'd got to replaying the raid over

and over; and thinking some more about Gail. It's a funny thing – but that's how some bits get inside your head. No matter what they've done, how they've pissed you off – they get inside your mind and there's just no shaking them out.

Now, I'm hardly wet behind the ears – I know all bits of stuff lose their shine after a while – but it's a fact that until that point in time arrives, and who knows when that will be, they are lethal. They get their claws round your billiards and that's that.

I made my way onto the main drag, well, what passes for it in Jasper's neck of town. The thing about Edinburgh is, it's not a big place – but it does have its distinct manors. If you stay clear of the New Town and the yuppie centre you won't go far wrong. Add to that the Old Town and the screeds of tourists there, you're laughing. Just about everywhere else has its charms, well ... for me anyway. I'm not a fussy bastard, I like a manor to have a few nice pubs, a few places to grab some scran and that's that. There were days when I thought about counting the building societies, points of drop-off for security vans and maybe even the odd bureaux d'change – if I was after some easy money – but not any more.

I found myself a nice old-school greasy spoon and ordered up a bacon roll and some coffee.

'Make it strong, mind ...' I told the waitress. 'I want to be able to stand my spoon up in it!' I'd missed this kind of patter inside. Funny that, how the day-to-day things get away from you. That's what the pound's all about though, dehumanising you. Depriving you of the simple acts of civility that make us people. I never got unsettled by it though; some radges inside will go crazy. Can't stand the confinement. Then you get the ones who've done fifteen years and they're more at home in a cell than they were on the outside. It's a funny thing, but y'know, no two cons are the same. Me, I can take it or leave it. It's a hazard of the job. But I'll tell you this, there does come a time in every robber's life when he starts to wonder when the Big Payer's going to come up.

It's a dream of course; stuff of legend. You get a group of cons together and they'll always be spraffing about the Big Payer. Not some five or ten grand counter jump, I'm talking about the hundreds of thousands, the millions. It was beyond my league. I was a raid man, working small firms. I'd never been asked to make the move upstairs. Well, until now that is.

Long Dong Silva's offer was, like the Londoner said, a tasty one. I knew it. Was understood.

My bacon roll and coffee arrived.

The waitress stood over the table, waiting for me to part with some poppy. I dug my hand in my pocket, there was a five-spot and some coin. I didn't need to look in the other pocket; I knew what was there. Silva's number.

I handed over the last of my cash and smiled.

Thing about Silva was, I didn't trust him.

I didn't like the look of him, flat out. There was something about him that said there was more going on behind the eyes than he would ever let on.

When you do a job, front the counter, you can tell straight off who the ones that will give you grief are. There's the lot that will empty till and take it in their stride. And then there's the ones that will try and give you a bag full of receipts or cheques – not out of some misguided sense of duty to the bank but because they get something out of fucking with people.

Silva was a past master of fucking with people. It shone out of him.

There was no doubt I had to go back to work, and soon. I couldn't rely on Jasper to keep me for ever. Sure, I could grab some work on my own but there was an offer from a decent firm on the table and I was seriously conflicted. I might not get another chance at the Big One.

I slurped the last of my coffee, took out my mobi and dialled Silva's number.

He answered on the third ring.

'Hello.' His London accent rattled me but I put it out my mind.

'It's Jed Collins.'

A pause on the line. I sensed his grin stretching out over those goldie teeth. 'Hello, my old son. Had a little think about my offer have we?'

He was lapping me up. I played him. 'Depends?'

He barked, 'Oh yeah ... and on what?'

I let him hang for a moment or two, replied, 'It depends on any number of things ... whether I like the look of the job, whether I like the team and whether I like my share.'

Silva laughed down the line. 'Let me tell you, mate, you'll be fucking cock-a-hoop ... Now, when can we meet?'

———✦———

I took a donner down Lothian Road and queued outside the ATM of the Royal Bank's big set-up. They seemed to be doing a roaring trade. Made me think. This lot, the bankers, had made a nice raid on the country's finances – took us all to the fucking cleaners. The sums were eye watering. Fuck me drunk, these bastards made the Brinks-Mat bullion job's £26-million take look like chicken feed. If I had the marbles I'd be on the other side of the counter. That's where the real robbery gets done.

My account was down to low double figures; depressing really, for a man my age. But that was the facts. I pulled a couple of Jimmy Denners out and headed up the road to a drinker I knew well.

The Drum was full of the usual Edinburgh crew you get in the middle of the day: barflies. A few bluenoses supping on that Hun piss McEwan's and a stack of dole-moles on the scrounge for whatever they could get. I took a stool at the bar; the barman had his back to me polishing a glass. I coughed into my hand and he turned around.

'All right, Jed ... when did you get sprung?' he said.

Broonie was a good bloke, carried a paunch like a darts-player now but hadn't changed much at all otherwise. 'Not long ago. How's tricks?'

Broonie slapped my shoulder, smiled his widest. 'Well, welcome back mate, welcome back!' His pub was referred to in the press recently as a "hive of villainy". I read that on the inside and it made me feel homesick. Still, looking around here, save a few schemie hoisters trying to flog some hot Hearts tops, there was little hard-core in evidence.

I tapped the bar. 'How about a pint of the black then?'

'No worries.' Broonie turned to the pumps, got to work on a creamy-headed Guinness for me. 'So, eh, what's the score then, Jed? ... You turning square-peg on us now or what?'

I scratched the side of my head, had a craving for a tab – this new smoking ban was a kick in the balls, made the pubs look pretty ordinary without the pall of Regal and Embassy. 'Well, you just never know.'

'Fuck off, mate. You can't kid a kidder!' Broonie laid down the pint in front of me. The creamy head glistened under the lights, thought it winked at me.

'Cheers, pal.' I downed a good belt. Leaned over the bar a bit, put my conspiratorial coupon on. Broonie took the hint, wised I was about to talk. 'Look, I need the run-down on a new player in town ... well, I say new, he's new to me.'

'Oh, aye.' Broonie turned his bar-towel over his shoulder, folded his arms.

'London *geezer*,' I put a bit of tone on the last word, paused then continued. 'Called Robbie Silva.'

Broonie leaned back, smoothed the edges of his mozzer, then whet his lips with a quick flash of grey tongue. 'Long Dong Silva ... Christ, what do you want to know?'

There was a rustle of shell suit at my back. I turned round to see a schemie with a filthy Burberry cap on holding up a Hearts top. 'Fancy a shirt, big man?'

I looked him up and down. There was a Mars Bar running from his mouth to his ear, a jagged and ruthless one that looked like a glassing. I raised my pint, pointed to the scar, said, 'You want a matching number on the other side?'

He didn't know how to take me, looked at Broonie – who dipped his head – then the schemie burst into a toothless grin. 'Aw, a fucking Hibee, eh? ... Sorry, pal, no offence, like.'

I turned away and heard him rustling off to try his luck elsewhere.

Broonie was back on his elbows, nodding towards the bar. 'Why you asking about Silva?'

I played it cool. 'Got my reasons.'

'Jed, you're a fucking blagger ... and Silva's about as far from that racket as it gets.'

I sighed. 'You know how it works, mate.'

Broonie shook his head, brushed the edges of his 'tache down again. He looked at me nervously. I noticed his eyes were ringed in red. 'If someone's put a bit of work up to Silva, you have to ask yourself, then why would he come to you? ... You're fuck all to him!'

I knew this. But I also knew Silva had an inside track on my abilities. I'd been going over things in my head, never a good idea, but I thought I had it figured out. 'Thing is Broonie, I did some business with a relative of his and –'

He cut in. 'Not that fucking cock-rag son of his ... Jesus

137

Christ.' He pointed to the schemie in the Burberry cap. 'Fucking Barnie wouldn't work with him!'

I flagged him down, 'No. Someone else.'

'Well that only leaves the daughter ... unless you're busy with his old lady.'

I edged Broonie away from this line of chat, said, 'Does it fucking matter, who?'

A shrug, more head-shakes. Broonie took a deep breath and turned away. He moved towards the optics and raised a glass to a bottle of Johnnie Walker, poured himself a large one. When he returned his cheeks were beginning to colour. 'What do you want to know?'

I put down my pint, pressed my palms together. 'Can he be trusted?'

'Of course he can't be fucking trusted. He's a top-drawer player, Jed. He's no blagger and you'll get no help from him on that kind of score.'

I kept my eyes on Broonie. 'That's not what I'm asking ... what I need to know is, if he has a job of work, can he be trusted?'

Broonie raised his wee goldie, drained the last of it. He grimaced, turned down the corners of his mouth. There was a glistening line of moisture on his lower lip when he spoke. 'All I can tell you is that Silva has shot up the ranks. If you're asking, is he of a level that would get a good bit of work put up – not some fag-coupon raid – then, aye. He's that level.'

I leaned back, said, 'You sure about that?'

Broonie nodded. 'Aye, I'm sure. If you'd asked me a year ago, before Big Andy and The Brothers went down, I'd have thought twice. But things change fast in this town and Silva's got the numbers and contacts.'

I got out my seat. Headed for the door.

'Jed,' called Broonie. 'Watch yourself, pal.'

I didn't need telling twice.

———— ✦ ————

As I headed back down Lothian Road I had the words of an old lag, a real Daddy of the Wing, ringing in my ears. He'd told me one time, after a discussion about the jobs he'd taken on in his day, that "if you have your doubts, leave it out". I thought at the time it sounded like good advice. But I'd never been very good at taking advice, or listening to my conscience; I knew if I had, then Jody would still be around.

I was crossing at the lights, just across from the Filmhouse Cinema, when my mobi started to ring.

I answered.

'Hello, Jed.'

I recognised the voice at once, but played up. 'Who's this?'

'I think you know who it is.' The old confidence was back; it was quite a difference to just a few days ago.

'Okay, well, if that's you Gail, then I want to know how you got this number.' I put a bit of a scare in my voice, but I didn't think it would do any damage to her. She sounded like she knew she had me in the palm of her hand. Kinda wished she had.

'You called Daddy ... I took your number from his phone.'

I didn't like the sound of that – Silva didn't look like the kind of man who'd let his daughter rifle through his gear. For a second, I felt a seed of doubt grow in my mind. Was she playing me? Was Silva?

Holy fuck.

My mind ran.

Had the whole raid on the fat Jambo been a plant – a fucking ruse to test me out? It was paranoia but something had put the thought there.

'Jed, you there?'

'Yeah ... yeah. I'm here.'

Gail giggled on the other end of the line.

'What's going on there?'

'Not getting all possessive on me, are you?'

'Give me a fucking break.'

She seemed to take a second or two to digest that remark, then, 'I want to see you.'

'Oh, aye.'

'Soon. Like, now ...'

I scratched my chin; there was a three-day growth there. 'Not likely, love.'

She arked up. 'And why not?'

'Because, to be fucking honest with you, I still haven't got over the last time we got together.'

She laughed out loud; I had to hold the mobi away. This girl was some piece of work.

'Not going soft on me, are you?'

'Not a chance.'

'Can't handle a bit of ... action?'

Action I could handle; Gail's idea of action, however, was another question. 'Let me think about it.'

She didn't like my response, but, fair fucks to her, the spoilt brat kept her cool. 'Okay-dokey, I'll give you a buzz later.'

'Yeah, you do that.'

'Oh, I will.'

I let the line die, pocketed my mobi and continued back to Jasper's pad.

When I got back to the flat, it was empty.

I was glad to have the joint to myself. My head was

numb with thinking things through. I was never very good at using my brain – I was always better at getting the kinds of things done that didn't require thought – physical stuff.

I knew who I was, knew my limitations. I also knew that at some point I was going to have to make a decision about Silva. I was either going to take his offer and go back to work, or I was going to have to look for an alternative.

I shrugged my shoulders. There was an ache setting up shop in my neck. I felt the tension mounting, gripping the tip of my spine and sending tingling pins and needles out to my flanks. Something had to give; another day of this and I'd be a fucking wreck.

I walked through to the kitchen and took out a tin of Stella, sparked up a tab. As the thick white smoke stretched towards the yellowed ceiling I stared out the window towards the city. Edinburgh was my home, always had been. Not always this part of it, but then the places I had been in the past I didn't want to return to.

I looked out at the tumble of tenements, the drying areas and the back greens. This town was the same wherever you went; this is how people lived. My people.

A young lad, no more than five or six, came running through the close bouncing a football. He was laughing and smiling to himself; a young girl about the same age came running behind him. The pair of them made me think of me and my sister at that age. For the first time in a long time I felt myself remembering a time in my childhood when we were happy; when Jody was happy.

And then my heart froze.

I looked away.

I walked through to the living-room and sat down.

In the armchair I shotgunned the can of Stella. The tab in my hand had burnt down to the filter tip before I remembered it was there. A long fossilised head of ash dropped onto the arm of the chair. I didn't even bother to rub at it.

I was miles away.

It was three days after my seventeenth birthday when Jody told me what he had done to her. I didn't believe her at first, thought it was a joke, a sick joke. Then she started to cry, her eyes blinking fast to wash out the tears as she told me he had done it for years. I couldn't take it in. I just couldn't.

'Before Mum ... died?'

She nodded.

'Did she know?'

'No!' said Jody.

'But how, how didn't she know?'

'Because I never told her.' She was trembling. Her eyes growing redder and redder. I wanted to hug her, to tell her it would be all right, but she looked so distant. Not just distant from me, but from everyone. I knew if I held her she would be stiff, cold. I understood then she had cut herself off from the world, from people.

I waited for Jody to leave the room and then I started to punch the sofa. I punched and hit out until I was sweating and my knuckles red, the skin cracked and bleeding. And then I slumped against the wall and slid to the ground.

I remember the crying; I remember hating myself for crying but the hatred was nothing compared to what I felt for him.

It had been light outside when I fell against the wall and wept, but it was dark when my father came home. I watched him staggering up the close. He flicked a cigarette into the gutter and I watched the amber sparks fly. It was as if they ignited something inside me; my heart pounded loudly in my chest.

When his key turned in the lock I felt my whole body

tense. There was a sharp spike prodding at my stomach. I thought I would be sick, but I held it in and walked to the fireplace.

The door to the living-room was mottled glass and as he turned the light on I saw him framed in the hallway. He was mumbling, drunk. I couldn't hear what he said, but it didn't matter. I was already way beyond words with him; nothing he could say would change what he had done.

When my father walked into the room I stepped towards him, the poker from the fireside was raised above my head. I let him get inside the door, turn on the light, and face me. For a moment or two he didn't seem to register anything unusual, it was just me, Jed, his son. But then his features changed and he looked up at the poker. I waited for him to say something, to explain, but he said nothing; he merely lowered his head and I brought the poker down.

I brought the poker down again and again. On his body and legs. I moved up and down his full length as he crawled before me, slithered away like a snake. I lost count of the number of times I struck him. He was already bloody and broken when Jody came rushing in.

'Jed!' she yelled. 'Oh, Jed. Jed ...'

She knelt down beside my father and touched his brow, and then she ran to the phone to call an ambulance.

I sat and watched the ambulance men work around my father but I didn't move from the chair. At some stage one of them must have called the police because in little or no time there were two uniformed officers standing over me.

I was remanded. A primitive fucking boot camp for bad boys. On my second month inside they told me my father had taken the easy road out, killed himself. My sister had been taken into care. On the third month they told me Jody had been moved to stay with a foster family in another town.

Jody never called or visited me. At first this made me

angry; I wanted her to be glad that I had finished off her abuser. But I know now she never saw it that way.

———✦———

I wasn't sure about this. You get a feeling for a job, call it what you like, superstition or whatever. I'd been in firms with blokes who had walked out because a black cat had crossed in front of the car on the way to a jump. There was one blagger, another fucking Londoner called Mad Mikey, who'd parked his motor down at Leith Docks and came back to see it covered in seagull shit, looked like a plasterer's radio, and that was it for him. Bird shit, at some stage, he'd decided was bad luck and he was Harry the Toff back to the King's Road calling the job "a write-off" and claiming we were in for "a fucking mugging".

I stood on the edge of the kerb; it was getting dark now. The street light fizzed, painting an orange glow on the road and the shop fronts. People were whizzing about, heading home after a few quick scoops in the howff. I wondered what it must be light to be a square-peg; to do an honest day's work for an honest day's pay. Nah, wasn't in me. Knew I wasn't wired-up right for that kind of patter.

The 26 bus showed, fucking old Jambo-coloured one, Jesus, what was that all about? I waited for it to hoy up close to the stop and then I got on and paid the Ted driver whose greasy-old quiff looked like it was about to drip on the wheel. The road out to Porty was chokka with cars and Joe Baxis, horns blowing all over the place. The days of going on the rob in this type of traffic were long gone. Not even with a fucking Suzuki.

At Abbeyhill the roads eased a bit and I watched the punters legging it down Easter Road, duckwalking to beat the rain that was starting up. Felt my stomach churning; had a lot on my mind of late but there was a chance that could all change.

You get a group of cons together and they like a good yak. They'll drive you round the fucking bend with tales of the one that got away. The Big Payer. I'd heard several versions of this story, the job that lets you retire on the proceeds and get the fuck right away from this rain ... Mexico, Costa. Doesn't matter. That kind of moolah and you're laughing.

I'd never had a story to rival the cons' tales of woe. Never been part of a big enough firm. When you do a post office or a building society, you're only clearing the take from the cashiers. If you're lucky, you'll net five grand. Splitting that more than two ways and you're going to need to pull a job a week. But I'm no different to anyone else at this racket – I fancy a slice of the big take. I wasn't scared of doing another stretch, and the thought of earning a nice Big Payer had me tempted.

The bus pulled round the roundabout in Porty, hit the main drag. I never much liked this end of the city – always reminded me of some skanky little Scottish town, one of those shit-holes in the west coast where all those fucking bluenosed soap-dodgers come from. Ones that looked like cast members from Zombieland, but with more scars.

Silva had picked out a drinker, The Arms. I spotted it through the bus window and got off at the next stop. When I got out it had started to spit down; there was a waft of effluent blowing in from the sewage outflows in the sea and I felt my stomach tighten again.

All I could think of as I walked down to The Arms was this better be fucking worth my time and effort – I'd vowed to hear Silva out – but sure as shooting the signs weren't looking good.

I rumbled through the door, had my who-the-fuck-you-looking-at-cuntybaws face on. An old soak at the bar turned round and eyed me, thought again, turned away. The barmaid was in her bad fifties, bat-wings and a corned-beef complexion. Her over-dyed black hair was scraped back in a tight scrunchie and showed at least an inch of grey roots; when she smiled at me I wanted to heave.

'What can I get you, love?' she said.

I was about to say something about looking for Silva when I felt my arse grabbed, both cheeks in cusped hands.

'I'll get his!' It was Gail.

'What you doing here?' I couldn't believe what I was seeing.

'Come on, you know ...'

'No, I fucking don't.' I didn't even want to contemplate the fact that she might be on this job; after our last outing the possibility seemed insane. Beyond insane.

Gail stretched round my waist, made an order at the bar. She had the hot-pants on again and was pointing her arse at me. She turned quickly, caught me checking her out and giggled. 'Get him a pint and I'll have a Bacardi Breezer.'

As the order went in, the door to the snug behind me screeched open. Inside sat Silva and the gimp with the mullet. I was ushered in with a tipping of Silva's head. As I stared at the pair of them, still conscious of Gail's hyperactive antics behind me, I felt like walking straight out the door. Figured I had about three seconds of standing there like a spare prick before I had to make a move, one way or the other.

You must've heard that phrase, hear it all the time, *my heart was in my mouth* ... That's where I was with these muppets. I knew the right thing to do was turn tail. Walk. I'd had first-hand experience of working with Gail and I sure as fuck wasn't for repeating it. The girl was so off-the-dial scripto I'd have to seriously consider giving her another balling. I mean, that type are as likely to have the billiards off you and hoiked in a handbag before you can say "thanks for the memory".

I started to feel myself sway a bit, don't know why ... was I gonna keel? Maybe it was the bad guts again, but before I could move a muscle, Gail – drinks tray in her hands – was shouldering me towards the snug. I looked down at her and got those big eyes flashed at me; they seemed to stare through me for a moment and then the hooks were in and I was being dragged to the snug.

The pub seemed cold, but in the snug it was warm. I remembered these sorts of places before the smoking ban; they were like fucking saunas – could hardly see two feet in front of you – you'd be padding about with your hands trying to find your pint on the table. As I sat down, Gail lifted my pint towards me.

Silva smiled, took up a wee goldie. 'You won't know my boy, Ben, will you?'

I looked over at the gimp in the Motorhead T-shirt and manky denims. He was a fucking greaser, real soap-dodger. I felt like dousing him with my pint and saying get a fucking bath, you tink! Instead I went with raising a brow in his general direction. 'Not Gentle Ben, is it?' I said.

He arked up, 'You trying to be fucking funny?'

I smiled; fuck, it was easy rattling his cage.

Silva slapped my back and picked up a bottle of Beck's from the tray, handed it to his boy. 'Here, get that in your fucking mouth ...'

'Like a dummy,' I said.

Ben rose. Put a stare on me. 'What did you say?'

'Oh, here we go ... toys out the pram already, are they?' He didn't know whether to piss his pants or poke his old man in the back and ask him to intervene. There was a stalled silence; the air in the snug seemed to have been drained and then Gail guffawed into her Breezer and I had to join in. 'Settle yourself, Benny ... I'm just pulling your chain!'

'Yeah, sit the fuck down and shut up, would ya!' said Silva. 'We've got serious business to discuss.'

The idea that there was serious business on the table with these chumps almost made me laugh again, but I kept it down; after all, I was a professional. And there could be an earner in this for me. Quite a good one. We'd have to get one or two things straight first though.

'From the off, Silva, why the fuck are this pair here?' I waved a finger at Gail and Ben.

Silva stretched out in his seat, sipped his whisky. 'They're family.'

It didn't fucking cut it. 'So?'

'So, they're my family and I trust them and that's why they're here.'

I wasn't buying it, leaned over, put my pint down on the table. 'I want to know who you're crewing this firm with.'

Silva took another little sip. 'This is it.'

I couldn't believe my ears. 'Are you taking the piss?'

He smiled, real wide one. 'Look, Jed, you don't know the particulars of the job yet ... I'm telling you, it's an in-and-out number and stone ginger to a man of your form.'

I looked away. My mind had filled with hot fucking air or something. I couldn't process a thought. Still, I'd come all the way across town and I had a full pint sitting in front of me so I thought I might as well hear him out.

Silva clasped his hands together, then separated them quickly as he twisted in his chair to face me. 'Okay, here's the deal ... I've got this contact. We'll call him Big Shug for the sake of it, right?'

'Go on.'

'Now, Shug works for one of these security firms, type that ferry money about all over the country ... you know the ones.'

I did. They were notoriously difficult to knock off, and the biggest take was twenty-five grand – unless you were blowing the fucking roof off them – because that's all the guards were insured to carry at the one time.

'I thought you said this was a payer, big job ...'

'Oh, it is ...'

'Sticking up a fucking security truck isn't.'

Silva smiled; it was that leering lip-curling one. I could see the gold in his side teeth once again. 'I'm not talking about blagging a pony-bag, mate. You see, my friend Shug knows something that I found most interesting.' He leaned in; the hands were moving again. 'Whereas, like you point out, mostly it's a 25-er you'd be lopping, there's this one special route that this one special van does once in a fucking blue moon and it's a long run from up north to down south, with Edinburgh smack bang in the middle ...'

Despite myself, I was warming to what he said. I got more comfortable in my seat, said, 'Keep going.'

'So Big Shug, he's on the inside in the Aberdeen depot and he's letting me know when the run goes ...' Silva dropped his grin, looked all serious. 'Not any run ... They're carrying anything from upwards of a couple of million ... in cash!'

My mouth dried over; I licked my lips. 'And how do you plan to get it out the van? Got some fucking Semtex, have you?'

Silva laughed, turned to his boy. Ben let out a whimpering little grunt, fired a look in my direction. I wondered how much effort it would take for me to wring his fucking neck.

'No need, squire ... no need! See, and this is the genius of it all. When I heard this I could have almost kissed Big Shug's Scotch fucking arse! The van only comes as far as Edinburgh before they stop off round about lunchtime at a very easy to reach Little Chef service station on the M8! And the fucking guards get out the van for a piss and a pie!

It's their little routine. There's none of this worry about is the chump in the van gonna drop out the bags because if you've got the lot, they've fucking got to open up or they're gonna cop their fucking whack!'

It sounded too easy. I'd learnt early on that when it sounds too easy, it's probably for a reason. 'How do you know the filth aren't all over this? Sounds like a set-up to me, bastards are known for it.'

I caught sight of Ben turning to his old man; the thought obviously hadn't crossed their minds. Silva flared, his cheeks reddened. 'Don't mug me off, Jed ...' He pointed a finger at me now. 'You think I'm some kind of cunt who hasn't done his homework?'

'You think I am? ... I checked you out, pal. I know armed-fucking-robbery isn't one of your regular earners.'

'Yeah, you're fucking right it's not. And normally I wouldn't touch it. You know why, because I don't fancy doing a life tariff for some small fucking change to me. But this is different. This is a quality job, a fucking good earner and we can all get a nice drink out of it.'

I shook my head. 'You haven't got the first fucking clue, mate.' He didn't like that, but held schtum. I fired in again. 'If you think you can pull this off with your raggedy-arsed boy and fruit-loop fucking daughter, then more power to you.' I took a sip out my pint and rose. Gail had those big eyes on me as I turned for the door of the snug. I felt a spike turn in my heart; she looked hurt.

'Jed ...wait!' She stood up. I was already walking but she followed me out.

On the street I stomped heavily back to the bus stop. The rain was coming down in sheets now.

'Jed ... wait!'

I heard Gail's heels clacking on the flags behind me. She grabbed my arm, but I pulled it away.

'Fuck off, would you?' I said.

'No, wait ... you didn't mean that, did you?'

'That job's a non-starter!'

'No, not that ... about me.'

I stopped, turned. The rain flattened my hair as I looked at Gail; she was shivering. I reached out an arm to her. 'Get back inside.' I saw Silva and Ben appear at the door of The Arms. 'Look, your family's waiting.'

'Ben's not *my* family ...'

'Well, your Dad's there.'

'Fuck him!' She'd raised her voice, to well within Silva's ear shot. 'You didn't mean that. You were just angry, right?'

I felt my throat start to freeze; she looked so felled by my words. I couldn't bring myself to hurt her; I'd hurt too many people in my time and always the most vulnerable ones. 'No, I didn't mean it.'

Gail reached out, grabbed my arm. 'I knew it.' The smile was back on her face. The rain was so heavy now that I delivered her back to the boozer.

Silva was sparking up a tab as we arrived.

'Jed, you don't want to be too hasty ... this is a nice bit of work. I've had it checked out. There's no fucking filth attached; I've had this van under obbo for the last three trips and I swear to fuck each and every time I was tempted to do it myself ... they're chumps. Two lardy-arsed melts who can't pass a fucking Little Chef without nipping in for a plate of egg and chips!' He was cringing at me, the creases in his brow and cheeks deepening with every new plea. 'I tell you mate, I've checked it out. I've checked you out and everyone I know say's you've got the minerals for this lark so what do you say?'

I watched Gail ease past her father in the doorway; she was dripping wet now.

'I don't know,' I said. 'I have a bad feeling in my gut about it.'

Silva took a drag on his B&H, cusped it in his hand, prison-yard style, then leaned over to me. 'Jed, this is a heavy bit of work. We're talking quite a few shekels here. I'd be fucking worried if you didn't have your doubts ... but don't go looking a gift horse in the mouth because your bottle's tested.'

I turned on him. 'Fuck off, don't give me that. There's fuck all wrong with my bottle. I'm a professional, that's all!'

'All right, all right ... you have your pride, and I admire that. So, to show I'm a fair bloke, I'll put you at the head of the crew.'

'What?'

'It's your say all the way. I'll fill you in on the recce I've done and all the ins-and-outs from Big Shug and then you can make the final call.'

I was far from convinced, but there was that part of me that always said fuck-it. 'Okay, and we split it 50/50.'

'I wouldn't have it any other way.' Silva flicked his tab into the wet night, reached out a hand to my shoulder and dragged me back into the pub. 'Welcome aboard, lad ... now let's get a pint down. Only one mind, got a big day ahead of us tomorrow.'

I looked him in the eye. 'What's on tomorrow?'

Silva grinned, 'The job, mate. The fucking job's on tomorrow!'

Jasper was packing a holdall when I got back to the flat. 'What's up, rent-man catch up with you?' I said.

'Eh?'

'Looks like you're doing a runner ...' I pointed to the bag he was stuffing with socks and jocks.

Jasper straightened himself. 'Got a bit of work on, going to be out of town for a bit.'

I nodded. 'You too?'

Jasper turned back to the bag. 'I'm off to sunny, sunny Spain.'

'Oh aye, Viva España!'

He finished packing, zipped up the bag and flung it on the floor. 'Not till tomorrow though.' He stood over the bag, kicked it under the kitchen table, then put his hands on his hips. 'What about you – picked up a bit of business, have you?'

I didn't want to tell him about the job – he'd only talk me out of it. 'Something like that ... fancy a pizza?'

Jasper's face lit up like a five-year-old's. 'Fucking right!'

Job done.

I called Pizza Express, got two large meat feasts on order. As we waited for them to arrive Jasper told me about his latest boat trip. Seems he was going out to pick up a load of gear that wouldn't pass through the proper channels. It sounded very last minute to me but who was I to question him on his business. Fuck me, if he'd asked what I was planning to do next it was sure as shooting he'd be poking holes in it. A hoor of a business.

When the pizzas arrived I fired into mine, but I didn't really have an appetite. The Silva job was bothering me. I knew it was all a big gamble, but I tried to shove it to the back of my mind because I knew life was all a gamble and living like a square-peg was no life at all.

Jasper cracked open a bottle of Chianti, said 'Suppose I better get used to this before Spain!'

I eyeballed him. 'That's from Italy, you muppet!'

He smiled. 'Oh, yeah? ... Well, they drink it there too.'

I shook my head.

Jasper poured out a couple of big glasses. 'You know, if I didn't know any better I'd say you had something on your mind, Jed ... that bit of stuff is it?'

'Silva's daughter? No danger.'

He looked eyes on me. 'Oh, aye? ... You sure about that?'

I was in no mood for this shite, and I knew I needed a clear head for the morning. I stood up, picked up the glass and drained a good belt, then, 'I'm turning in, got a big day ahead tomorrow.'

'Come on, I'm only pulling your leg – have a bevvy with me!'

I turned away. 'Another time.'

'I'll be in Spain!'

'Well, when you get back then.' As I went through to my room I hoped I'd still be around when he got back, and not banged up after another performance by Gail.

I kicked off my Timberland boots, dived onto the bed. I lay there staring at the ceiling as a little light crept in from the street signs. It was still raining – suited my mood.

I couldn't put my finger on it – I swear for the life of me I couldn't – but there was something about the way this Gail bit looked at me that made me think of Jody. My sister was gone, but the look she used to have in her eye when I'd come back from that garage, that first fucking job I had as a grease monkey. She would put those eyes on me, those big staring, pleading eyes like she wanted to tell me something, but ... well, she did in the end, but I almost wished she hadn't.

When I found out what had been going on, what my old man had done to her, everything changed. I couldn't live with myself in that borstal. I was fighting everyone, even the screws, and I was still only a lad and they were grown-up. I just hated the world and it had holed-up in me. My only comfort was that I had Jody; she hadn't visited ever, but I knew she was there. Well, I thought she was.

I don't know how long it was after they told me Jody had been moved to another town, with the foster family, maybe six months, maybe a year, but that was when the sky came down.

They put two screws in the room with me when they broke the news.

'Sit down would you, Jed,' said Mr Parker, he was the Governor, he was a doctor and wore a white coat sometimes, but not today; he had a tweed jacket on, I remembered the elbow patches on it, leather, brown leather they were, and frayed at the edges. I wondered who had sewn them on for him. Funny that, the things that stick in your mind sometimes.

'Why?' I didn't want to sit.

'I think it would be better.'

I knew now why he was telling me to sit, but I was too young then to get the picture. He sat beside me on the bed, then turned to face me. I tried to face him but my mind was on the screws and what they were up to. I didn't want to be jumped by them. I thought it unlikely with Mr Parker – Old Nosey they called him – around but you couldn't be too sure.

'What is it?' I said.

'I'm afraid we've had some bad news today.'

I shrugged; I wasn't following him.

'Yes, some bad news ...' I smelt aftershave off him he was so close. Years later I found out it was called Tabac and came in little white bottles; I've never liked it since. He went on, 'I'm sorry to have to tell you that your sister, Jody, has died.'

155

The words hit me like a boot to the gut; I swear I doubled over. 'No. It's not true,' I said.

'I'm very sorry. They found her this morning, there's no doubt.' He stood up. I felt his hand on my back for a second but I pulled away. The screws moved in at that point but Old Nosey flagged them down.

'How?' It didn't make sense; she was younger than me.

He hesitated; I watched him remove his glasses and rub at his eyes. 'Your sister ... your sister took her own life.' He put on his specs again. 'I am dreadfully sorry, Jed.'

As I started to cry they left me alone.

My memory of this time is patchy now, always has been, but I can still recall rocking to and fro on the bed for ages, the springs squeaking and squeaking. At some stage I must have fallen asleep and I awoke in the middle of the night. It was a clear night and I saw the moon in the sky through the bars on the window. I thought about Jody and then I couldn't look at the sky anymore. As I pulled my gaze away, it fell on the light-bulb dangling above my bed and I rose and unscrewed it.

The glass bulb smashed easily as I tapped it against the wall. I selected the largest shard and stuck it into my wrist; the blood flowed freely and I repeated the process with my other wrist.

As the blood spilled I wanted to get away from it; I didn't want to have any of my father's blood in me. It was foul, tainted.

'You killed her, you bastard.' I said this over and over to myself. I wanted him back, so I could kill him myself. If I had killed him, it might have saved Jody; I knew she blamed herself for his suicide and she just couldn't live with it. I could have got by with her hating me for killing him, but I couldn't get by with her hating herself.

When I woke my wrists were bandaged and they had me

in a straitjacket; I was pumped full of tranquillisers. I felt gutted to be alive.

The flop was a deserted farmhouse on the edge of Midlothian. The place looked like it hadn't been lived in for years. Silva seemed quite pleased with himself to have found it, but Gentle Ben was shivering and snivelling, complaining about the cold and Gail was complaining about the smell.

'What is it? I've never smelt anything like it!' said Gail.

'It's the smell of fucking poverty, gel,' said Silva. 'And the reason you haven't come across it before now is I've fucking silver-spooned you.'

I looked away. Ben was poking at the grate in the fireplace. 'I think I'll get a fire on.'

'Think again, cuntybaws,' I said. 'You want to send a smoke signal to the filth, do you?'

He threw down the poker and stomped out the room.

Silva was sparking up a tab, running his fingers through his Brylcreemed hair.

'We need to have a little chat,' I said. He looked nervous; I didn't need anyone nervous on this job.

'Yeah, yeah ... all right, through here.' He nodded me through to the next room, the kitchen. On the table was a large Lotto sports bag. He walked over to it, unzipped. 'Take a look in there.'

I wandered over to the table, stuck a hand in the bag. I saw the wooden handle of a gun. As I reached for it I saw there were two more of the same. I took out the shooter; it was an old hammer-cock shotgun. It looked ancient. 'The fuck is this?'

Silva looked scoobied. 'Guns, innit?'

'I said I wanted decent shooters ...' I held up the hunting

weapon; it had a single barrel that looked about three-foot long. 'How the fuck are we going to manoeuvre with these?' I had visions of Gentle Ben tripping on his at the moment of truth.

'Hang about.' He reached in the bag, removed a small handgun; it was a snub-nose Colt. 'I got this for the girlie. We'll be mustard.'

I shook my head in disbelief. 'We can't use these shooters. They're a fucking joke.'

Silva stirred, pointed a finger. 'Now look.'

'Don't fucking look me – you'll have to saw the stocks off.'

'We haven't got fucking time, or a fucking saw.'

I opened the gun; it was empty; I threw it on the table. I knew a bloke in Leith that would hire you old shooters for a ton-a-time. They were manky old things held together with gaffer tape but I'd have sooner had them on the job than this lot.

'Let me call a pal.'

'No!' Silva roared. 'Not on my job!'

I tilted my head. 'I thought this was my job.'

'I said you could plan it.'

He'd changed his tune, but it was too late to argue. 'Well I'm planning to have different guns.'

He seemed to find some calm. 'Look, I know these guns like the back of my hand, and so do the kids – I taught them how to shoot with them. They're mustard! Trust me.'

I felt time ticking along, I sensed this was not a battle I was going to win, said, 'I'm not happy with this.'

'The guns look the part, that's all that matters ... they're for putting a scare out.'

I took a deep breath, picked up the shooter and put it in the happy bag. 'Call the others.'

Silva nodded, went to the door and summoned Gail

and Ben. They trotted through like sullen teenagers a few seconds later. As we stood round the table I told them how I wanted the job to go, what their roles were and who they took their orders from.

Ben huffed.

'You got a problem?' I said to him.

His huff turned into a sneer. 'No.'

'Good.'

Silva started another tab. He was smoking like a fucking lum.

I tapped a finger on the table. 'This should be a simple job, if you all do what you're told, when you're told. I've got it timed to six minutes and I'll be clocking it at that. If we go over the six minutes I want all of us to pull back. Got that?'

Silva nodded first, then the others.

I continued, 'Now, this is a heavy bit of work, and we know that, so it has to go like clockwork or we're fucked. Gail, you're gonna be our bag man – I want the money bagged and booted fast as you can.'

'Okay. Got that,' she said.

'Now, the old fella is gonna stay in the car, soon as the doors shut – you boot it.'

'Got ya,' said Silva.

'Ben, you and me are doing the frightners. That means noising up the security guards, shaking them up. But remember – first and foremost – get them to open those boxes. There'll be bangers and dye packs in there and you have to get them to take them out ...' His eyes wandered. 'You hearing me?'

'Yeah, yeah ... only bag the money, no other shit.'

'Right ...' I scanned the group. They were fuck-all but I knew my own abilities and figured I could hold this together. 'Now, one last thing. Do not fire off those shooters.'

'What?' said Ben.

'You fucking heard, I've not been on a job yet that needed gunfire and I'm not fucking starting now.'

'But what if they try it on?' said Ben.

I locked him down. 'Leave it to me. No fucking shots, right. You start firing off rounds and the filth will be on us quicker than a fucking rat up a drainpipe. We need all the time we can muster to get back to the flop and I don't want to be playing dodgems with plod.'

Silva started to nod and the others followed suit.

I checked my watch. 'We've got an hour and a half before we go. Be ready.'

As we were getting into the Toyota that Silva had sourced, Gail leaned over and placed a little kiss on my cheek.

'What was that for?' I said.

'Luck, or something.'

'I'd sooner something ... we don't want to be relying on luck.'

Gail winked. 'Well, go for something, then.'

We drove out of the farmstead. The road was rough and ready but the car cleared it no trouble. Silva had a tab in the fingers of his rope-backed gloves. I kept an eye on him; he was nervy, but I think he was more worried about the rest of us than himself. My main concern was how Ben would go; Gail, I had experience of and I think she had learnt her lesson, but this gimp was a mystery to me and I didn't like unknown factors on any of my jobs.

The day was clear, not exactly sunshine but as close as you get in Scotland. There was a low cloud covering but I didn't expect rain. That was good, making a getaway on wet roads was not a great idea. Tyres spin and cars lose control.

At the by-pass Silva flicked his tab out the window. The others were quiet. I could feel my pulse calming as we got onto the M8; I knew I was readying myself for the job. Some people, they get edgy; me, I get fucking Zen. I'm never calmer than when I'm on a bit of work.

As we cruised along the road, no-one spoke. It was getting hot in the car and Gail opened her window a little. I felt a few spots of rain coming in now, but it was nothing to worry about – didn't even require the wipers on.

'There she is,' said Silva. He'd spotted the service station up ahead.

'Ease off the peddle,' I said. I looked out to see if I could spot the security van but there was no sign. One or two cars were parked out the front of the Little Chef but there was no sign of the wagon we'd come to target.

'Where the fuck is it?' said Ben. His voice whined and grated. I felt like giving him a backhander.

'Easy. We're ahead of schedule,' I said.

'But they should be here, surely.'

'Not necessarily ... might have been heavy on the roads.'

Silva put on the blinkers and pulled the motor up at the edge of the carpark, facing the exit junction.

When the car came to a halt, Gail spoke. 'What now?'

'We wait.'

'For how long?'

'Long as it takes.'

It didn't take too long. I'd no sooner uttered the words than the big dark van pulled in. It was a heavily-armoured job. I couldn't see the driver's face but he drove cautiously, passing a spot at the front of the Little Chef and reversing into another one at the side.

'This their routine?' I said.

Silva was fiddling with the strap on his gloves. 'Yeah,

yeah ... hang about, you'll see the bloke in the driver's side come out first.'

The driver's door of the security van opened. He was a short bloke, squat. He walked to the back of the van, stretched a bit and then did a 180 and tapped on the side as he walked back towards the front.

Silva stirred, went to grab the keys in the ignition.

'Wait!' I said. 'Not until the other one's out.'

The second door of the van opened up and a slimmer figure got out. It was a woman. I could tell by the shape. She had long red hair coming out the sides of her helmet. This looked like bad luck to me, but it was too late to back away.

'Right, masks on! Gun the engine!'

———————— ✳ ————————

There's cons on the inside will tell you, looking back, these things happen in slow motion. Not for me they didn't. It was all happening at 100 mph.

The tyres of the Toyota screeched to a halt as the two guards headed for the Little Chef. It had all gone to plan. We were between them and the van; they had nowhere to run.

I was first out. Had the pair in my sights as I stared over the long barrel. 'Get your fucking hands up!' I sensed Ben and Gail running beside me but my vision was blurred through the ski-mask.

'Fucking move it, you cunts!' Ben had come from nowhere. He pointed the gun at the woman's head. He was close enough to blow her fucking nut right off, helmet and all. She started to scream.

'Shut your fucking hole!' roared Ben. He was side-stepping, dancing on his toes. The woman kept spinning. The whole scene made me dizzy.

'You. Get the fucking van open.' I grabbed the stout

bloke by the collar and marched him back to the van. He rattled keys as he went.

'Fucking move, faster.'

Gail kept at my rear as we went. We left Ben with the other guard but she was screaming her head off. I turned to Gail. 'Shut her the fuck up.'

As I glanced back I saw Gail turn and look at her brother. He was slapping the redhead about. His gun was pushed right up in her helmet now.

I roared at Gail again. 'Fucking hell … sort that out!' She looked back at me and didn't seem to know what to do. The stocky bloke stood at the back of the van; he dropped the keys. I knew it was all delaying tactics. I pushed the gun into his gut. 'What are you fucking playing at?'

'You haven't thought about this, have you?' he said.

'What?'

'You'll do thirty years.'

I gave him a slap, bust his nose; it started to bleed. 'You'll not see another fucking day if you don't open that fucking van and get the money on the street.'

He wiped the blood away from his face and kneeled down to retrieve the keys. I looked at my watch; we'd already wasted three of our six minutes. 'Hurry the fuck up!'

'What's going on up there?' shouted Silva.

It was chaos.

The redhead was still screaming.

Silva was revving the engine.

I kicked the guard in the gut. 'Fucking move it!'

'I'm looking for the keys.'

I saw the keys on the ground; he'd shoved them out of his reach. I grabbed him by the collar and yanked him up. Gail was back at my side; she bent down and got the keys and gave them to me.

The van door had a pin-combination pad and a lock. As the guard stood there contemplating the situation, he said, 'You don't want to do this.'

'Fucking open it or I'll put your brain across the tarmac. Don't fucking test me on that.'

Silva revved again; he was in a panic. 'Come on ... get the fucking thing open.'

I turned to see Silva but my attention was grabbed by Ben. He had the redhead in a head lock and was dragging her to the back of the van. The gun was pointed in the air as he pushed on with his awkward load. 'What the fuck's going on up there?' he yelled out. 'Where's the fucking money?'

He was level with us before I could speak again. The redhead was white with terror, whimpering and crying. When the other guard saw her it was like a bolt of bravery shot through him.

'Now, look here, leave the woman alone!' he said.

Ben stared at this fat fuck like he was ready to put a bullet in him. I knew things were spiralling out of control. I stepped in, grabbed the guard again. 'You stupid fucking cunt, open this door and get the money on the street or I will put a fucking bullet in your head sure as I fucking stand here.'

He froze. Looked at the crying, whimpering woman. 'I can't do it.'

I didn't believe this was happening. We'd turned up the one guard in the world who was prepared to duke it out with armed robbers.

I looked at my watch again: we had hit five minutes. We didn't have enough time to unload the van. I turned towards the car. 'Right. Let's go!'

Gail trooped beside me, but Ben stayed.

'What the fuck are you doing?' he yelled.

'Get in the fucking car. Now!' I beckoned him back

but he was twitching and jumping like a lunatic. The idea of missing out on his take was high on his mind. I knew there was no chance of him listening to me. I was ready to dump him but as I turned to Silva I knew the chances of him leaving his boy behind were nil.

'Get in the fucking car.' I yelled at him again, but it had no impact. I knew I'd have to drag him. As I turned tail, headed for Ben, he got even jumpier and started to wave the gun about.

'Get back!' he said.

'What? ... Put the fucking gun down.' I held out my hand to him, but he was gone and I knew it. I kept walking towards him. He sensed I was almost on him when the gun went off.

The redhead fell in a heap.

A pool of dark red blood spilled out from beneath her head.

'What have you done?' I said. The words seemed meaningless.

I felt a rush at my back and saw Silva had got out of the car. He raced towards the scene and took it in. Ben had turned from us all and had the gun on the second guard now.

'No, don't!' I said.

'Okay. Okay ... I'll open it, I'll open it,' said the guard as Ben forced his shooter into the back of his neck.

How we made it back to the flop, I have no idea.

When we ditched the Toyota and got into the changeover car there were sirens wailing all over the shop.

We'd fucked up, and I knew what that meant but the others had no idea.

Silva had taken Ben into the back room as soon as we got to the farmhouse. I stayed in the front with Gail. She looked shaken.

'You okay?' I said.

She didn't answer at first, just stared at her fingers, then, 'Did you see all that blood? ... I've never seen blood like that.'

I put an arm round her shoulder.

'He's an animal,' she said.

I presumed she was talking about her half-brother. 'What do you mean?'

Gail started to cry. 'How could he do something like that?'

I grabbed her tighter. All the while I was wondering how long we had before the filth started trawling for us. We were in serious shit now. I wanted to take my share of the money and get moving, but I didn't want to leave Gail behind.

'Look, things haven't turned out right,' I said.

'No kidding.'

'We can't stay here now, it's not safe. I know someone who can help us, he's a friend and ...'

She wasn't listening. As the door from the back room was opened and Ben strolled out, she got up and started to beat on his chest.

'You fucking arsehole, you fucking idiot!' Gail slung punches and slaps as Ben ducked; Silva appeared at her back and dragged her to the sofa, dumped her.

'You fucking stupid bitch!' yelled Ben. He had scratch marks running down the side of his face. I was ready to add to them.

'You've some bottle haven't you, considering your position?' As I spoke, Ben patted his cheek with his shirtsleeve.

Silva turned away from Gail, faced us. He noticed I had

the long gun barrel pointed at his son's head.

'Now watch what you're doing there, Jed,' said Silva.

'Shut the fuck up. His card's marked,' I said.

Ben's colour changed. His eyes seemed to drop further into his head as he realised I had no intention of letting him off the hook. He looked at me for a moment, then his gaze darted towards his father and his sister. Somewhere inside that fucked-up head of his he had a notion: he wanted to wound me before I finished him.

'He fucked her for years you know,' said Ben. His top lip quivered; a line of sweat formed on his forehead. 'She didn't tell you that, did she?'

Silva sparked up, 'Ben ... what are you doing?'

'Ask them, he said ... it's true. Father and daughter. What do you make of that? Still got a thing for her now, have you?'

I looked at Silva; he had guilty eyes. Gail had her face in her hands. She was in tears again.

My heart started to pound.

'You're making it up. You think I'll bite on that, you're mistaken.'

Ben started to giggle. 'It's true! It's true! ... I used to see them. He made videos too.'

I remembered what Jasper had said about Silva"road-testing" his porn starlets himself.

'Shut up!' said Silva.

I put the gun to Ben's head. 'You are one sick fuck.' He had known about the abuse and did nothing. He could have stopped it, saved her. I would have done anything to save Jody – I wished I had killed my own father to save her.

Ben was laughing as the gunshot came. As he fell back a black mess appeared on the wall behind him. At its edges there was red blood and indiscriminate brain matter.

After the gun's discharge the room was silent, except for

the ringing in my ears. Nobody moved for some time and then Silva ran for me with his arms out.

I smacked the gun barrel off his head and he fell on the ground, moaning. I started to reload the shooter.

Gail rose up. As I looked at her I suddenly understood why she reminded me so much of Jody. Then I knew what Ben had said was true.

Gail looked down.

I wanted to see her smile.

I wanted to see her sigh, in relief.

I wanted to see her run to me, open arms, shower thanks on me.

But she cried.

'Gail,' I said. I put the gun down on the sofa, went to her. Silva writhed on the floor.

'Gail, why the tears?'

She couldn't find words. Breath was a trouble. She raised her hands to her face. 'He's in pain.'

'So fucking what?' I said.

Silva slapped about on the floor, grimaced in agony.

She started to pat her cheeks, make bellows of her face. 'He's in pain.'

'So fucking what?' I repeated.

I stomped past her, picked up the gun again and shoved it in Silva's face.

He yelled out: 'You're fucked, Jed Collins!"

I smacked the gun off his head; I wanted Gail to see him in agony, the way he'd seen her in agony – I hauled her down.

'Look at his face. Remember that ...' I grabbed Silva's hair; he screamed as I smacked at his head. 'See the way he's squirming, trying to get away?'

She looked.

'See him?'

I wanted her to see her father in pain, but more than that I wanted her to see him in terror. The kind of terror he'd inflicted on her. I was full of an anger I didn't know I possessed.

'Gail, see him ... ?'

She froze. I think she understood. I took the shooter and aimed it at Silva, but thought it was too easy a way out for him. I threw the gun down, roared at him. 'You dirty fucking bastard. Your own daughter ... your own daughter. *How?* You fucking animal.'

I knew the words I wanted to say; they came easily. They were the same words I'd wanted to say to my own father.

'You dirty bastard. You dirty fucking bastard ... your own daughter.'

I was crying. I watched my tears falling on Silva's chest. The look on his face was defiant though; he couldn't care less what he'd done.

He smiled, laughed at me. 'You dumb bastard ... the whore loved every minute of it!'

I was motionless as the gun went off behind me. I felt my ears ring. One side of me went numb. I turned quickly to see Gail holding the shooter; she was motionless. Her face cold, firm.

Dark blood pooled on the floor under Silva's groin.

'Is he dead?' she said after a few moments.

'Yes.'

She looked at me; her look had changed. 'What now?'

I grabbed a deep breath. 'We take the money.'

'Where?'

I looked out the window; it was starting to rain, said, 'I hear the weather's nice in Spain.'

'*Spain?*'

'I know where there's a boat leaving. If we're quick ...'

London Calling

There's a time and a place for this shit. Now isn't it.

'You're not cool with this?'

'Answer me this, Don, do I look fucking cool with it?'

Don curls his lower lip, bites down. It's not a pained look, but I'm thinking, not far off it.

'A beer?'

'Fuck your beer.'

Frowns.

'It's the good stuff ... Stella.'

I raise myself from the Ikea cowhide chair, comfortable as a bastard anyway, and cross the laminate floor. The first thing that comes to hand is the purple and red lava lamp. It smashes like the One O'clock Gun as I take it over Don's head.

'It'd take a truckload of Stella for me to be cool with you fucking my girlfriend, Don.'

London Calling comes on the iPod plugged into the Bosch speaker unit on the wall. I think, bollocks, Jonny Ladd isn't going to like this turn of events.

First I see of the bloke is Don knocking seven bells out of him in The Wheatsheaf shitter. He's a suit. Banker-type or something, I'd say ad-man maybe, but like I'd know how an ad-man looks ... I sell a bit of Bob Hope for Don. Need to get a new line.

'Don, what's this shit?'

He looks up, still kicking the crap out the poor guy. His new Kickers have blood on them, he spots it, removes one, starts slapping the fella about the head with it.

'Look what you've done to my shoes, y'prick!'

'I'm sorry ... I'm sorry.' He raises his hands, waves them about his head in a, it must be said, girlie manner. I laugh out loud.

Don clocks me in hysterics, falling into one of the cubicles, and starts up himself. It's quite a sight. I'm hoping no one else comes in when, bang on cue, the door swings open.

'Jonny,' says Don.

I drop the laughter. Calm it. Feel my feet slipping as I ease onto the toilet seat and make myself invisible. Dealing for Don's one thing, mixing it with the likes of Jonny Ladd is another. Not got my sights on the Premier League, unlike some.

Jonny speaks, 'This the cunt?'

'Aye, aye,' says Don, 'That's him all right ... clocked him with the blonde bird out the estate agent's office ... one with the big tits, yeah.'

Jonny Ladd says nothing. I can see him in the mirror, out the gap in the door. His face is a roadmap of hard lines, look like they've been cut in with razors; maybe some of them have. He gives the guy on the floor the once-over, I think he might speak, but he walks past and touches Don on the arm, motions a thumb, 'Get him the fuck out of here.'

'Where?'

'Your gaff, there's a brasser on the way to meet you ...

Make sure you've got your camera. I'll tell you where to send the shots. Now get a fucking jig on.'

'You got a hold of it?'

'Aye, I've got it.'

The box is cardboard, not fit for the job.

'He's gonna come out the bottom, Don.'

'It'll be fine, it's just two flights.'

Two flights up an Edinburgh stairwell like this is not easy going. In the Old Town's twisty, windy stairs, it's a near impossibility.

'I'm telling you, he's gonna fall out!'

Don drops his end, as if to prove a point, and the banker slumps out. The blood smeared over his face, from a nasty nosebleed, leaves a streak on the newly painted white wall.

'Och, for Christsake, Don. I told you this would happen.'

Over the edge of the banister there's a female voice, sounds Oriental, 'Hello, is suck-suck, yes?' It's the pro, she's Thai or something, anxious to get to work. We're real multicultural in Edinburgh these days.

Don shouts back, 'Aye, aye ... just a minute.' He reaches down, gives the banker a slap, he starts to come around. Mumbles. Don jumps a few steps, turns, fishes in his pockets for the keys to the flat, and says, 'He'll walk from here, drag him. I'll get opened up ... set the scene!'

I pick the guy out the box, balance his arm around my neck. I hear Don slam the door of the flat.

The banker speaks, 'You have to help me ...'

'Y'what?'

'I know what this is all about.'

'Yeah, you pissed off Jonny Ladd.' That's a no-brainer in my book.

'No. It's nothing to do with me ... it's my girlfriend!'

I'm scoobied, feel my mouth droop, then Don opens the door, and hollers, 'Get a shift on down there.'

When I turn back, the guy's passed out again.

'So, what's the deal here, he owe Jonny Ladd some?'

Don looks at me, scrunches his brows, 'Fuck no, it's for a bit of fun.'

'Come again?'

'The blonde, y'know, one with the big tits, Jonny's got a bone on for her.'

I don't follow, say, 'I'm not with you.'

'Look, the idea is, we get a few photos on this fuckhead with his pants around his ankles, maybe some munter going down on him and the blonde suddenly has a change of heart.'

'That's low.'

'It's a living.'

I didn't agree. For a while now I'd been thinking there were better ways to make a living than dancing to Jonny Ladd's tune, or dealing for Don for that matter. Ange had said it ... there's more to life, change is good, or some such shit.

'What's with the shake of the head?' says Don.

'Nothing.'

'Nah, you don't approve, do you?'

'It's not that.'

The brasser moves on the couch, points to the banker who's coming around again. She goes over to him, starts to loosen his tie.

'No, fuck no ... it's his pants you take off, here ...' Don directs her to the belt buckle, walks back to me, starts to play with his camera-phone. He says loosen up, get over Ange leaving, and ... am I cool with him putting the moves on her?

Fuck no.

He tries to ply me with a beer, Stella Artois ... Funny, I think, Ange never liked beer, but lately she'd been big on Stella.

I feel a rush of blood to my head.

Miss Suck-Suck lets out a scream when the lava lamp explodes. She jumps up as Don hits the floor. I raise a hand, say, 'It's cool ... we're all cool with this.'

She goes back to work. I say, 'No. No. There's been a change of plan.'

'Explain, please?'

'This fella here,' I turn Don over, start to undo his belt, 'you want to get your gums round him instead.'

'Okay-dokey.'

As she goes to work, I take up Don's camera-phone.

The banker's coming around as I snap away, 'Don't worry about us mate, we'll be out of your hair in no time.'

He keels over again.

'Wise. Get your head down.'

'Okay-dokey,' says Miss Suck-Suck.

I laugh, 'No you're doing fine, love.'

The Clash on the Bosch speaker unit get me moving, *London Calling* sets the mood as I fire off some more shots, get in some arty ones.

I'm thinking, now here's maybe my new job. Christ knows I need one now.

I wonder if Ange will approve? I think this as I locate her number on Don's phone, and press 'send'.

Hound of Culann

He was your typical 'Troubles are over, my arse' Ulsterman. Tats. Sovereign rings. A swagger you could dry clothes on and a number-one to the nut. They were ten a penny in the city now. Usually, I'd have sent him packing with a brick up his hole but the well-used Webley in his waistband said he meant business.

I knew right off what he was here for.

I knew right off I didn't have it.

There was a crowd of say, eight, nine people between us. Good ol' boys sucking back stout, stocking up for a shot at the local hoors. None that would move to pull a greasy stick out of a dog's arse, or a lit firework for that matter.

'Any service going, mate? Murder a beer.' I stood up to meet the barman as he rose, slapping the local rag down on the bar-top.

'Beer?' he said.

'Yeah, two ... one for me and ...'

He lifted a hand, I thought he was flagging me shut-the-fuck-up, 'What kind?'

'Come again?'

'Look, lad, I've got beers and beers.'

The hard-nut was two yards off, homing in on me, 'Right, right, eh ... the Deuchars'll do.'

The barman softened. Ironed out his creased brow, said, 'Good choice.'

I watched him slide off, caught sight of two scab-cracked elbows poking through his flannel. The fuck was I doing here? I had Marie now, waiting. I'd promised her.

A sovereign-ringed hand pounded the bar.

Culann had said take it easy, but take it. I remembered the words because I'd followed them to the letter.

'Time and place is all I need,' I said.

'You'll get a call. Don't miss it. Don't question it. Don't even respond. You got it?'

'Sure mate, no need to boil up yer piss.'

Culann had the appearance of what he was, a parasite. A fat fuck. A lazy, loose-moralled – scrub that – amoral, piece of shit. He let his heavy lids hang on his bloodshot eyes for a moment or two then he flashed his tongue like a lizard, 'You straight?'

'Mate, you know I am ... I fuck up you go medieval on my arse, Culann, that's not happening.'

I had him. The eyes sunk back in his fat head. His face played that moronic expression he wore most days. Only this wasn't most days for him, or for me.

I felt a tap on my shoulder. Not gentle, but a lot less than I was expecting. These big guys, all talk and no trousers. It's the size, the sheer scale that usually excuses them from any kind of conflict. Pound to a pail of shite, the jaw's never been tested. I mean really tested. As I turned, suddenly, I wasn't for trying the theory.

'Gilmour.'

'Who's asking?'

The knuckle-dragger removed his hand from the bar. Put his dark eyes on me, 'That wasn't a question.'

From the pocket of his cheapo leather he produced a picture of me, dropped it on the bar. I could hardly look, I was with Culann; I'd never wanted out the life more.

'Looks like you got me.'

A nod. No change on his face though, that ancient Scots' wisdom thing going on. I tried a smile. Nothing.

The barman arrived with the Deuchars. 'Get them down ye!'

'Cheers, mate.' I picked up the pints, offered one to the big fella.

'I don't touch alcohol.'

I knew at first sight of him that he was probably pumping his arse with steroids, so should have sussed he wasn't gonna touch the cold stuff.

The barman was appalled. 'That's a fucking good beer you're turning up, boy!'

'No worries, won't go to waste,' I told him.

The pug disagreed, said, 'Oh, I think it might.'

He picked up the pint glass, snatched mine with his other hand, then smashed them both together, right in front of my face. Shards and beer splashed over the floor.

The place fell silent.

Then, 'Get your fucking arse out to the car, Gilmour.'

The call had come at 2.20 a.m.

I took the details and climbed out of bed. I had an old Golf GTi, never failed me, purred into action first turn of the key.

The streets were quiet heading out through Liberton. I'd rented a bungalow in Corstorphine to keep everything as low key as possible. Was ready to cut and run after a couple of days but stuck it out to get the job done. Right down to the 9–5 appearance, suit from Markies, the lot.

The call dropped me the details of a Midlothian gaff, out near Straiton. I needed to push the Golf to make the time, but I'd been cruising the suburbs so long, figured the burn would do it good.

When I pulled in there was a set of pimped-up 4X4s in the road outside, Toyotas with the full chrome roll-bar kits. My instructions were simple, take the crate from the local boys, the one marked Edinburgh Airport, and bring it back to Culann.

In and out.

Pass GO and collect two grand.

If only it was so simple.

'So, that's the crate?' I asked the homeboy, Nike cap on backwards, barely a tooth in his gob.

'Yeah, mate ... that's Culann's beast.'

'Y'what?'

'In there. The dog!' He seemed confused, a look that said he'd just been anally-probed. Something told me he preferred doing the probing himself.

'You're shitting me, yeah? No one said a thing about a dog.' 'Mate, why do you think there's so much interest ... it's a fucking champion in the pit.'

I put a torch on the crate. Sure enough there was a livestock stamp and clearance papers attached.

'Well, bugger me ...'

The two shit-heads laughed, started to slap each other on the back, then, 'Mate ... this hound's a fucking killer.'

I pulled the top layer of the paper covering the crate and steadied the torch. There was a little movement inside. Then two yellow eyes flashed for a second and the dog threw itself at me, snarling and barking. The fucker went ape.

'You sure about this?'

'Bloody right!' said the mouthy one. He took off his cap and scratched his head, then, 'Look, I got the word on this coming through from America ... I work the airport, greased its arse you might say.'

'But it's a fighting dog.' Culann had pulled some shit, but bringing in beasts like this was a new low, even for him.

'Mate, Culann's putting on the fucking fight of the century!'

'So why haven't I heard about it?'

"Cos if you had, maybe some mad bastard would get the idea of stealing the fucker.'

The pair of them laughed themselves stupid. It didn't take long. I couldn't watch. The two grand seemed like small potatoes when weighed against the fact I'd be reading about this beast tearing some toddler's arm off sooner or later. Then there was the bigger picture and the opportunity it presented me.

'Boys ... you have a point.'

The laughter stopped flat. 'What?'

The pair looked like I'd just torched the 4X4s sitting behind us. I guessed there'd be plenty more opportunities for them to make a killing cherry-picking the cargo bays, but this deal, I decided, wasn't paying them.

'On the road.'

'Y'what?'

I took the shooter from my belt. 'There's been a change of plan ...'

'So, how do I know you're who you say you are?'

The pug didn't even blink, in a flash he had me pressed

against the driver's door of the Golf, an armlock so tight you could jack-up the car with it.

'I didn't come here to be fucked over ... there's a time factor and not to mention the limits of my patience.'

I'd been hardballed before. 'There's also the fact that I'm the one with all the cards here ... now get your fucking mitts off me or there's gonna be one thirsty, hungry dog gnawing at the confines of a crate till it keels.'

He twisted harder, said, 'Anything happens to Culann's dog ...'

'You'll what, break my arm?' I let him get the taste of that for a while, then, 'What do you think it is today, about four-below? ... Fucking cold out for sure. Beast'll be lucky to survive the night.'

'Okay, what do you want?' said Culann's lump.

'Just what we agreed.'

He loosened off his hold. Stepped back. I could tell he thought I was making a mistake. That I'd be lucky to see the week out. But my conscience was clear. I was doing the right thing; Marie would agree. I'd already queered the deal for Culann, put my arse in a sling, there was no going back now ... I needed reassurances.

The pug pulled down on his collar, looked out to the horizon. 'Culann's losing patience.'

'You know what I want.'

'Gilmour. You're out. No bastard will work with you now ... Just don't get any ideas about a challenge, that would be fatal. He dropped his chin and laughed. 'I'd be going far, far away ... I hear Tasmania's nice.'

'And the cash?'

He pulled a Jiffy-bag from inside his leather, 'You're paid up.'

I ripped open the seal. All sound.

It was getting colder. I shielded my eyes from the wind, brushed a layer of muck from the top of the Golf.

'Come here,' I said.

He followed me round to the front of the car. I wet a finger on my tongue, started to draw a map in the bonnet's grime. 'The dog's tucked up in an old barn about three miles from here ...'

He left so quickly, looked so gladdened, I never had time to utter the words, 'Sorry I broke the cunt's neck ... But, fair play, it had gone for me.'

Pretty Boy

The slot-machine's lights flickered off the blood-splattered floor as Stauner came round. He lay in a mix of piss, blood, fag-dowps, shattered glass and ... hair. Lots of blond hair.

'The fuck's this?' he said.

Stauner touched his head.

'No ... the bastards!' They'd shaved his head. Not a scalping, but a fine going over with the number one.

'No. No. No,' he yelled out. He slapped palms on the pub floor, tried to gather up as much of his long locks as he could.

'The bastards ... the fuckers, this is out of order.'

The blond curls unfurled with every touch; already caught up in the shards and blood, there was no way back for them.

Stauner rose.

He looked around: it was The Moorings. He could pick the place any day, his old stomping ground. Pulled some gash in here, he thought, he'd even renamed it, The Hoorings after his successes.

'How the fuck'd I get in here?'

The last thing Stauner remembered was handing the Adidas holdall to Monique. She'd kissed him, bloody hard he'd thought, even for Monique. Then she'd grabbed his crotch and asked what he'd been feeding that bad boy on.

'French lassies!' Stauner said.

'You are teasing with me, darling. Always you are teasing, no?'

No teasing about it, he'd thought. He meant every word he said: 'I'm your man, hon … happy to supply the meat for a wee French roll anytime!'

She liked that, he thought. She spun round and flicked her long black hair in his face. He could still remember how it smelled as she backed onto him, grinding in her 'petit derrière'.

'Later, mon amour … I have to take this to safety. You did well, yes? No one was hurt?'

They were in the clear, there was a phrase, 'Went like clockwork,' he said.

Monique snapped: 'How much?'

'Like we thought, hon, ten-large.'

Hurriedly, she unzipped the holdall, tipped her head towards the contents and tucked her shiny black hair behind her ear, all in one smooth, and very French, motion.

'Ah, it is all good,' she said.

'Told you.'

She leaned forward, touched Stauner's chin and adjusted his glare towards her, 'Always you are looking to the ladies!'

'Only one lady for me, hon,' he said, reaching out to place a slap on her behind.

She smiled coquettishly, leaned in even closer, 'My ladies' man,' she said, then ran off, slinging the holdall over her arm.

Stauner steadied himself on one of The Moorings' Formica-topped tables. His head spun. There was a metallic taste in his mouth and his ribs ached from a solid, sustained beating.

Somehow, he found the ability to negotiate the darkness towards the bar, and put on the lights. The brightness made him feel like acid had just been flung in his eyes. He felt his guts heave, then he hurled violently all over the bar counter.

'Fucksake ...'

Stauner put his hands out, seemed to settle. There was a McEwan's bar bucket full of water with some melting ice. He raised it, tipped the contents over his head in a oner.

'Hell's fire ...' he said. The chill rose on his neck, pushed tributaries down his back. In a few seconds, however, it had the desired effect: he was beginning to function again.

He recalled getting into Franklin's motor. Franklin, fuck me, he thought – Frank the Plank, Frank the Wank – or any other of the hundred-and-fifty piss-takes he'd came up with for the wee poof over the years.

'Where you off tae, Stauner?' Franklin called out.

'Eh ... the station, how?'

'Jump in, I'll give you a fastie. Save waiting for the bus, eh.'

'Eh, aye, suppose.'

If he'd been smart, he'd have smelled a rat there and then. What the fuck was Franklin doing given the likes of him a ride for fucksake, thought Stauner. Christ, he'd been done for riding the guy's wee sister when she was thirteen or fourteen. Couldn't see him forgetting about that, even though it was when they were back at the school.

'So, what's the Hampden Roar, Stauner?'

'Nothing, why?'

'Just asking ... bit edgy there aren't you?'

He looked at the Next Man carriers Stauner had stuffed at his feet, the other side of the gear stick. They were chock-full of new clothes ... for Paris.

'Splashin' out, Stauner?'

'Not really.'

'Next, though ... had a win on the ponies?'

'Business is good, y'know.'

Franklin laughed, 'So I hear.'

That's when Stauner realised they weren't heading to Waverley Station; then he felt the Nylon rope round his neck.

Stauner grabbed a glass from behind the bar, pushed it under one of the optics and filled it up with Famous Grouse. The whisky burned on his cut gums, but the feel of it surging down to his stomach was pure bliss.

He hit the optic again, settled another score with his cravings. As he looked around The Hoorings, Stauner saw the place was a tip. It looked like a bomb had hit it, as his old mam would have said. The curtains had been pulled down, ripped to pieces. Hardly a stick of furniture was left standing. The slot-machine had a table leg through the front, and worst of all, the sin of sins, the pool table's baize had been slashed to pieces.

'What is this?' he said. 'I must be missing something.'

He'd been worked over. Got that bit. Properly robbed, understood. But dumped in The Hoorings – the place, trashed – had him scoobied.

Stauner belted down another low-flying birdie, then staggered towards the door. Sure as shite, he wasn't hanging about. His bags were gone, and the ticket; but, Paris was still on his mind as he tried the door handle.

'Christ!'

It was locked. Bolted and shuttered from the outside.

'Fuck. Fuck. Fuck.'

Stauner kicked out, slammed his boot into the door. He managed to keep it up for about a minute till he realised that he didn't have the strength to dislodge the shutters.

He leaned against the wall, the bare plaster felt cold against his back. He felt his knees buckle, and then he slid down towards the floor. Through the window he saw headlights coming, illuminating the car park. Then he heard the sound of tyres on the gravel.

Stauner stood up. Hit at the door again, but it didn't budge an inch. He ran to the other side of the bar, tried to lift a window, but they were all painted down.

What'd the fucking Health and Safety have to say about this? he thought.

He could hear footsteps running up the path to the front of the pub. Panic jumped in him. He felt his chest start to heave. His mouth dried over. His head was a furnace.

The remains of a chair was to hand, Stauner picked it up and threw it at the window. It smashed as loudly as gunfire, instantly covering the floor in glass.

He could hear the keys turning in the locks, and voices.

'Fuck ... c'mon!'

Stauner tried to reach out, to open the shutters, but his hands were too big – wouldn't go in. He was trapped, like a fucking big rat, he thought.

As the pub door swung open two old pugs the size of brick shithouses walked in and stood, square-footed, before him.

'What's this?' said Stauner.

The pugs didn't answer. Didn't utter a word. Then in walked Rab Hart. The Wee Man was the last person in the world Stauner wanted to see.

Hart walked slowly, his expensive shoes crushing glass beneath his every step. When he came level with the pugs, they took a step backwards, stood behind their Guvnor and clenched fists.

For a moment no words passed between them, then Hart spoke: 'Slight matter of ten grand of mine to discuss, Pretty Boy.'

Stauner tried for words, but none came.

'Robbing off me's one thing ... messing up my boozer's quite another. You'll be lucky to get out of this alive, Stauner.'

'No, Rab ... you don't understand, it was the French lassie, she fucked me over.'

Hart laughed: 'Fucked you over ... that not your style, Pretty Boy?'

The Wee Man's laughter hit off the walls, sending blades into Stauner. The pugs joined in, their vast chests making tremors that set layers of bling jingling.

Hart tipped back his head, he removed his glasses, and one of the pugs suddenly halted all laughter and rushed to his side with a hankie.

'Fucked you over ... I like that, no, I do, really I do,' said Hart.

'But, you don't ...'

'Understand? Is that what you were going to say? Oh, I think I do.'

Hart nodded to Stauner, and the two pugs sprung like thoroughbreds, 'Understand this – you'll see a good fucking now, laddie!' he said, 'bastardin' sure you will.'

Killing Time in Vegas

Man, I was itching. The temp' was up at 90-plus, but *Christ,* the humidity was the killer. Collar and tie weather it wasn't. Shit, you carry about a 55-inch chest in this – I was bench-pressing 500lbs and upping the reps daily – comfortable you ain't.

My suit was linen. Navy blue, bought from Hugo Boss back in New York. Not by me, *uh-uh.* This was a thrift store job. Time I can buy Hugo Boss off the rack I ain't coming back home to Vegas for work.

'Can I help you, sir?' Blonde with diddy eyes and the whitest top row of teeth I'd ever seen. Bottom row lagging behind, must've been waiting for the top's payment plan to finish.

'Francis Jarman,' I told her, 'I'm here for the instructor's job.'

'Excuse me?' She looked vacant. Like the chick on the Minute Maid ads, minus the smile.

'The, eh, fitness instructor ... for the gym.'

She still didn't get it, pointed me sit with a long red fingernail. When she picked up the phone I heard her get my name wrong, called me 'Farnham'. I shook my head but I only got a look, one that said, *'Purleeze*, like I give a shit'.

I sat back down and saw her cross her legs away from me, tug her skirt over her knees. Always makes me smile when chicks do this around me. They see the muscles bulging out all over and think I'm a real player. But I ain't; chicks don't pop my trunk.

'Stay seated, Mr Farnham,' she said slamming down the phone, 'there'll be someone to see you presently.'

'Presently!' I said too soon, then realized I'd put the heavy-hitting intonation in there. I'd been blurting a lot lately.

She dipped her head, looked at me over long lashes, 'That's right away,' she spat.

I smiled one of my widest, Jonny calls it my stage school smirk, 'Thank you so much, mam.'

I could hardly wait to meet my interviewer; just a joy to be dragging ass across state for this kinda shit.

———✱———

Five'll get you ten this guy's a homophobe, I thought. Had queer-hater written all over him as he came in: Brooks Brothers' shirt open at the collar, Gap khakis and sweet loafers: Timberland or Sebago, something like that, way outta my price range.

He blanked me big time as he popped an iPad on the desk. A good ten minutes of office chat passed between Mr Big Shot and Blondie as he tried to tell her to fish out something from the mail he wanted 'upstairs on my desk by five'. She smiled and giggled. That ain't all he was getting upstairs on his desk later, I thought.

I was ready to bail when he finally turned to me, dropped eyes on a clip-board and said, 'Mr ... Jarman?'

'That's right.' I stood up, tried to keep my size outta the picture, but I dwarfed him into shadows. ''Pleased to meet you.'

'Would you walk this way, please.'

I was thinking if I could walk that way I'd be buying size

32 khakis off the rack too, as my thighs chafed together on every step.

'Take a seat,' he told me. I still didn't know the motherfucker's name. *Shit!* Bad manners, that's always been a hatred of mine. I don't allow myself prejudices, but bad-mannered people I just hate right out. I needed the job, though, so I battened it down fast.

'That's some heat you got today,' I said, going for the small talk angle.

'This is Vegas,' he said, shooting a look that told me he wanted to end the sentence with *'fuck-head'*.

He handed me over a form to fill out. On grey paper, real thick too. I fired through; when I handed it back it looked like I'd been mopping up by the sweat marks all over.

'Sorry, I'm real hot,' I said, spluttering, 'I mean, the heat, y'know it's hard being in the heat when you're used to New York.'

I was screwing up. I knew it. Could see the signs, but I'd have been way off the mark if I had to pick his next question. I didn't see it coming in a month of Sundays.

'Mr Jarman ...' he paused, leaned over the desk and locked his fingers together in a tent, 'are you a ... homosexual?'

I felt my breath stop. I suddenly went from hot as hell, to ice. I wanted to say, 'Can you even ask me that? Is it legal?' But some defence mechanism kicked in, an old one, probably learned in the schoolyard. I said: 'No. *Shu-u* ... no way!'

I wanted to spit after saying the words. Could see Jonny's face and there was shame in his eyes as he looked at me.

He raised his eyebrows: 'Interesting. Your resumé doesn't say if you're credentialed.'

'*Credentialed* ...' Shit. 'I thought you said ... I mean, I misunderstood.'

Big Shot rose. He leaned over the desk and collected up his pencils and papers, shuffled about a bit, then, 'I think we're done here.'

'That it?'

'Excuse me?'

'I mean, I came all the way from New York ... it seems hardly like five minutes since I got in here.'

His hand went in the pocket of his Gap khakis, there was a dip in his brows, hard to spot, but definitely there, 'We're very specific about what we look for in suitable candidates.'

Suitable candidates? I heard that and was ready to snap his neck like a breadstick, but there was still a chance; I couldn't jeopardize it.

'Well, I hope I'm a good fit,' I said.

'Thanks for dropping by. We'll let you know.'

I grabbed his hand, I knew I was holding it too tight. But I let that grip linger for a little longer, just long enough for his brows to lift back up his damp forehead.

I took a motel just off the Strip. I dropped my bags and swapped the Hugo Boss for a set of beach shorts and a black T-shirt. With my wraparound shades I looked like I could ride point for a biker gang.

I sent a text to Jonny about the interview – lied and tried to sound hopeful. I switched off my cell after that to avoid the retread he'd take me through. I was sore as hell and I knew it'd only mean a beat-down for me on getting home if I kicked off again. I couldn't hurt him either, he'd been through enough when I lost my job and we started going behind on the rent. The guilt smacked me again like acid bile rising in my gut.

I hit the casino bar with brass-knuckles. I was cooling down nicely, on my second bottle of Bud, when some torn-assed old butt-surfer started hitting on me.

'That's a work-out paying off, I'm thinking,' he told me.

'Yeah, well ... nothing for nothing, huh.' I tried to be polite, wanted to tell him to ditch the shit and leave but he was way older than me and looked lonely.

'What you bench-press?'

'I dunno ... 500lbs or so.'

'Man that's a work-out!'

'I guess.'

He looked me up and down, watched me every time I raised the neck of the bottle to my lips.

'Want another?'

'Look, I ...'

'Hey, it's just a beer ... no harm in a man buying a stranger a beer is there?'

I nodded okay, said, 'I guess not.'

Soon enough he was buying me margaritas and slapping my back. We laughed away and were getting on just fine, but then I felt his hand linger a mite too long on my thigh.

'Take it away, pal ...' I warned him.

'Wha-a-at ... this here,' he rubbed his hand harder into my muscles, grabbed the flesh beneath my shorts, 'There's no harm in that, surely.'

In a flash I'd grabbed his fingers and crushed them in my hand. I knew he hadn't done anything that wrong, but outta nowhere I was a race car in the red, I'd been on a slow boil since the interview ... since a lot longer than that.

'Arg-g-g ... you son-of-a-bitch!' he yelled, 'you son-of-a-Goddamn-bitch!'

I saw the barman getting edgy, the old hom' was making a scene. I stood up and grabbed my keys off the bar.

'Look at you, standing there like an ape! I knew the second I saw you you was a jackass ...' he yelled at me, 'whenever someone bulks up like you, it's because they're building over something!'

He was still hollering as I walked out of the bar, into the casino lobby, and a whole other world of shit.

Outside the elevator a fresh ruckus was underway. A busboy was taking heaps from some corporate-type who'd tied a few on. The jerk was swaying and holding onto a bottle of pink champagne, pockets stuffed with chips, another victim of the Vegas flesh-pots who should've stayed home.

It was late and I knew better than to intervene but I was being pushed, call it whatever, I didn't want to see anyone else take any grief.

'Okay, sir, you've made your point, now leave the kid be,' I said, as I put myself between the busboy and the second big shot of the day I'd had cause to tussle with.

'Fuck you!' he spat.

At first, I thought nothing of it. Hell, I'd worked doors, this was *'fries with that?'* to me. But there was something about the voice that came with a knife-edge. Then I saw it, staring me in the face, the name on the swipe-card attached to his lapel: Mike Clarkson.

'I'm going to ask you to re-evaluate that response ...' I said.

'What?' He looked up, but he didn't remember pushing me around in high school, he'd no memory of the way he and his Jock buddies used to ride me, bitch-slapping and calling me Hom'-Boy and such.

'You have no idea have you ... really, no idea!' I could feel the alcohol racing in my veins, mixing with the adrenaline and one hell of a sore mood. 'I'm Francis Jarman.'

It took him a while but the slow-blink on his face turned to register the information.

'Francis ...oh yeah, I remember you.'

'You bet your sweet ass you do.' I put a heavy finger point into his shoulder. In New York it would have been enough to get you put inside – just contemplating it would be – but I was past caring here. Call it an out of town thing. I'd lost the Vegas vibe.

'You've, er, changed some,' he slurred.

'Oh, yeah ...' I was enjoying riding his fear. It was a classic turn of the tables. Would take a few revolutions more to get even with this bastard little queer-hater, though. 'Why don't I just walk you to your hotel, *huh*?'

'Eh, no, no ... I'm, er, staying here, at the casino,' he said waving the bottle. 'I've got a room just upstairs, that won't be necessary.'

I wanted just one shot. One clean crack at his face to remind him, to let him know how it felt to be bullied by someone stronger than he was. Man, this rage was lapping in me. But I chilled. I grabbed his shoulders and spun him towards the elevator. 'Word to the wise, Mike ... lay off the busboy!' As I stepped back from the elevator I could tell he'd learned nothing in the time since we'd last clapped eyes on each other.

'I'll bear that in mind ... *FAG-SIS*!' he yelled out to the whole place.

I was at the doors, fists at the ready.

As the doors pipped me to a close, he stood laughing, waving that Goddamn pink-champagne bottle at me like it was his dick.

❈

The red button wouldn't open up the elevator again. I gave it a few good shots but it wouldn't shift.

I hit the stairs.

I moved fast; despite my size I was still agile. I'd kept up the cardio' too. There was only one floor, but shit, this was Vegas, everything was fast, the elevator beat me to the punch, dislodging Mike before I could grab hold and tear him a new asshole.

The down light was already on when I got there, just in time to see him staggering off to his room, bottle still in hand. At the door a couple of hookers were hanging out, butt naked, save a long white feather-boa they shared between them.

If there was a time to settle down, think about doing the right thing, this was it. I gathered myself and slumped on the wall, my sweat-soaked back sliding me all the way to the floor.

My cell phone fell out and I switched it on. I'd missed a call from Jonny, I cursed inwardly and played the voicemail message:

'I saw through your text message, Francis. Look, this is about as much as I can take. I'm going back West so don't expect me to be around when you get home. I can't live hand-to-mouth with you anymore, I put a box with your hormone shit and needles and whatever in the stairwell by the dumpster, if you're so desperate for it, it'll still be there in a couple days.'

The message went quiet but the little clock still ticked off the seconds; he started again:

'No, scrub that last bit ... I'm putting it out with the trash! You know, you'd still have a job if you didn't take that shit! It's fucked with your mind, I mean what did Mr Hernandez say to make you fly at him like that! He was your boss, you can't go round hitting your boss and keep your job. Oh, Christ, like you care, go screw yourself, Francis ... go fucking screw yourself!'

I threw the cell at the wall and it bounced right back, smacking me upside the head. It hurt like a bitch and I jumped right up and stamped it into the floor.

My heart was pumping black blood to my head. I was past the break-point now. Adrenaline raced in my veins so much that I could see red tinges in the corner of my vision. I couldn't hold myself back anymore – I turned to the nearest target.

The carpet to the door of Mike's room felt thick under my sandals and made a swish-swish noise that annoyed the fuck out of me. I ripped the sandals off and tore them apart in my bare hands as I strode, steps like explosions, all the way to the end of the line.

I thought about knocking, but the door looked flimsy enough to need only a couple of shoulder barges. I was wrong; it took only one.

The hookers screamed as I ran in. I grabbed one by the wrist and yelled at her, 'Get the fuck out of here, now!' The other raised her hands to her face and screamed louder, I slapped her and she dropped like a stone. Her buddy wasted no time on help though, turned tail and shot out that door like a scalded cat.

Mike lay naked on the bed, save a white towel round his waist, the bottle of pink champagne still in his hand. His mouth was a wide `O' but there was not a sound coming from him as I grabbed his hair and turned him over on his front.

'What was that you called me?' I yelled at him.

'*What*?' his voice was a pathetic whimper.

'What was that you called out to me?'

'I-I-I don't ...'

'Yes, you Goddamn do! Think, what was that shit you said?'

'I-I-I-' Every time he spoke I felt my rage pitch up a

notch. He was riding me. Just like he always had.

'You fucking well know what you said, you fucking well know ... say it, say it, you fuck, say what you said to me.'

'I didn't say ... when?'

'When? When? ... Eighth Grade you motherfucker!'

I reached down for the towel around his waist and pulled it clear of his butt-cheeks.

'You know what it is with guys like you, don't you?'

He twisted his head to see what I planned to do He was crying now, full on tears like a baby. *What are you going to do to me? What are you going to do to me?*

'I said, do you know what they say about guys like you ... always attacking us, calling us queer! You know what they say?'

'No. No,' he yelled out, 'I don't know, please, please I have a family.'

'They say you're the queers! It's suppressed in you ...'

'No, please, please,' he whimpered.

I pushed his face into the pillow and grabbed up the phallic looking pink champagne bottle.

There was still plenty of fizz left in the bottle, as I pressed it into his ass it sprayed about like a power-hose.

I could listen to those screams all day, I thought, they sounded like, no, they fucking told me, the world was mine now.

They must have stopped for a time before I noticed the bed had turned black and damp and the bottle was no more than a shard of glass in my hand.

The last I remember was the hooker scrambling for her purse and the sound her .45 made as she pumped a round into me. I don't recall feeling a thing, but then, a 55-inch chest carries plenty padding.

The Long Drop

Sometimes it was the thing to do.

There was no keeping the needle under seventy; eighty was a trial, but the lights went out when the grille clipped the dumpster. These dark country roads called for careful driving; stick in the dirt from the slips and the wet – and the fact that this was the night luck ran out on us – we were always going to go to shit.

The Toyota came to rest on its roof; Craven watched the wheels spinning and shook his head. He tried to crack his backbone into place. 'The car's fucking finished. We're finished.'

'Oh, y'think?' said Lois. She had a deep cut above her left eye, it looked like jello when she dabbed it with her shirtsleeve. As her flannel rode up I saw the SIG Sauer was still tucked in her waistband. That was something.

'You need to get rid of that,' said Craven, "we're finished!'

She turned to me, gave a slight sigh, then looked back to her shirtsleeve. 'Oh, I'm good for now.'

Her tone was enough for Craven to fire up. 'Someone's been killed. We're fucked.'

He strode forward and flagged his arms like he'd lost control again.

Lois didn't like that. The way her lip twitched, the way she narrowed her eyes ... I could almost smell her anger.

She removed the pistol.

I knew to look away.

For a second, the spinning wheels of the car were lit by the muzzle flash.

I'd met Craven at NA, it was three weeks after my split with Pam, two weeks before Lois crossed the dark divide into the long drop that was my life.

Craven was an old hand at kicking; he was wrapped far too tight for the real world and meth was his crutch. I liked to think I had the edge on him in that regard. When I used, it was because I was bored. Or working a job.

'So, how'd you end up here?' Craven collared me at the coffee counter; he twitched and oozed sweat from his heavy brows. His hairline was receding and some freckles on his crown looked like they were ready to slide down his face.

'Do I know you?'

He shot up his hands. 'Whoa, easy cowboy!'

'Don't call me that, please.'

'You object to being called cowboy? Or, you're just not real friendly?' The tone was queer, but I didn't have him down as a homosexual. Either way, it had taken less than two minutes for me to tire of him. 'I don't like people messing with me.'

'Well, fuck you!' He made a dramatic flourish with his coffee cup; some grey liquid spilled on the floor. A few heads turned.

I moved off, found a vantage point by the doorway – it seemed a good place to assess the crowd. I soon had them sussed. The room was full of trembling, bug-eyed losers, all except the one. I watched over the cold decaf as Craven made a bee-line for her.

I wished I had his courage – Pam had taken that.

The lot held only two vehicles, three if you included the trail bike a group of kids were using to burn doughnuts on the asphalt. I watched them from below a to-let sign hung over the door of a long-vacated HoJo's. The neighbourhood had lost its sparkle. Brownstones were being boarded-up left and right; cops kept clear.

'This'll do,' said Craven.

'You sure?' I said.

'Oh, yeah ... these Toyotas, can't kill 'em with an axe.'

I took his word. Watched him approach with his steel rule outstretched; it didn't take him long to make the ignition kick, then the engine purred to life.

I ran to the passenger's door. Craven gunned the gas.

As we drove he lit a Montecristo; said it was 'his thing' on a job. I didn't question it – I had met a lot of guys with strange rituals and superstitions. This wasn't any take down, though. We'd moved up a league. The thought made me edgy.

'Hey buddy boy ... you keeping it together there?' said Craven.

I turned to face him, 'Me?'

'You think I'm talking to Mr Magic Tree? Fucking-A I mean you.'

'Don't worry about me.'

His voice dropped, took on a mocking tone, 'Oh but I do buddy boy ... I do.'

'Cut the shit, Craven ... just spit it out, where you going with this?'

He started to laugh. He laughed me up. 'I ain't going anywhere ... and neither are you! Isn't that what your little woman used to say?'

I felt a rush of adrenaline enter my veins; I grabbed the SIG and pushed it in his throat. 'Pull this fucking piece of shit over now.'

His face changed colour, dropped several shades. His mouth turned down towards his chest, as he grabbed for breath his words came falteringly. 'Jesus ... I'm, I'm ... only messing with you, man.'

I moved the gun from his throat to the middle of his temple.

'How many times do I have to tell you? I don't like people messing with me ... Pull the fuck over!'

The job was bloody; I never meant for it to be that way. I knew Lois wouldn't approve; she had insisted on one thing only – no body bags. We'd cleared the city, made the highway in good time but Craven wasn't in any kind of condition. I took the wheel from him but I wasn't in much better shape. She was only a girl.

'Man, this is wrong, dead wrong,' Craven whined.

'Shut the fuck up!'

'Why was she in the middle of the road?'

'I said shut the fucking hell up, Craven. He rocked to and fro on the passenger seat. Tears streamed down the sides of his face as he tugged at the few tight red curls that sat above his neck. I could see the streaks of blood where he'd cradled her head on the front of his jeans, it had already dried dark on the pale blue denim.

'What was she, man ... six?'

I couldn't listen anymore. It was his fault; he rolled out

way too fast after we cut Pam loose. Craven had fucked up twice now – tested our luck – and that was fucking fatal. If I had to produce the gun again I'd fire it in his face; make that two body bags.

'Craven, listen ... now listen. Are you listening?' I needed him to chill out; for all our sakes.

He sobbed louder, brought his knees up under his chin.

'We have to collect Lois from the drop ... if she has the money, we can still make this work. Do you hear me? We can still clear out ... go our ways like we planned. Only richer, a hell of a lot richer.'

Craven didn't answer. As the wind and rain picked up, and the sky darkened I started to think of Lois. It had all been her idea – the kidnapping. I had never had a thought to it; not even when Pam had turned me out without a dime, not even then. There was something about that line of business that brought nothing but bad luck; that's what the old boys said. But Lois was certain we could pull it off ... 'You don't need to be part of the gig ... just feed us what we need to know,' she had said.

I never believed her. I knew better, but Pam had taken something from me and I wanted to take something from her. Christ Almighty, my mind was ablaze. I was full of thoughts of the past, the present meant nothing to me, and Lois had this way of making me believe anything was possible. Anything at all.

———✦———

Craven pulled the Toyota into the side of the street. The SIG started to feel heavy in my hand; my palm was sweating. If he had made contact with the mark then we were finished before we'd even started. We were skating close to the edge on this job as it was; it would take one look from Pam, one hint that I was back in her ambit and her father would have her locked-down by security. Billionaires are funny that way about only daughters.

'What the fuck do you know about what Pam used to say to me?'

Craven knew he'd fucked up. He had set about riling me, taking me for a ride … but he hadn't thought it through properly. He didn't see where his joking would end.

'I … I … didn't do anything.'

He looked pathetic, his eyes looping in wide circles, searching for some answer that was never going to come.

'*I didn't do anything* … Is this fucking kindergarten? … Am I playing with you, here?'

'No. No … I …'

I smacked him with the gun. His cheekbone opened up, a little blood spilled out. 'Tell me now … when did you speak to her about me?'

He turned to his lap, looked at his palms. 'In the diner.'

I hit him again, the force of it sprained my wrist. 'What did you say to her?'

'She didn't know me … she didn't know who I was … I just sat next to her at the counter and she asked me to pass the mayo … we started talking and she said something about an ex she had. I just put two and two together … that was it. I promise. She had no idea who I was … she'd never know me again. I promise. I promise you …'

I took the SIG in my other hand, I was ready to blow his fucking dumb head through the window.

'Craven, you stupid motherfucker. You stupid son of a bitch … you never heard of tempting fate?'

If I had been anything like the man I once was I would have pulled the trigger myself, but he was gone. Pam had turned me around, made me believe I could change ... and I did. I had changed so much that I wasn't capable of living the life anymore. I'd grown soft; that's what the meth was about. It was recreation to begin with, a break from carrying shopping bags in Beverly Hills, some kind of reminder of the old days, the old kicks. I knew I'd taken it too far. Pam knew that too – or maybe she was right when she said I was never going anywhere.

'What the fuck happened?' Lois yelled. Her blonde hair was tied back tight from her face, it made her look harder than usual, her features seemed severe as she squinted through the falling rain.

'Get in! I shouted.'

'What the fuck's going on?' She looked at the dent on the fender, where Craven had hit the girl ... throwing her little body in the air.

'What happened?'

I let her get inside the Toyota, she looked at Craven rocking to and fro and yelled at me again, 'Tell me what the fuck is going on ...'

'Take this, keep it on him. She took the SIG Sauer from me.'

'What is this?'

'Never mind ... Did you get the money?'

Lois wrestled the rucksack off her back, stayed calm. 'Every dime ... let's hope we get to hold onto it.'

I gripped the wheel tighter. I was already upping the revs as we sped into the rain. Lois spoke. 'Now, what happened back there?'

Craven was stirring, 'We're finished ... the girl. That poor fucking girl.'

'What's he on about?'

I tried to keep the needle below eighty but I was desperate to put some distance between us and the scene.

I felt a cold gun on my ear, 'I'm not going to ask again,' said Lois.

'We killed a fucking little girl ... she was in the fucking road!'

Lois turned back to Craven, he was still cradling his head in his hands as I yelled, 'You fucking killed her ... you dumb bastard! You killed that girl when you spoke to Pam in the diner.'

'No. No. No.' Craven mumbled and sobbed.

'You burned our luck ... You fucking burned us!'

Lois couldn't take it anymore; she exploded. 'You spoke to her? You fucking spoke to the bitch!' She levelled the gun at him. I turned, saw her eyes widen, her breathing stilled. I tried to grab the gun – her shot broke the windscreen – I went to right the wheels but the car was on the verge already. I pumped the brakes but it only made matters worse. We fell into an uncontrollable skid.

The second the car turned over on its roof, I thought we were all dead. As we rolled to a stop I wished I had died. Outside I tried to find the courage to go and take the SIG from Lois but I knew Pam had been right about me all along, I was going nowhere.

A little girl had died, but I did nothing.

Sometimes it was the thing to do.

Daddy's Girl

Ben the gimp racked up another bottle of Bud, leaned over the bar, real conspiratorial, then blurted, 'He was fucking her for years, y'know.'

I thought, not again. Some guys see you with an eighteen-year-old in hot-pants, they get off on this shit. I grabbed the Bud, watched a white head of grog float over the edge and caught it on my tongue.

'Straight up,' said Ben. He eyeballed me real close, even let a fly settle on the bar, blinked at it, thought about a swipe, thought again; watching me was obviously more interesting to him.

I slurped the beer. Ben's jaw jutted, a jagged line of crooked teeth poked up like fence-posts ... and, what was that, drool? He was drooling as he waited for me to go postal. Riding me for a move; the signs were more subtle in the Joint.

'So, you, eh ... you know? Gonna take care of it?' he said.

I'd been out just long enough to know what passes for shit-stirring on the street. If I was cracking heads through, Ben was topping my list right now.

I lowered the Bud.

'You wouldn't be making trouble, would you, Ben?'

He swatted at the fly. Missed. Moved back from me real

fast and flicked a bar-towel over his shoulder. 'Fuck off! Trying to be a mate that's all.'

He did the petted lip thing, my little sister Kimmy used to do this when she was about eight, nine ... no later than ten, for sure. I still remembered her ways.

'A mate, eh?'

'Too right, try and do a man a good turn and what do you get?' He didn't know what he was saying; he was still pumped on the rush from the job.

'I dunno, Ben, you tell me ... what's a good turn?'

He got that faraway look in his eyes. Slapped palms on the bar, leaned in again, 'I'm telling you straight down the middle ... that girl bangs like a truck stop door! She's my sister, I should know ... there's more to being in this crew than lapping about in my old man's Mustang.'

He wrapped the bar-towel round the pumps; the fly settled down on the bar again. I swatted it with the heel of my hand; showed Ben the blood and guts, little legs still twitching.

He turned down the corners of his mouth, dropped brows.

'That's fucking gross.'

'You want gross, Ben?'

There was no one in the bar to see the muzzle flash, hear the shot or Ben's cry as the bullet lodged between his ears.

The Mustang started first time. Beautiful set of wheels. Always loved these old cars.

'It's junk,' Angie had said when her old man offered it to me.

'Junk ... girl, this is quality. Genuine piece of American history, this is!'

She flicked her hair back, those dark-blonde curls making waves like the ocean behind us, 'I'm hungry, let's eat.'

I took her to Maccy Dees on the Point, out by the auto-mart. I liked to listen to the crickets at this time of night, smell the imported eucalyptus breezing in over the burn of gas and burgers.

'What do you want?' said Angie.

'I'm good, thanks.'

'Not even a Coke?'

'Maybe a Coke, small one.'

She smiled as she spoke into the clown's nose, ordered herself a Big Mac, sprung for the 'Go Large' option when she was asked. As she leaned over she exposed her lower back above her trackies ... how did she stay in shape and eat all that comfort food?

We drove to the back lot. Gulls were scratching on the nature strip. Angie devoured the burger and fries, then set about washing it all down with the Coke.

'Daddy has some work for you?' She wiped her chin as the Coke dribbled down the side of the cup.

'Oh, yeah.'

'Yeah, says it's something you'll like—' she opened the cup, took out an ice cube.

'*Like?*'

I liked two things, playing the ponies and the other ... Angie climbed over the stick-shift, popping the ice-cube in her mouth.

'*Mmh-hmh,*' she said, fiddling with the cord on her trackies, and passing the ice-cube from her mouth to mine.

Was it all just a game to her?

I was making good time on the highway. The Mustang took its time lapping in the 'burbs, but out on the proper roads – no problem. Had the needle touching 70-mph. Always made me jumpy travelling at speed on the way to a job. Never on the way back. Amazing how some sirens, few Mars lights, helps you get your shit together.

I felt hot, must have been a 30-degree day, in country LA, you remember those with a fondness, mostly.

The sides of the highway, the verges and trees, were burnt yellow. Not even a bird digging for a feed. Out the back of the car a trail of dust kicked up.

I could feel sweat forming on my spine. Drops ran down my forehead, got in my eyes. I took the sleeve of my shirt and wiped.

I was coming into Venice as the cell phone rang on the passenger seat.

'Yeah, it's Jonny here ...'

The voice on the other end was one I recognised straight off.

'Why the fuck are you not where you're supposed to be?' said Patto.

What was I gonna tell him?

I'd thought of blowing him out?

That it was a last-minute change of heart?

I went with: 'I got ... side-tracked.'

Patto roared. I could hear the Irish coming into his voice; most parts, I'd say it was left in the old country, but now and again it came back ... usually when he was about to go Ned Kelly on someone's ass.

'Now, you listen here ye little gobshite, I will permanently end your ability to play the hard fuck by removing your tongue and any other protuberance I find to my feckin' fancy if you are not at exactly where you are supposed to be in the next fifteen minutes ... do I make myself feckin' clear?'

Those Irish, real way with words.

I clicked the cell to end the call.

Patto saw me pulling up in the Mustang and burst a blood vessel.

'You dumb Yankie fucker, what the hell are you bringing that piece of shit for?'

I wound down the window, it played on his nerves, kind of accentuated the car's vintage. 'It's your car.'

'I know it's my feckin' car ... holy mother of God, that's why ... look, fuck it!' He called over to his feckless son, yelled at him: 'Ben, get those feckin' plates changed ... and stick a feckin' rocket up yer arse would ye!'

We were late already. Later now, with the plates change. I gunned the engine.

Patto and Ben sat silently in the backseat; Patto running a hand over a Mossberg 12-gauge. I thought it looked a very sexual movement. Wondered what Freud would say? I saw Ben and Angie watch him too; they didn't seem to have the same feeling as I did. They didn't see it as sexual ... it was *fear* I saw in their eyes.

The Mustang was a noisy car to take about town. The revs attracted glances.

'This will never feckin' do,' said Patto.

I pushed him, 'Want to back out?'

He put the shooter to my head, 'Don't feckin' rile me, laddie.'

Ben placed an open hand on his father's shoulder, 'Come on, calm it! We got a job to do, right here and now.' It had the desired effect; Patto settled. I knew I never had that level of influence on my father. If I had, maybe Kimmy would still be with us.

I screeched the tyres to a halt.

We dived out – masks on.

Angie was the first. Fearless. I guess she felt she had the least to lose.

The driver of the security truck had too little time to react before Ben put a round through the gap in his visor. He turned to his father grinning like an imbecile as the man twitched in his death throes.

'Drop the fucking box!' yelled out Angie. The second guard stalled, his eyes fixed on the dead driver where he lay, head contents spilled on the asphalt.

'I said drop the fucking box!'

This time he complied. Angie took the box and keys from his belt, then led the way back to the Mustang.

Inside of five, we were done.

I drove back to Patto's bar.

After the gunshot Patto came running through from the back holding the Mossberg out in front of him. I had my Glock aimed on his shoulder, dropped him easier than tagging cattle. Angie appeared at his back, fists full of dollars from each hand fell all over him as she looked down.

I wanted to see her smile.

I wanted to see her sigh, in relief.

I wanted to see her run to me, open arms, shower thanks on me.

She cried.

'Angie,' I said. I put the Glock in my belt, went to her. Patto writhed on the floor, tried to get to the shooter. I picked it up. 'Angie, why the tears?'

She couldn't find words. Breath was trouble. She raised hands to her face.

'He's in pain.'

'So fucking what?' I said.

Patto slapped about on the floor, grimaced in agony.

She started to pat her cheeks and make bellows of her face. 'He's in pain.'

'So fucking what?' I repeated.

I knelt, put the Mossberg in his face.

Patto yelled out: 'Arggg, Jonny ... you're fucked!'

I wanted Angie to see him in agony, the way he'd seen her in agony – I hauled her down.

'Look at his face, remember that ...' I grabbed Patto's hair, he screamed as I smacked at his head, 'see the way he's squirming, trying to get away?'

She looked, her eyes wide. All colour left Angie's face. She was white as an angel, just like Kimmy, in her coffin.

'Angie, see him.' I wanted her to see her father in pain, but more than that I wanted her to see him in terror. The kind of terror he'd inflicted on her since she was a child.

'Angie, see him ...' She froze. I think she understood. I took the shooter and aimed it at Patto, but couldn't pull the trigger. I threw the gun down, it was too easy a way out for him.

'You dirty fucking bastard, your own daughter, how could you ...? Your own daughter. *How?* You fucking animal.'

I knew the words I wanted to say, they came easily. They were the same words I'd wanted to say to my own father when Kimmy died; before he took the easy way out to avoid the back-lash.

'You dirty bastard, you dirty fucking bastard ... your own daughter.'

I was crying. I could see the tears falling on Patto's chest. The look on his face was defiant though, he couldn't care what he'd done.

He smiled, laughed at me, 'You dumb bastard ... the hoor loved every minute of it!'

I couldn't move as the Mossberg went off behind me.

I felt my ears ring.

One side of me went numb.

I turned to see Angie holding the gun. She was motionless.

Her face was cold, firm.

Dark blood pooled on the floor under Patto's groin.

Enough of This Shit Already

Shopping is, like, my way of getting over Steve ... until the meds kick in anyway.

I'd been to Wal-Mart buying stuff I don't need or want – picked up my fourth pair of Ugg boots for Chrissakes – had them under my arm as Brad Johnson squeezes beside me in the elevator to math class, starts his shit again.

'Been trappin'?' he says, leaning in close enough to let me know he'd sprung for a second chilli-dog at lunch.

'Excuse me.'

'What Dad calls it when my mom comes back all bagged up like a fur trapper,' a laugh on his last word, like, for no reason. This jock shit has me weirded out, but I've got good cause.

The elevator jolts and Brad rocks forward on the heels of his Nike Airs. I get a feel of his semi and I'm thinking, whoa ... that stuff about me putting out is such fiction already. But my heart's racing. Pounding and pounding because this is my first day back after ... The Incident. Brad and I haven't even spoken about The Incident.

'This is my floor!' I say, edging away real fast, I'm sweating, shit, this is too full-on.

'Your floor, my floor ... I don't mind one bit!'

That's not even funny. Six weeks past, at Trish Jacob's

party, Steve caught Brad on top of me, doing stuff. I was way out of it, can't remember a Goddamn thing. But Steve and me are so over now. And Brad, I just feel way too strange around him. Real strange.

I'm shaking as I turn to push the button and he smiles at me, moves in close, all slimy-like. In the polished elevator door I see him eyeing my ass, pursing his lips and flicking out his tongue like a snake or a lizard or something. It's all for his jock buddies, they high-five, and I want to hurl. No shit, I want to throw chunks here and now.

Brad's hot hands grab my hips, pull me back. His semi feels more like a hard-on now. I can't move, I want to say something but I'm too choked, what a wimp-out!

'You remember this, Alana?' he says, smiling, laughing.

My heart goes from flat-out to stopped in a second. I feel chills all over me. But I remember nothing.

Ding! The elevator stops – a judder passes through me.

I shake off Brad's hands and run out.

I'm in such a rush I nearly drop my new Ugg boots.

'Hey, someone's been to the stores, let's see,' says Louisa. She comes running over and takes my bag with the boots, 'Oh my God, Alana, these are so awesome!'

I'm too pissed to respond, my heart is, like, racing as I think of Brad and his buddies laughing at me. What the hell were they saying?

'What the fuck is this?' cries out Louisa, she holds up a little white box I took from the pharmacy. I mean *took*, I'd never stole before but I couldn't bring myself to buy it. I'm acting real strange since The Incident.

I snatch back the box, tuck it away. 'It's ... you know, a test.' I whisper on the last word.

Louisa's eyes widen, she drops her voice lower than mine, mouths the shape of the word: 'Pregnancy?'

I nod.

Louisa rolls her eyes, 'But, you and Steve ... I thought you never did it!' I can take hearing his name from Louisa, she's my friend, she makes me laugh, but I still don't like it.

'We never.'

Louisa sticks her tongue in her cheek, rolls up her eyes again, 'Oh.'

I don't think she understands.

Shit, I don't think I do.

I sit through math but I don't think I'm learning a frickin' thing. My head is full of Steve and how I'd promised he'd be my first and the way his face looked when he said about catching me with Brad. He roared and cried and said I was like all the other dumb chicks jumping in the sack with an asshole just because he gets Daddy's Porsche on weekends.

I cry, too, when I see the little white stick go blue. I cry and it hurts because I don't know why I'm crying. Is it because that's my life, like, over already? Or is it because I've done one more thing to hurt Steve? I don't know anything anymore.

'Alana, you dumb bitch,' I say. I've been sitting in the girls' john for an hour; it took me so long to build up the courage to pee on the little white stick but now I have the answer I wish I didn't. I wish I was never born, Christ, how did this ever happen?

I pull up my panties and take Mom's gun from the strap thing on my leg. Mom loves this little gun; she saw it in a movie once and Dad bought it for her, strap thing and all. She laughed and laughed that day. That was a long time ago.

All the happy days seem a long time ago now. I look at the gun, it's small, says Beretta on the side but Mom calls it her Bobcat, like, why? I dunno. I don't know anything. I don't even want to think about anything.

I put the gun in my mouth and close my eyes but I can't pull the trigger. All I see is, like, my mom and dad and grandpaw crying and crying and crying and the tears are just too much. I don't want to cause anymore tears. I didn't want to cause any tears, ever.

'Hey, Alana ... how 'bout a replay?' shouts Brad to me.

Am I, like, underwater or something? My mind feels all fuggy, could be the tears but I feel changed. My thinking just doesn't work. Dr Morgan said I'd feel different when the medication kicked in, but I don't think this is what he meant.

'Are you talking to me?' I shout back.

Brad's jock buddies slap him on the back, there's white teeth lighting up the whole corridor as all the queen bitches stop to stare and you could hear a fuckin' pin drop, like they always say.

'That night at Trish Jacob's place was, ehm, y'know ...'

I sure as hell don't know.

'Was what?'

More back slapping, one of the goofballs gets so excited he drops a folder, papers swirl about when the door to the schoolyard opens and the breeze takes them.

Brad puts his hands out. 'What, you don't remember?'

I shake my head. I'm just so glad Steve's moved to Lincoln High and can't see any of this.

'Well, how about I give you a re-run tonight?'

This is, like, tennis or something, eyes flitting up and

217

down the hallway to catch what I'm gonna say next. I don't even know, only, I've said it before I realise.

'Okay, sure.'

The silence breaks into uproar.

'Woop-woop-woop,' carries down the hall and Brad's buddies try to lift him up. The noise brings out Mr Martinez from the history department and he smacks his hands together to get everyone to shut the hell up.

Soon all I hear is the queen bitches slipping past me and muttering 'slut' over and over.

Like I give a fuck, now.

———✦———

The black Porsche 911 is sat outside our front porch for, like, maybe a minute before Brad's hitting the horn and yelling.

'Who is that?' asks Mom.

'No one,' I say.

'Don't you lie to me, missy!' She goes to the window, pulls back the drapes. 'What in the name ... who do you know drives a car like that, Alana?'

'No one!' I'm pulling on my Ugg boots and then I'm running for the door when Mom starts to flap.

'Now, just you hold on a minute my girl ... I know you've been a little out of sorts but remember what Dr Morgan said about taking things easy!'

'Mom ...'

The horn again.

'Alana, I don't think running about all over town is the way to get your head together.'

'I'm not running about, Mom ... I'm just ...'

'Alana, I never ... I didn't mean that.' She looks concerned, starts to undo her apron strings at her back, then moves towards me with her hands reaching for my face.

'Mom, please.'

She clasps her hands round my face, her eyes are all misty as she says, 'You're such a pretty, pretty girl my darling ... You could have anything you want, anything in the whole world.'

I want to say, 'Anything?' Like it's a real choice or something, but I know it's not. I can't have Steve.

I pull away and run for the door.

I can hear Mom yelling after me as I get into the Porsche.

We drive, like, forever. Brad talks and talks about a whole heap of crap, what the Dodgers need to do next, how his daddy knows President Obama, his vacation in France and England and wherever. Eventually, we're parked out by the flats. They have crags and rocks out here and they say some serial killer used a scope-gun to shoot kids who were making out way back. I dunno if that's true, but it's what they say. I think about that a little as Brad turns off the engine and swivels round to face me. He has that shit-eating grin of his on. I never noticed before now but the grin's crooked, too.

'So, here we are,' he says.

'Yeah.'

He sits on the edge of his seat with his crotch facing me, like maybe that serial killer's scope-gun once looked.

He touches his lips, sways a bit. Goes on and on. Says Steve's name, like three, maybe four times, I lose count. I'm, like, hearing Steve,

Steve,

Steve,

Steve, and I'm thinking, why? Why's he keep on him?

Enough. Enough already.

All the while I just look into him and want to hear this is all, like, a nightmare or something. That my life's a bad dream I'm soon gonna wake from. But I don't hear it. Nothing like it.

'Hey, c'mon, you know I wanna fuck you again, Alana, and I know you ain't getting none from old loverboy Steve, so I'm guessing you could do with the action.'

This is the best he can do?

I'm tuned in to what he's saying and I'm, like, is that it? We done? You had your say already?

He reaches out and tries to pull me towards him but I pull away.

'Oh, I get it.'

'You do?'

'Yeah, you want some stuff.'

'Stuff?'

Brad goes into his jacket and pulls out a baggie, I can see a little white powder in the corner. He takes a few pinches and lays out a line on the dash and offers it to me.

'Go on, it's what you want.'

I shake my head.

'Go on, go on.'

'I don't do drugs, Brad.'

Now he does the eye-roll thing and looks through me. 'Oh, yeah.'

'What do you mean, oh yeah?'

He starts to tie a knot in the baggie, tucks it back in his pocket.

I ask him again, 'What do you mean, oh yeah?'

'Nothing, I mean, well ... you were pretty out of it back at Trish's place.'

I feel my heart beat fast again.

'Yeah?'

'Hell, yeah.'

He leans in again. I feel him start to breathe close to my neck. He starts to kiss me, then his hands move over me.

Touching and grabbing.

'Where did you get the coke, Brad?'

A laugh, then, 'Connections.'

I feel his tongue come out, it runs up and down my neck, onto my chest. He starts to unbuckle his belt. It seems to take him, like, forever to draw down his zipper, but when I look up at his face I see he's grinning and trying to tease me or something, yeah, like he was some strip-joint dream boy, I don't think.

'Your connections, they can get you anything you want?' I say.

He's on top of me now, pops it out, starts grinding, pulling at my panties. 'They can get me anything I want, baby.'

He's grinning and acting like some frat boy who's just got the town slut in the back-seat of his daddy's Buick. I lay there feeling my head pushed against the door and my ass jammed against the stick shift and I want to scream but my voice is so weak I can hardly get the words I have to say out. 'Like Rohypnol?'

He puts his hand on my ass, says, 'You know, Steve ain't coming back, Alana, why don't you relax?'

He moves fast, now. There's no, like, struggling with buttons or straps or whatever, he's ripping at me.

'Stop!' I tell him.

'What?' He looks pissed with me. 'I can't stop now!'

His hands move fast but mine move faster as I slip the Beretta out of the leg strap and point it at his crotch. As he feels the cold metal touch his balls his face looks white as death, but that might just be the moonlight. He's sure as hell stock-still ... until I pull the trigger.

Blood splatters the window behind him instantly. I move the gun about and I'm firing and firing until there's smoke everywhere, so much I can taste it.

For a moment, I lie there.

I can feel the gun smoke burning my throat.

My lungs fill up and I start to cough.

Brad's mouth isn't crooked anymore. It flops open and his lips spill blood on me. I'm like, yeuch. He's a dead weight on top of me as I slide out from under him. I wonder, does he know why?

Oh yeah, like I'd care if he did.

Too Close to Call

Marie had been at me for close to an hour when I flipped. Dropped beside her on the couch and cracked a knuckle on her brow. She flopped like a deflating sex doll.

'Well, what do you expect?' I said. 'Jesus Christ!'

Pedro rose, put a greasy paw on her cheek. 'She's cold.'

'No shit ... tell me something I don't know, huh.'

He went back to his window seat and lit a Lucky. The neighbour's Schnauzer started barking.

'Dog don't like it none,' said Pedro.

I took up a football trophy and aimed it at his head. 'You want this?" I'm only saying, bro ... No need to go all bugeyed on me.'

I slammed down the trophy, said, 'Just shut up and give me a smoke.'

Pedro smiled, his yellowed teeth looked like little fossils inside his old head. It was all his fault, this mess. I wanted to smack his teeth off the four walls. Bitchslap him a hundred times harder than I'd just done to Marie.

Pedro tossed the pack. I sparked a match and put the Lucky to work. The taste came like old dreams as I tipped back my head and sighed.

'So, what's next, brother Mitch?'

'We sit tight.'

'We've been sitting tight for an hour now, Mitch. Cops gonna be coming by soon. Real soon.'

He was riding me. In the Joint they tell you, someone starts riding, you take a breath. I took another belt on the Lucky. I wasn't ready to go back to beating off buttfuckers and an orange jumpsuit. Pedro knew this. He was clean – as clean as any wino crackhead motherfucker in Dodge. But my card was already punched. I rubbed my knuckles. They hurt like hell, sitting up in points like a row of KKK hoods.

'Well?'

'I'm thinking.'

The Schnauzer barked like bad news. A beige saloon went past the window in slow-mo.

'Don't take too long.'

I turned to eyeball Pedro, expected to see him grinning, perhaps perched on the end of a cigarillo like Eli Wallach in his most famous role. That's what the three of us were – The Good, The Bad and The Ugly. My mind ran amok ... I heard some of Eli's lines: *There are two types of spurs, Blondie ... The type that come in through doors and the type that come in through windows.*

'Get to the back of the fucking house,' I roared.

'What?'

'You heard me. Get off your ass and check the back's secure and lock the Goddamn door.'

'Are you for real?'

'Fucking A.'

'No door's gonna stop Mr Nightstick coming in.'

I lost it. Ran towards him and yanked him by the collar. On his feet, I spun him and rabbitpunched the back of the head. His shoes flew out behind him, he stumbled out to the back door.

As Pedro left, Marie let out a low, barely audible mumble. I bent at her side. She looked like she was coming round.

'Yo ... Marie, honey, you with us?'

A groan.

'Guess not.'

'Mitch ...' she said.

'Yeah, honey. I'm here.'

'What happened?'

'I hit you. I'm real sorry.' I was aware how pathetic I sounded.

'You hit me. Why did you hit me, Mitch?'

'I've got a bucket of adrenaline racing through me and you flipped out. It was just instinct.'

'Mitch, you've never hit me before.'

'Honey, I'm sorry. I'll never do it again. I promise. Are you okay?'

'I guess.'

I propped Marie up on the couch. She touched her head. I could see a red leaf-shaped stain forming on the skin. The contusion would be berryblack inside an hour. I felt time ticking away. We needed to move.

'Where's Pedro?'

'I sent him out back?'

'The money?'

'Still in the trunk.'

'Mitch, those cops didn't just come from nowhere.'

I hoped she wasn't starting to push my buttons again; I knew the cops had been fed a line by someone and I'd lost my edge.

'They were tipped off,' I said.

'Who?'

I looked to the door. 'Dunno.'

I heard Pedro hammering down the window frames, it set the Schnauzer in the yard off again.

'Mitch, we've got to get out of here.'

I looked to the window; the sun streamed in, painting an oblong block of yellow in the centre of the floor.

'Mitch ...'

From where I sat I could see the car, front fender bashed, back window shot out. I was no wheelman, but I'd lost them. It wasn't meant to be like this. Simple job. In and out. Just stick to the rules. But they were waiting – two cops – for a bank job. Shit, these days a motorcycle courier forgets to take his helmet off and there's choppers overhead.

'Mitch, we have to move, now.'

I turned back to Marie, her face was torn in misery, her upper lip trembling. If I didn't act soon, she'd need hosing down again.

I wiped her brow, said, 'You good to go?'

She nodded.

'Then sit tight, I've one more thing to do.'

I stood up, walked through the door. In the hallway, I heard Pedro. He was whispering, or trying to, into his cell phone.

'I didn't know he could drive like that. How was I to know? You should have chased, chased ... the money's still here. Out front.'

I reached round to the .45 tucked in my waistband and took off the safety. My heart pounded, I felt sweat gather on the back of my neck. This was my ticket back to the Big House. Even bent cops refuse to turn a blind eye to this kind of thing. I tasted the Joint's gruel and grits again, the smell of stale sweat, Bubba's necklock in the showers. I wanted to apologise to Marie once more.

Fuck. Why did this shit keep happening to me?

As the .45 clicked in his ear Pedro lowered the phone and turned. He looked at me as if I'd just beamed down from Venus. His lips drained of blood and turned grey. I wagged the .45 towards the phone. He moved his thumb to 'end call' and dropped the handset on the floor.

I gave him a second for words.

None came.

My nerves shrieked, I felt the blood surge in my veins as I raised the gun to his head.

'Oh sweet Jesus, please, no ...' pleaded Pedro.

'He's not gonna save you now.'

I blindsided him. Put my left through his eye, opening it up like a welt, the white shot through with red. He fell. I kicked him in the head. A flap of skin tore clear of his brow. More blood ran out. Lots this time. It looked like a coathanger abortion. He put both hands over his head.

'You made a mistake, Pedro.'

I put the .45 to his head.

He crouched, as if in prayer. I swear, he whimpered. I'd expected more of a put up.

'What else did you give them?'

'Nothing ... Nothing... Nothing ...'

'Horseshit.' I slapped him with the gun.

'No, I swear ... They don't know nothing.'

'My name?'

'No. I would never.'

Somehow, I didn't believe a word of it.

'You lose, Pedro.'

'What?'

'The Game of Life.'

He screamed like a loose fan belt. The Schnauzer kicked off outside the door. I hoped it would drown out the sound of the gun's discharge.

I left him flat on his back. Dark blood covered the floor like a slaughter house.

In the hall, Marie ran to me.

'Come, on,' I said.

'But?'

'Not now, get in the car.'

I grabbed her arm and led her through the front door. Sunlight burst like an explosion all over the burnt-yellow lawn. I felt my guts begin to heave, felt for sure I'd hurl but somehow I kept it all in.

My hands trembled, I couldn't get a grip of the keys, but Marie leaned over and helped me locate the ignition. God, I didn't deserve her, did I?

I got the car started, and then suddenly, the Schnauzer came running, stopping still on the lawn. He turned his head to the side, made that dog look, one that says a million things and nothing at all.

I pulled out on to the street.

'You good?' said Marie.

'Yeah, fine.'

I took one last look in the rearview mirror, caught sight of the Schnauzer again.

I could have swore the damn dog waved at me.

I gunned the engine.

Eat Shit

'He said that to you? ... I don't, you wouldn't shit me on this, Eddie?'

Miami Mike carried two Buds back from the bar, he swayed a little – nights with old Eddie from the block could turn pretty tasty.

'He said it, I tell you now, God as my judge ... it's what he said, Mike.'

Mike slammed down the Buds; white froth flowed down the sides and onto the table top.

'Whoa, calm the fuck down, man ...'

The beer spill pooled on the chequered paper tablecloth, a red candle in a dancing-girl statuette, her hooters glowing from within, trembled in prelude to a fall.

'This kinda shit, it's way outta line,' said Mike. ''Run this by me again, from the top, don't leave anything out ... and I mean anything.'

Eddie picked up his Bud, ran a hand over the bottleneck and slugged deep. His lips twitched. Nerves on edge and out there for all to see.

'Well, you asked ...'

'She's at it again, the fucking Party Queen,' said Gloria. Eddie struggled to the edge of the bed and wiped the sleep from his still-tired eyes. 'You're kidding me.'

'You can't hear her?'

'Honey, I took a bucket of Moggies, how else you think I sleep here.'

Eddie slapped palms on his face, shook his head; it seemed like the neighbourhood joined in, 'Oh yeah, now I'm hearing ...'

Gloria stood at the window and looked out with a face ominous as thunder. She tugged at the heavy drapes and light flooded into the bedroom.

As he smarted, Eddie noticed the Lucky in her fingers; she'd started smoking again. It was the stress. He knew it was all wrong. They were being held to ransom in their own home.

'I can't take much more of this,' said Gloria, 'this is some kinda retirement!'

Eddie rose, went to her side. He tried to take the Lucky from her; Gloria snatched her hand away.

'What are you going to do about this? We can't live like this anymore, Eddie ... we can't!'

Gloria yanked open the window and roared: 'Turn that fucking music down you crazy fucking bitch! Turn it the hell down or I'll come over there and wrap that fucking boom-box round your scrawny motherfucking neck!'

'So that was the start of it, huh?' said Mike.

'Yeah, like I say ... since we moved from back East, all we had was like, y'know ... parties from the get go.'

Mike leaned in, stroking the base of his Bud like it was a lapdog, 'She's round the clock with this?'

'Hey, buddy ... let me tell you, when we was growing up back in the old brownstone, we had it peaceful compared.'

Mike looked thoughtful. Eddie scoured his mind for the word to describe him; he thought it might be contemplative.

'What're you thinking, Mike?'

He rose, tipped back the rest of his Bud. 'Thinking it's your turn to get the Buds in, pal.'

Eddie made the run to the bar. On his return he was careful not to spill any beer like Mike had done last time.

'Well, I'm all ears.'

Mike played with the edges of his moustache, greying now, but the jaw was still firm. He was carrying none of the meat Eddie was. 'Then what happened?'

'The bitch's daddy came round, he's some big-ass lawyer, slapped a stack of papers on me and next I know I've got a restraining order and he's saying I harassed his daughter.'

'That it?'

'No, man ... he's suing my ass.'

'You spoke to this girl of his?'

'Man, yeah, 'course ... but nice, like ... fuck, this is Miami, I ain't looking for no aggravation. I had enough of that thirty years renting Pintos to fat ass out-of-towners.'

'This restraining order ... what did it say?'

Eddie sighed, lowered his eyes, rapid-fired on the Bud, 'That's the worst.' He put down the beer and stared at his palms like the answer was written there. 'Claims I *sexually* approached her.'

Mike banged the table. The dancing girl fell over. The candle went out. 'The low motherfucker!'

Eddie stayed silent. He looked at his oldest friend, his one remaining relic from childhood. He knew the look on his face, he'd seen it before. It was like back in '68 when he took the Louisville slugger to the basketball court, took down five, six guys who'd welched on a drags bet.

'Eddie, here's what you do – the next letter he sends you, you wipe your ass on it.'

231

'*What?*'

Mike grabbed Eddie's arm, there was darkness in his eyes, Eddie had never seen this look before. The thirty years that had passed before they'd hooked up again held some blind spots ... he understood that now. 'Okay, okay ... but, then what?'

Mike released his arm, 'I'll keep you posted.'

A pool-side party was in full swing as Mike pulled up outside Eddie and Gloria's condo. It was a neat set-up, he thought. Sun-dried adobe brick, bit of a hacienda feel happening. Nice. He could see why Eddie had sprung for the condo, made their old stomping ground on the Lower East Side look just like the hell on Earth it surely had been.

He lowered his mirrored Ray-Bans and scoped his friend's home. Looked quiet; drapes shut. No one home? Or, if they were, keeping totally out of sight. No way to live, thought Mike. Not at all. Not for an old friend of his.

He retrod the times Eddie had shared his lunchpail with him when they were kids. Mike could still remember how it felt to have an empty belly. But he'd worked out of that world; so had Eddie, he deserved better.

There was some dance music playing. Loud as all hell. Mike was five-hundred yards from the pool but he could still make out every line of Marky-frickin-Mark's *Good Vibrations*. It was obviously a track daddy's girl enjoyed. 'Yeah, do it, do it ...' said Mike.

Pullman appeared: 'You want I should grab the slut?'

'Slut?' said Mike.

'Yeah, she's a slut, look the way she's dancing ... that's filth, man!' The girl was groin-grinding two beach bums, surfer-types with blonde bangs and over-tanned complexions. 'She's gonna have those guys dicks out like two ski-poles any minute, wait see.'

Mike took off his shades, 'She's some piece of work alright.'

'Look, now ...' She took off her bikini top and tweaked at her erect nipples, the surfers poured beer on her breasts and she encouraged them to lick it off, 'See, I fucking told you!'

'Sexual suit, huh?' said Mike.

'Come again?'

Mike put his shades back on and walked to the SUV.

'Yo, boss ... you want I should snatch her?'

'What for?'

'Take her to the border ... make her suck Mexican dick for a month – fifty cents a throw! ... See how loud she wants to play fucking Marky Mark then.'

Miami Mike gunned the engine and motioned Pullman to get in.

---※---

Daddy had a practice on the sweet side of the street. Old colonial mansion, painted white and bathed in sunlight. If there was royalty in Miami, they'd keep a joint like this. But Mike knew there was no royalty in Miami. Not the type with crowns and robes anyway. The royalty he knew carried Mossbergs in the trunk and hired people like Pullman to fire them.

The lawyer wore a light linen suit, black shirt beneath with a flower-print tie. He topped the outfit off with red-toed cowboy boots.

'That's our man,' said Mike.

'You sure?' asked Pullman, 'Motherfucker looks like Boss Hogg!'

'That's him.'

Mike didn't need to say anymore. Pullman got out the SUV and crossed the street. As he went, Mike watched his muscle-bound factotum walk towards the sidewalk.

The SUV's windows were blacked out, they kept Mike's identity hidden from the street as Pullman grabbed the lawyer round the neck and wrestled him to the ground like a steer. It was a carefully-practised manoeuvre, all over in under a minute.

The lawyer squealed like a stuck pig in the back of the vehicle. It took two raps on the side of the head from Pullman to quieten him down.

They drove out to the flats. It was hot, topping eighty Fahrenheit. A dust trail blew up behind them.

When Mike stopped the SUV, he slowly turned to face the lawyer for the first time.

'Do you have any idea who I am?' said a crumpled suit, covered in blood from a fierce nosebleed.

'Do I look like I care who you are?' said Mike.

The lawyer, flustered, raised a finger. 'I will, t-tell you ...' Pullman grabbed the finger, snapped it back. The lawyer shrieked then folded like a knife, cradling his hand.

'Look, boss he's crying ... Straight up, he's crying like a fucking girl. I never seen that before, you seen that before, boss?'

Mike turned away, spoke quietly, 'Yeah, I've seen that before.'

'W-what do you want from me?' screamed the lawyer.

Pullman laid a hand on his chest, 'Boss, let me ass-fuck him, please, huh?'

Mike turned front again, watched Pullman in the rear-view, he saw him eye the lawyer up and down, grab his thigh ... 'Go on, Boss ... I ain't gave no one a good ass-fucking for the longest time.'

Mike laughed. The lawyer seemed to let out a whimper, then wet himself.

'Man, he's pissed in his pants!'

Mike stopped laughing, 'Get this piece of shit out of here.'

Pullman opened the door and kicked the lawyer off the seat. He landed face down in the dirt.

'I think he lost some teeth that time,' said Pullman.

The lawyer tried to run, his arms and legs splayed out like a newborn foal struggling on fresh limbs. Mike let him get a hundred feet before sending Pullman to the trunk.

The first shot from the Mossberg stopped the runaway in his tracks.

It was the strangest thing, thought Eddie, it had been quiet for days. Party girl seemed to have shipped out, then the 'For Sale' sign went up.

A knock at the door amidst the silence startled him.

'I wondered if I may ...'

It was the lawyer again; Eddie's heart sank.

'I ain't got a Goddamn thing to say to you, what is it now? You got a new suit to slap on me?'

The lawyer raised his hands, 'No, no ... q-quite the reverse.' There was something strange about him, and it wasn't the Band-Aid above his eye, he seemed ... different, quieter somehow.

'Please, may I come in?'

Eddie opened the door.

Inside, the lawyer politely asked to sit. He produced a bottle of twelve-year-old Scotch from his briefcase, 'I wanted to, *a-hem*, er, I wanted to offer my sincerest apologies for my daughter's over-exuberant behaviour ...'

Eddie rose, ranted: 'You fucking roach! You tried to sue my ass ... you filed a restraining ...'

He intervened: 'I-I know ... I was very misguided, it would appear I was misinformed ... may I offer my sincere apologies, and if I may also, I would like to compensate you.'

'*What?*'

'I did some calculations, you've been here for three months, is that correct?'

'Yeah. What the ...? You know I have ...'

'These condos attract four thousand dollars a month rental and so I thought twelve thousand would be ...'

'Fifteen,' spat Eddie.

The lawyer fumbled for words, looked startled, his bead-eyes narrowed some more then seemed to wet up, 'But ... y-yes, of course. Fifteen thousand.'

Mike's advice was playing to a tee, but Eddie wondered about the next part. He was ready to let it slide, accept the cheque and kick the guy out on his ass.

But then lawyer daddy spoke up. 'I believe you have a letter of mine, if I may have it returned I w-would be most grateful.'

Eddie went to the dresser where he kept the letter. He returned to the lawyer, slowly taking the document from its manila envelope, then he presented it: brown streaks of his own shit lined the length of the page.

Slowly, trembling, the lawyer accepted the offering. He stared at it for a moment and then tore it with his teeth and began to chew on it.

'All the way down,' said Eddie.

'Y-yes, yes of course.'

'Eat shit!' said Eddie, smiling, 'Eat shit, you motherfucker.'

I Want Candy

I'd been working homicide for twenty years, but this kind of thing, you just didn't see every day.

'It's the pits, Jake.'

'The pits, that's it, that's what you got for me?'

Billy's mouth dropped, but I wasn't finished.

'A pregnant woman, hacked to death with her child cut out of her, the strays in the alley eating her guts ... and that's all you've got to say?'

'Jake, I ...'

'Forget about it!' I hit out, could have taken down a wall with that one.

Billy didn't see it coming. Fell on the asphalt and shook his head. He got up and walked, grimaced and flashed hurt blue eyes as he spat blood at me.

Two days later they took me off the case. The next week it was my badge they took.

Now I'm doing security in a 7-Eleven in Buffalo. Earning minimum wage and sending half of it back to my ex-wife upstate. You'd think life couldn't get any worse. But, maybe I was the guy lying in the gutter looking at the stars.

'Jake! Jake! Get your goat-smelling ass out here.'

I swear that bastard tries to bigfoot me one more time,

I'm popping' a cap in his wide old ass. I walk through to the front counter, with the Irish in me rising like a rain cloud.

'You want something, Mr Delago?'

''Course I damn well want something. Think I'm hollering for my health? Help this lady out with her groceries would you ... And put them in the trunk, too.'

He turned that greasy head of his towards her, spat out one of those lousy piranha smirks of his: 'Always glad to help a lady,' he said, adding slyly, 'especially one so fine.'

Delago got a smile back, but her eyes were on the roll of meat spilling over his belt. 'Much obliged to you, kind sir,' she said, turning tail and wiggling her ass at us both.

Please. I mean, was anyone still falling for this Daisy Duke shit? I slung arms around the groceries and followed her out.

'I'm the Caddy,' she said, smiling, 'pink one.'

I nodded and headed off in the direction of the shiny phallus, trimmed in chrome. All the while I could feel her eyeballing me, as she rolled a cherry liquorice between her lips.

'You look like you've been working out there, fella.'

I'd heard all the lines, but most times, I hadn't been on the receiving end of them. As I popped the trunk I felt her hand stray onto my hip and knew I'd scored for sure. Perhaps this wasn't going to be such a hard stretch.

I didn't tell Candy about my having been a cop.

'This place sucks,' she said.

'What do you expect? The sign outside says *Rooms by the Hour*.'

'We should've went to the Holiday Inn, at least they've got a pool.'

I sat up, reached for my pack of Luckies on the bed-stand. 'I didn't know you wanted more exercise.'

She smiled at me, climbed on top and stuck her hooters out like a cowgirl at a rodeo. 'Give it to me.'

'Honey, you're going to kill me.'

'The smoke, wise-ass.'

I could tell she was restless. Always that look in her eye, darting off somewhere, searching for the next big adventure. Shit, that was the last thing I needed dragged along on, I'd way too much on my mind.

'I've got to get back to the city,' she said.

'New York?'

'Of course, where else?' She rolled off and parted her legs in the birthing position as she blew smoke-rings to the ceiling. 'This place hasn't got any action. And I *need* action.'

I took back my smoke. 'You're not a big hometown girl, are you?'

'Shit no, I outgrew Buffalo long ago ... I'm here because I have to be.'

'And why's that?'

She slit her eyes as she stared at me, changing tack again. 'You're a city boy, don't you miss the action?'

'This suits me fine. The less action the better.'

'Horseshit!' She sat up, shook the bed as she threw back her long blonde hair, 'You're just like me ... you're primed.'

'Get out of here.'

Candy got up and jumped on the bed like it was a trampoline. My Lucky went flying and I landed on my ass, staring up at her from the floor as she stomped up and down like a five-year-old. 'Jake, I'm gonna rock your world,' she yelled.

I didn't doubt it.

———✦———

Onetime there wasn't much could butter my muffin, but these days, I'm not doing too good keeping a lid on it all. Say what you like about me, and some have said plenty, but what sets me burning is the injustice of this world.

Delago was riding me: 'Jake, Goddamn, how many times? How many times? Get that fucking deadwood away from the dumpsters.'

He was talking about the winos. Most were there because they couldn't help themselves. But the point was missed on Delago.

'Have I got to get a bat and break their fucking heads myself?' he said, pointing at me with the chocolate shake he'd brought back from his second trip to Wendy's today.

I held it together by a thread. 'Mr Delago, what you're proposing goes against the law.'

'Against the law ... hold on, remind me when you got out of Harvard Law School, Jake ... *Huh*, c'mon, remind me.'

'I'm only saying ...'

He cut me off, waddled over and slapped a wet paw on my face, 'You ain't saying nothing, you'll do as ...'

I tried counting to ten – by now I knew I had serious anger issues – but I only got as far as two.

I took Delago's shake in my hand and squeezed so hard a chocolate-coloured volcano erupted all over him. His eyes turned black. He threw down the cup. There was words, loud words, but they bounced off my back as I walked.

The sight of the winos scattering made me look around. I spotted Candy at the edge of the lot, blonde hair blowing wild as she leaned on the fire escape, sucking down a can of Sprite.

'Now, I know you're ready for some action,' she hollered.

Does everyone become what they despise? My father had asked me that in high school. He probably had a reason, some incident, some mistake I'd made, whatever it was I didn't remember it now.

'Just sit tight honey-pie,' she said, 'and when you see me come running round that corner, you gun that motherfucker till she screams, y'hear?'

I heard alright. I just didn't have the words. Dropped a vague nod.

'Good boy.' Candy leaned over, placed her wet red lips on my cheek and smiled. 'You'll do just fine.'

As she left, her aroma lingered in the Caddy. That French perfume she wore, the smell of her hair, her scent. She was the whole package for sure. And right to think that most men would do anything for her. She wrapped them around her little finger to get what she wanted. She was used to getting what she wanted, regardless of the consequences.

The bank was two blocks from where we'd parked. The back way out led right onto the alley where I sat drumming my fingers on the wheel – like a teenager hot to take the family sedan for a first spin. Time was lost to me. Could have been a half-hour, could have been minutes. But I was so keyed when I heard the gunshots, I had to open the door and heave my guts on the sidewalk.

This was serious. What the hell was I doing?

I tried to fix my thoughts, get in line. But I was shaking so hard I couldn't make the engine bite. Then I saw Candy, running.

'Start the fucking car!' she yelled.

I couldn't get my hands to work.

'Start the motherfucking car!'

I don't know where it came from but I found a thin

dime's worth of cool, suddenly the Cadillac purred to life and I made those tyres screech louder than bush pigs fucking.

Candy dived through the nearside window and waved me to burn the road up: 'Get the fuck out of here.'

I heard the sirens now, saw the Mars lights speeding along the highway. I turned through the alleys. There was a drill for these things. I knew what the cops would be doing. I just had to hold in my guts and drive, slow and steady.

'What the fuck was wrong with you back there?' said Candy, climbing into the front seat and checking on the loot.

'I don't know.'

'You don't fucking know, no shit! That's exactly right.'

'Look, I ...'

'Don't go saying sorry to me, you know I hate men who say sorry. Man, you're one fucking candyass bastard to be taking along on a job.' She seethed with white-hot anger.

'I ...'

'Enough already. I told you, didn't I tell you?'

She was hyped, madder than hell, the adrenaline twisting her face. I hardly recognised her now. Truth told, I hated this person and what she'd got me into; even if my intentions were pure.

She turned on me. 'Man, you are one weak bastard, Jake ... I should have known better. That was nearly a repeat of NY, I didn't have you down as a Lottie Tanner, no I didn't.'

That name sang like a pay cheque to me. '*Who?*'

'The bitch on my last job, turned yellow on me, wanted to split before we sealed the deal ... She got hers.'

I looked at Candy, she had a twisted smile as she counted the cash, 'How?' I said, my voice a soft plea.

She turned to me, wiped off the smile. I swear that look in her eye came closer to evil than I'd ever seen. 'I carved her.' She made a slashing move with her arm. 'But I still delivered, I got the job done.'

Candy looked back down at the cash, her mouth counting out the reams of bills.

'That name, Lottie Tanner ...'

'Yeah.'

'Think I might have heard it before.'

'Oh, really ...'

'Yeah, she came from Buffalo didn't she?'

Candy looked up, her tone rose higher. 'You knew Lottie?'

'Only of her. And only professionally.'

'What the hell are you saying, Jake?'

'She was my last case.' I looked her in the eye. 'I was a cop ... some days I think I still am.'

Candy's lip twitched. I saw her reaching into the bag for her Colt but my foot was already on the brake. Her head hit the windshield like a ten-pin strike.

I stopped the car. Leaned over to Candy, put her hands behind her back and took off my belt to tie them.

The words felt worth the wait, the work I'd put in. 'Time for a trip downtown, honey.'

Also published by McNidder & Grace

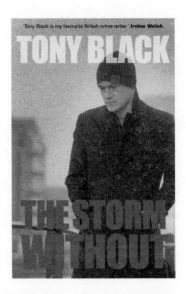

Still recovering from the harrowing case that ended his police career, Doug Michie returns to his boyhood home of Ayr on Scotland's wind-scarred west coast. He hopes to rebuild his shattered life, get over the recent failure of his marriage and shed his demons, but the years have changed the birthplace of the poet Robert Burns. When Doug meets his old school-day flame Lyn, however, he feels his past may offer the salvation of a future. But, Lyn's son has been accused of murder and she begs Doug to find the truth. Soon Doug is tangled in a complicated web of corrupt politicians, frightened journalists and a police force in cahoots with criminals. Only Burns' philosophical musings offer Doug some shelter as he wanders the streets of Auld Ayr battling *The Storm Without*.

The Storm Without, ISBN (9780857160409).

'another masterclass in Tartan Noir.' *DAILY RECORD*

'this is an elegaic noir for the memory of a place, delivered in a prose as bleakly beautiful as the setting.' *THE GUARDIAN*

'this is the Great Scottish Novel, got it all and just a wee shade more... Classic.' KEN BRUEN, author of *HEADSTONE*

To be published by McNidder & Grace

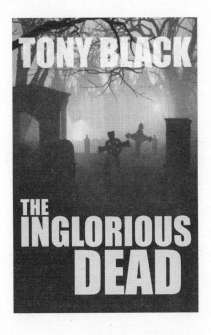

Doug Michie will return in the follow up to
The Storm Without in
The Inglorious Dead in 2013.